To Michelle,

With regards for your

birthday,

Bethany Askew

I Know You, Don't I?

Bethany Askew

I KNOW YOU, DON'T I?

First published in 2020
by Wallace Publishing, United Kingdom
www.wallacepublishing.co.uk

Typesetting courtesy of KGHH Publishing, United Kingdom
www.kensingtongorepublishing.com

For Anthony, with my love and thanks.

Carly

One

"I know you, don't I?"

"No," she says, "you must be mistaken…"

"Caroline," he says firmly. "Caroline Westminster…"

She shakes her head but he's seen the flash of recognition in her eyes.

"I used to teach you," he says. "At East Devon College. Maths. You were very good…"

He's older, of course. His hair is greying and there are laughter lines around his eyes, but there's no mistaking him. This is her moment to correct him.

"I'm not Caroline," she should say. *"I'm Carly. Carly Spurway."* but the moment's gone and she finds herself shaking hands with him automatically. "Mr. Exton…" she says politely.

"Mark, please." He laughs. "What're you doing here?"

She glances around at the pictures on the walls.

"Not here, literally." He laughs again and she can see now that he's a bit nervous. "I mean, here in Taunton?"

"I live here. Well, only just. I've been here a few weeks. You?"

"Oh, we've been here for years. I'm teaching at Wyvern's now. The sixth form college."

The 'we' isn't lost on her. Married, obviously. Well, of course, he would be by now. He must be, what, early forties? He was probably only a few years older than them when they

7

were in the sixth form, though he seemed so much more mature, not long out of university; the good-looking Maths teacher that all the girls fancied and all the boys wanted to emulate. He's still good-looking, despite the slightly greying hair. More confident now, though. Slim, athletic-looking. Clearly he looks after himself. He senses her examining him and his dark eyes hold hers. Embarrassed, she looks back at the painting.

Someone pushes past them, jogging his elbow so that his red wine spills slightly over the back of his hand. He bends his head to lick it off and says, "It's getting crowded in here. Why don't we go through to the bar?"

"I've got to go," she says quickly, glancing at her watch for authenticity.

"Oh, please," he says. "Just a few minutes. I don't often bump into former students. You've all moved away…"

She knows she shouldn't. This goes against everything she's moved here for. But he doesn't know who she is. He thinks she's someone else. She doesn't have to see him again.

The bar is crowded too, but a couple are just leaving a table, and Mark pulls out the chair for Carly almost before the woman has picked up her jacket. The woman's glare at his perceived rudeness softens as he smiles charmingly at her. The charming smile lingers on his face as he sits down opposite Carly.

"I didn't realise it would be so busy," Carly says.

"So you were telling me. You've just moved here…"

This is the last thing she wants to talk about, so she says again, "It's busier than I expected. I don't know any of these artists." She gestures to the paintings above her head and on the opposite wall. "I was sent a flier."

The Brewhouse Theatre and Arts Centre is within walking distance of work. It was easy enough to pop in before she drove home. Going to art exhibitions was one of the things Graham had hated.

"They're local," Mark says, "but I've seen that one before. In an art gallery in Minehead, I think…" He gestures to the black and white painting on the opposite wall: a girl standing on a pavement somewhere in France, her short hair ruffled by an unseen breeze. "Paul Ashton. He's good, isn't he? Unusual style, the monochrome. But I don't know the others. There's a play on tonight as well. That's why it's busy."

"You're going?" she asks.

He shakes his head. "You?"

"No."

"Would you like another drink?"

She's scarcely taken a sip of her orange juice and he still has half a glass of red wine, so she shakes her head.

"It's some sort of am-dram tonight," Mark says, picking up the programme and leafing through it. "You were always in the school plays, weren't you? The lead roles as I remember..."

Carly remembers seeing Caroline in a play in their final year at college—*King Lear*. It was an open-air production. Her long dark hair was loose down her back, a gold coronet on her head. She must have been Cordelia.

"Yes," she says, nodding. "A long time ago..."

"Twenty years, maybe? No, longer. East Devon was my first teaching post. I was so nervous. You haven't told me what you're doing now..."

"Optometrist," she supplies. "Pender and Brown. In North Street."

"Glad you put the Maths to some good use..." He tips his glass of wine towards her in silent tribute and she smiles.

"And your parents?" he asks. "How are they getting on?"

It's always a shock to hear her parents spoken about so casually by people who don't know what happened. She takes a quick sip of her orange juice to steady herself before answering something vague, but in her consternation, it goes down the wrong way and she starts coughing and choking. Tears stream down her face and she waves away his attempts to pat her back.

"Please... I'm fine..."

She stalls for time, finds a tissue and takes a mirror from her handbag to wipe the mascara streaks from her face.

"I read about his retirement in the Gazette," Mark says in an obvious effort to cover the awkward moment. She's back on safe ground: Dr. Westminster was well-known in Tiverton. "Lovely place for holidays," he goes on. "D'you get there often?"

She nods vaguely, still coughing, sniffing, and wiping her nose. The door to the side of them opens and a fresh group of people flood in with the cold breeze. She sees him look up expectantly. Of course. Only people like her go to exhibitions on their own.

"Are you meeting someone?" she asks.

He reddens. "A friend. Not coming, obviously."

This is another one of those moments. She could say, "I've got to get on..." They would part. Caroline Westminster would be relegated to the deepest depths of his mind. He would get back to, well, whatever it is he's up to. She would get on with her new independent life. But she doesn't. Something shifts between them. A decision is made. They both know where they stand.

"So, where are you living?" he asks.

"Bishops Lydeard. The health farm. I've got a flat..."

"Quantock Manor? I didn't know you could live there."

"It's a well-kept secret." She laughs. "There are only ten flats. We can't go into the health farm itself but we can use the outdoor pool, and the grounds are lovely. How about you?"

"We've got a house in Sherford."

She nods even though she doesn't know where that is.

"Children?" she asks. She may as well know everything.

He nods, draining the last of his red wine. "Twins. Chloe and Sam. They're fourteen. That awkward age." He rolls his eyes at her. "You don't have any, do you?"

She shakes her head. A woman would pursue this. *"Didn't you want any...? Are you planning on any...? There's plenty of time..."* But he's a man. He accepts it without question, doesn't need to know more.

There's a brief pause, then he says, "I'd love to see you again. If you'd like..."

Everything tells her to say "No", but what harm can it do? She can always back out later. "Yes," she says, smiling at him. "Yes, I'd like that."

He feels in his pocket for his phone.

She sees him start to type *Caroline.*

"I've changed my name," she says quickly.

"Married?" he says. "Yes, of course." As if he's expecting it.

"No, I mean, yes. Divorced."

An expression of relief flits across his face. *So much less complicated,* he's thinking.

"My first name," she says. "It's Carly now."

A puzzled look crosses his face, followed by a frown. Is he remembering Carly Spurway? But why would he? She wasn't as brilliant as Caroline Westminster. She didn't have a well-known GP for a father. She wasn't as pretty, as popular, as vivacious. Then just as quickly, the frown is gone. Obviously he thinks changing her name is just one of those strange whims that women have.

"A fresh start," he says.

She nods and smiles, relieved.

"So. Carly...?" he asks, waiting for her surname.

"Anderson," she supplies. She hadn't changed her name back when she'd split up with Graham. She had always hated the name Spurway. And it was easier for work.

"Well, I'd better be off," he says, reaching for his coat.

She stands as well, picking up her coat and scarf.

"Can I walk you to your car?"

She's drunk a glass of orange juice, it's a twenty-minute drive home, and she's dying for the loo, so she shakes her head. "I'll just..." She gestures vaguely.

"Okay," he says easily. "I'll be in touch..."

She watches him make his way through the crowd, turn, and wave at the door.

There's a long queue for the Ladies'. There are never enough loos in theatres. As she shuffles forward, snatches of conversation drift past her:

"I told you there wasn't time..."

"She was in that last play, wasn't she...?"

"Do you think we should've ordered a drink for the interval...?"

The three-minute bell for the performance rings whilst she's in the cubicle and by the time she comes out, the last woman is desperately drying her hands on a tissue before she hurries out and slams the door behind her. Carly catches sight of her reflection in the mirror as she washes her hands: she can see why he thought she was Caroline. She has the same colouring: dark hair, blue eyes, pale skin. Caroline was slimmer than her at eighteen, skinny almost; everyone was envious of her. *"How d'you stay so slim?"* they'd ask as she tucked into cakes and biscuits, or chips from the chip shop. But Carly lost weight during the divorce; all that haggling over money and wrangling about which piece of furniture belonged to whom, and who bought a certain book or DVD. She was pleased to find jeans and trousers feeling looser on her. She found it easier to be careful about what she ate with no man around to tempt her into biscuits, cakes and puddings.

The cold air hits her when she gets outside. For a moment, she wishes she had accepted Mr. Exton's— *Mark's*—offer to walk her back to the car: the windscreen may be iced up, the car may not start. As she gets in the car and drives home, she realises these are the sorts of things that make her miss Graham.

It's the same when she gets home. The novelty of solitude has quickly worn off. As she heats up and eats her supermarket meal-for-one, she reminds herself that this is what she longed for when Graham was asking her what was for dinner every night, and she was nagging him about not helping her or not emptying the bins.

As she does the washing up, she stares out the window

above the sink, where she can just about make out the shapes of the trees against the dark sky. A few stars twinkle and it's a clear night. There'll be a frost tonight, but tomorrow is forecast to be sunny. The walled garden looks lovely when it's frosted and sparkling. There's a narrow balcony running along the front of her flat and in the spring, she'll put tubs of flowers out there. Also chairs and a table, a sun lounger maybe, though she doesn't sunbathe. She can take all her meals out there, when it's warm enough.

She loved this flat the moment she saw it. A 1980s brick-built block of flats in the grounds of the health farm. It's only a fifteen-minute drive from town and it's everything she needs: private, self-contained, with the old house nearby and the landscaped grounds making it feel special. She has one of the smallest flats: just one bedroom and a lounge-diner, both rooms overlooking the private walled garden. She didn't need to change the magnolia walls and the cream carpet, and when she furnished the living area with pale cream furniture and a glass table, she relished not having to consult Graham about the price or the style.

It's very quiet here: she can just about hear the hum of a distant television. All the other residents must be in their seventies at least, and there's a rule that says no children under sixteen can be residents. That's one of the reasons she chose it. True, it would be nice to have someone nearer her own age to chat to occasionally, but she's said "Hello" to some of the staff who live in the health farm—a large old house around the corner from the block of flats—so maybe she can invite them in sometime.

The girls at Pender and Brown—Hannah and Madison—are much younger than her: big boisterous girls, always talking about diets and new outfits; only interested in clubbing, boyfriends, hair colours, manicures and beauty treatments. She's glad they haven't asked her to join them on their nights out (she knows she looks younger than she is, but they probably still think she's too old). She's added them on

Facebook, but only because they pushed her into it (they're young enough to be competitive about the number of 'friends' they have), and so that she can say she's seen their latest 'pics': the inevitable selfies, that 'awesome' new dress Madison bought, Hannah's latest chap, or the hot new man that one of them pulled on Friday night.

The original optometrists—Jean Pender and Tom Brown—are long deceased, although the practice, well-established in the town, has retained their names. The new partners are Bob Gray and Lesley Simms, in their mid-forties and early fifties respectively. Bob is prematurely balding; a whippet-thin man with piercing blue eyes. He has dozens of photos of his children on his phone and he produces them regularly, along with stories of them that only he finds amusing. Lesley is a nervy lady with short, iron-grey hair. She has grown-up children—one of whom has 'special needs'—and a dread of missing some ocular abnormality that would lead to her being hauled up by the General Optical Council or sued by a patient. Both work between this branch and the firm's other two branches in Wellington and Chard. Beyond the usual "Where are you living?" and "Where did you live before?", none of them have asked much about her. Maybe the Practice Manager, Rachel, has warned them that she's newly divorced and doesn't want to talk about it. Rachel is briskly efficient—she doesn't like them chatting, especially on the front desk. When they hear her coming out of the back office, Bob and Lesley scuttle into their examination rooms. If Carly could be friends with anyone at work, Rachel would be the most obvious choice. She's probably only a few years older than Carly. She's tall, slim, and wears her fair hair tied back for work in a thick swaying ponytail. The customers call her "Miss Warren", she doesn't wear a ring of any sort, and never mentions a man's name or talks about "us". Carly suspects she's also a divorcée. She was certainly very sympathetic when Carly told her about her divorce at the interview. It might have even swayed Rachel's decision.

"I was brought up in Tiverton," Carly had explained. "I just feel I need to be back in the West Country. Like coming home..."

It wouldn't have made much difference to Bob, the only partner at the interview. (Lesley couldn't come due to urgent family issues). He was only interested in Carly's professional expertise, but Rachel had nodded understandingly.

The interview had gone well. They offered her the job almost immediately, though it took several months before she could start there, what with moving and all the other things that were going on.

When Carly started work there and looked at the bookings, she realised that they had actually been desperate for another optometrist for some time, as there were no free appointments for weeks. Apparently, it was hard to get optometrists in the West Country. Most people wanted to work in the London area or the Midlands. Carly wasn't too bothered why they took her on, she was just relieved she'd managed to escape her old life without anyone prying too much.

The staff had been important to her though. She didn't want to find herself working with another manager like the one she'd had at Optimum Vision, but she had taken to Rachel instantly at the interview. As for Bob, well, he was one of those opticians happy enough to stay in the background and do his job, rather than interfere with the day-to-day running of the business. While there's the odd obligatory work get-together, and maybe a drink after work with Rachel if she asks her, Carly can't imagine making friends with anyone there.

In the old days, she used to have lots of friends. But since the divorce, the inevitable had happened: Graham had told all his friends that everything was her fault and they, in turn, told their wives the same. She had kept in touch with a few people, but most of them lived so far away that she was unlikely to see them again. No, she had to accept she needed to make new friends. The health club was so expensive and in any case, she found using the gym boring, but maybe she could find evening classes, yoga or Pilates.

She has a quick shower and changes into leggings and a top, then takes out her laptop. She should be searching for Pilates classes but instead, she finds herself on Facebook.

A flutter of excitement runs through her as she types Mark's name into the search box. She's not surprised when she can't find him. He doesn't seem the type to upload pictures of his children, and it's not as if he's in the sort of profession where he needs a Facebook profile to advertise what he does.

It takes her an age to track down Caroline. None of the Caroline Westminsters are from Devon, let alone Tiverton. She's probably listed herself under wherever she lives nowadays. Next she tries her old school friends, scrolls through the lists of their friends, and tries every Caroline. Names she hasn't seen for years flash up before her, and she can't help stopping to see what they look like and what they're doing. Frustratingly, some have their privacy settings set too high for her to get more than a cursory look. Then one name makes her pause longer than usual: Vicky Fraser. The name seems familiar, yet she can't quite place it. Then in a flash, it comes to her. Vicky Watts. She had been a friend of Caroline's. Vicky must have married Jason Fraser. They'd been together since they started college and it amazes her that they still are. Quite a few of them had long-term relationships in the sixth form, but none survived past university. In fact, Caroline was one of them. She had gone out with someone in their Maths class. They had always sat together and had been inseparable.

She clicks on to Vicky's page. Luckily for her, Vicky isn't bothered about privacy. There are posts of her and her two children, and her house and garden. Carly clicks on to 'Friends', types in 'Ca', and there it is: *Caroline Lee Pitt (Caroline Westminster)*. The picture shows a smiling, short-haired woman. Surely this isn't Caroline? She clicks on to her. Caroline is another person who is unfazed by, or unaware of how to stop people prying on her. Carly scrolls down the timeline, studying post after post, picture after picture. Ironically, Caroline Westminster's long, dead straight dark hair—the dark hair Mark Exton so obviously remembered—is now cropped elfin short. Apart from the blue eyes and pale skin, she and Carly could never be mistaken for each other nowadays. Caroline's nowhere near as pencil-thin as she was at eighteen either: the tops of her arms are rounded in her sleeveless tops, her jeans stretch over her thighs. As Carly scrolls further down, the reason becomes obvious: first a child of about four, then a chubby toddler, and then finally, a babe-in-arms appears in the pictures, sometimes accompanied by a proud-looking bearded husband, tagged as Damian Pitt. There's another boy in the pictures too: tall, broad-shouldered, thick dark wavy hair, late-teens maybe. A friend's son? A nephew? Or maybe Damian Pitt was married before and it's Caroline's stepson. She shrugs inwardly. This isn't what she's looking for anyway. She jumps from the timeline to "About". East Devon College is there, of course. After that comes Aston University in Birmingham, where she studied Business Studies. She hasn't listed any places of work but Carly is relieved to see her home town is listed as Solihull, so there's absolutely no reason why she'd ever turn up in Taunton. She clicks on to the photos. There are albums of skiing holidays. And beach holidays where the toddler (Harry, apparently) is making sandcastles, a floppy hat on his head, or paddling in the sea holding his daddy's hand. Mysteriously, the teenage boy is there too. The caption underneath identifies him as Joshua. Several pictures show Caroline arm-in-arm with an older dark-haired girl, sometimes with two children and a man in tow. The girl looks vaguely familiar. Was she at college with them? She's tagged as 'Emma Mitchell'. Carly can't remember an Emma, but then she can't possibly remember everyone and apart from Maths, Caroline did different A-levels from her. She clicks on to Emma's page out of idle curiosity.

"To see what she shares with friends, send her a friend request," Facebook tells her.

Carly returns to Caroline's page, scrolls through the photo albums, and finds what she's really looking for: 'Chez Mum and Dad'. She double clicks to open the album. Older, fatter and greyer versions of Dr. Westminster and his wife stand either side of a smiling Caroline, her short hair hidden under a baseball cap. They all look tanned, relaxed and happy. There's a pool behind them, a table and chairs, and a distant blue vista of hills and trees. She clicks through quickly: pictures of the house, tiled floors, white walls, the family eating, playing, little Harry in the arms of the good-looking Damian Pitt. Emma Mitchell is there too, sometimes with the children and the man, other times arm-in-arm with Caroline or her parents. Then suddenly Carly realises she has to be her older sister.

Frustratingly though, there's nothing to tell her exactly where they are. Then, finally, a random comment from a friend:

"Looks lovely. Where is it?"

"Veyrignac. In the Dordogne."

Carly could kiss the unknown Jessica Woods who made the comment.

She clicks on to her own page. She's never been the type to post loads of photographs and now she systematically deletes the ones of her sister, Tina. Getting malicious pleasure out of saying 'yes', when the question asks her if she's sure she wants to delete them. If only she could delete Tina from her life altogether.

She closes her laptop and switches on the television to watch the news, then picks up her book to read for a while. These are the times she misses Graham the most: the quiet evenings. No one to talk to—just herself and her all-too-perfect flat. Nothing out of place: no newspapers, magazines or keys lying on the glass coffee table; no DVDs or controllers on the arms of chairs; no shoes littering the floor. It's worse in bed: the double bed yawns emptily beside her.

It's been ages, she tells herself sternly, she must get used to it. It's dangerous to dwell on the timescale, because other anniversaries spring to mind. The date they met, the date they married, the date they split up; all stubbornly refuse to be forgotten. At least here, there are no shared memories like there were in their house in Reading. She must stop looking back, start to look forward. She has resisted checking her phone all evening, but now she allows herself to look. Her heart gives a small leap when she sees the message:

"Great to run into you tonight. Would love to see you again. Will be in touch, M." Followed by a smiley face.

Her first impulse is to reply. She composes a quick message in her mind, she even starts to key it in. *"Lovely to see you too. Look forward to hearing from you."* But she stops even before she's finished it, deletes it letter by letter, and turns her phone off so she's not tempted to start again.

Two

Carly wakes up with a feeling of excitement. Something has happened. What is it? Then she remembers: Mark Exton. She reaches for her phone almost before she realises what she is doing. No new messages. Obviously he doesn't want to appear too keen.

She dithers about what to wear that day, just in case he turns up at work, though the chances of him doing that are infinitesimally small. She does her make-up and hair carefully too and it must show, because Madison says "You look nice today" when she arrives. Carly blushes and looks at herself in the mirror when she gets back to her testing room. Madison's right. There's a glow in her face, a sparkle in her eyes. All this for a man she's only just met, and she's not sure whether she wants to see again after today. But this is why people have relationships, isn't it? For the excitement at the beginning, not the tedium that comes with familiarity.

She lets a day go by and is just composing a reply to Mark's message when another one arrives:

"Fancy meeting up for a pub lunch? I can pick you up if you let me know where and what time."

"Thank you, I'd like that," she replies. *"Thursday okay? I can meet you at one fifteen. The car park by The Crescent?"*

***

She usually wears trouser suits, but today she puts on a dress and jacket, new pale tights and high-heeled shoes. And instead of tying her hair back in a low ponytail she just clips it up at the front, leaving the rest loose down her back. She slides a bottle of perfume and a tube of hand cream into her handbag.

She remembers why she wears trousers and boots the moment she steps out of the front door. An icy wind is blowing and dark grey clouds threaten rain. Her legs feel exposed in the skirt, and the heels of her shoes skid on the damp path.

When she arrives at work, it's Bob Gray who notices this time, giving her a low wolf whistle as she walks past the reception desk. By mid-morning, they've all worked out she's meeting someone.

"You could at least tell us who the lucky man is," Bob quips for the umpteenth time.

"Leave her alone," Rachel says. She smiles as she says it, but the underlying tone in her voice manages to convey the fact that she doesn't want her new optometrist complaining of harassment.

It's the first time they've shown a real interest in her and with interest, comes tentative questions.

"Do you know anyone down here?" Hannah asks.

Carly shakes her head. "No, but I went to school in Tiverton."

Tiverton is too much of a backwater compared to Taunton, and won't be of interest to Hannah or Madison.

"Your family still lives there though?" She goes on.

"No. My parents moved to France when they retired." How easily the words come out. She almost believes them herself.

"Wow, that sounds lovely. D'you go there often?"

"As often as I can. It's beautiful. They've got a villa with a pool in the Dordogne."

Hannah probably hasn't a clue where that is but in the background, Carly senses Bob's ears pricking up.

"Got any brothers and sisters?" Hannah goes on.

"A sister. Emma. She's older than me. Lives in Manchester." This much she did get from Facebook. "I don't see her much," She goes on. "Except when she comes to France with the kids to see Mum and Dad."

It's so satisfying to erase Tina from her life and it all sounds so much more glamorous than the truth.

Back in her testing room, waiting for her next patient, it crosses her mind that Hannah or Madison might look at her photos on Facebook to see this new exotic life she's conjured up for herself. Maybe there's a way she could download some of Caroline's and put them on her page? Or take down her own profile and upload a new one? The idea's appealing. A new profile. An alias. She could put Caroline's maiden name on, then add photos of her parents and sister. Then she dismisses the idea. What about the friends she has on Facebook already? They'd wonder what the hell was going on. In any case, Hannah and Madison are far too caught up in their own lives to bother with hers. Best to keep it simple.

By lunchtime, their curiosity has waned anyway: Hannah has had a text from her latest boyfriend. Whatever it says has clearly upset her. She manages to pull herself together when Rachel or any patients are around, but the rest of the time she's sniffling into a tissue with Madison comforting her.

"He didn't mean it," she's saying. "You know what men are like…"

"Don't I just?" Carly thinks. Yet here she is, spraying on perfume, checking there are no mascara smudges under her eyes, putting on lipstick. Bob is safely in his room. Only Rachel sees her leave, checking her watch as usual to make sure Carly comes back on time, nodding a brief goodbye as she reaches to answer the telephone.

The cold hits Carly again as she steps outside. She walks as fast as she can in her high heels, as she heads towards the car park.

"I've got an Audi," he had texted, adding *"Silver,"* presumably in case she knew nothing about cars. She tells herself not to be nervous but her stomach fizzes with excitement. It's years since she's felt like this and she can't deny it feels good. She feels alive again. She's almost there when she hears a car drawing up behind her. Mark leans over to open the passenger door. She sees his quick look of appreciation as she slides into the passenger seat. Then his eyes are back on the road.

"I thought we'd go to the Cross Keys," he says. "Since we don't have much time."

She drives past the Cross Keys every day on her way to and from work. There are always long queues at the roundabout.

"I've got a patient at two fifteen," she says, remembering Rachel's glance at her watch.

"Don't worry, I've got a class full of seventeen-year-olds just *dying* to learn all about calculus. I'll get you back in plenty of time."

In the ten minutes it takes to get there, they chat easily about the weather, the traffic, the patient she had this morning, his late-night marking session. The car park is nearly full, but he manoeuvres the car easily into a parking space that Carly would have struggled with. As he gets out of the car with her, walks to the pub and finds them a table by the window, Carly wonders if he's worried about being seen with someone other than his wife, but he seems unconcerned. Maybe he has rehearsed a ready excuse:

"An old student of mine," he would say with a laugh. *"We just bumped into each other."*

While he queues at the bar, she studies the menu with a sinking heart: scampi and chips, haddock and chips, steak and kidney pie and chips. She's trying to keep off the weight she's lost. She turns it over, hoping to find a salad, but there are only desserts on the back. The chalked "specials board" offers Duck à l'orange and Lamb Shank, which they don't have time for.

"I think they do sandwiches," Mark says, maybe seeing the look of dismay on her face. He puts his glass of red wine and her apple juice down on the table. "Or soup, if you fancy something hot? I'll find you the snack menu."

They settle for a sandwich each and he sits down opposite her.

"So, tell me what you've been doing since you left Tiverton," he asks.

Aston—where Caroline went to University—also run a course in Optometry, but he might know Birmingham and she's never even been there, so she tells him about her course at City University ("I always wanted to live in London. But it wasn't as glamorous as I expected!"); her pre-registration year at Hudson Opticians, on the outskirts of Reading (where she met Graham. though she doesn't tell him that); followed by her years working in Optimum Vision in the centre of Reading. Here she becomes less confident but he doesn't seem to notice. Like everyone else, he assumes she left because of a painful divorce that she doesn't want to talk about.

She notices him watching her as she talks. This is what she's missed, what she needs: someone being interested in her, being nice to her, admiring her, appreciating her.

Now it's his turn: he talks about his job, how much harder it is to be a teacher than it seems, the preparation, the reports, the Open Evenings.

"Everyone thinks it's just school hours and long holidays," he says. "Well, of course, it's true we *do* have the long holidays. But we don't just go home at four o'clock, and we have to start early.

He tells her about the twins. Sam and Chloe turn out to be a boy and girl: the boy is a typical acned teenager, morose and moody, either out with his mates or cocooned in his bedroom with his earphones in; the girl is experimenting with hair and make-up, always in the bathroom when he needs it.

"Do they get on well together?" she asks.

"They used to. Not so much now they're older."

"I'm so lucky with my sister," Carly says, injecting what she hopes is an affectionate and wistful note into her voice.

"I didn't know you had a sister."

She nods. "Emma. She's three years older." This is just a guess. "We've always been close. Everyone used to think we were twins when we were younger. We don't see a lot of each other nowadays but we're in touch all the time." She gestures to her phone.

"Another one like you," he says with a smile, his eyes holding hers and making her blush. "You two must have been popular. You had a boyfriend at college didn't you, Caro?" The name comes as a shock, but she doesn't correct him. She has a distant memory of Caroline being called Caro, and she rather likes the new name to go with her new life. "Greg something-or-other," he goes on. "You used to sit together. Bit of a slacker. He used to copy your homework. I could always tell…"

"Foster." The surname comes to her out of the blue. Tall, skinny guy. Not especially good-looking. Always messing around and playing the fool. He could do a really good impersonation of Mr. Exton, complete with confident swagger and stern voice. She's smiling as she thinks of him. Maybe Mark thinks she has fond memories. "It didn't last," she says. "We were at different unis…"

He's nodding, understandingly. "Do you keep in touch with any of your old school friends?"

She shakes her head and says, "Not really. Well, a few are friends on Facebook but we don't speak or anything. You can just keep half an eye on what they're up to. Are you on Facebook?"

"God, no. No reason to be really. I'm not into all that social media stuff."

He mentions his wife, of course, but only in passing. His smile vanishes as he does so, his face tightens. Her name is Paula. She's an estate agent with Hardy's in High Street. Carly remembers them sending her details of flats in the area.

Maybe Paula was one of the many people she spoke to on the phone.

By some sort of secret unwritten code, Paula can now disappear into the background and they can pretend she doesn't exist.

Back in the car, he pauses before he starts the engine, and looks around quickly. She knows what's going to happen.

"I've been thinking about you a lot," he says.

She looks over at him. They move together like magnets. It's a short kiss. Short and gentle. Almost loving. She wants it to go on longer but he pulls away, and she remembers with a little thrill of excitement that they have to be careful.

"I'll be in touch," he says when he drops her off.

"Good lunch?" Bob says with a wink when she gets back.

"Lovely." She smiles. Suddenly she doesn't care what they think anymore.

Hannah has calmed down. The recalcitrant boyfriend has sent another text and she's all beaming smiles. "Did you go somewhere nice?" she asks.

"Only the Cross Keys," Carly replies.

She's saved from any more questions by the telephone ringing, and the rest of the afternoon is so busy, no one has time for chat.

Carly checks her phone in between patients, her heart leaping at the sight of a text from Mark:

"Lovely to see you. Can't wait till next time. Be in touch soon. xx"

Her fingers hover over the phone, wondering what to reply. Then she decides to leave it for a while. Make him wait.

There's a missed call too: Tina, but no voicemail. Why does she always call during work hours? She knows Carly can't talk then.

She calls again in the evening, just after Carly has finished eating. Her first instinct is to let it go to voicemail, but then she'll only have to ring her back, so she may as well deal with whatever it is now.

"I called earlier," Tina starts sulkily.

"I was working," Carly retaliates. Why do they always have to start bickering like this? *I bet Caroline isn't like this with Emma.* "How are you?" she manages to go on more levelly.

"Oh, you know…"

Of course she does. There's always some drama in Tina's life.

She carries her plate to the kitchen in one hand, holding her phone to her ear with the other one. She'd put it on speakerphone but Tina is incredibly perceptive: she'd hear the echoed sound of the kitchen, the clatter of plates, and the rush of water running into the washing up bowl. She'd know she was only being half-listened to while Carly got on with the things she had to do. So with the phone still clamped to her ear with one hand, Carly lets the hot water run gently into the bowl, adds washing up liquid, and washes up as quietly as possible, while Tina recounts a long story about someone at the hospital who offended her by saying something inoffensive.

"Did you report it?" Carly asks in the brief moment that Tina stops to blow her nose. She's crying, of course.

"No, well, I can't really, can I? It'll make me look silly."

Carly pours herself another glass of wine, carries it back to the sitting room, and mutters vague "uh-huh's" and "Yes, I see's." into the phone.

Gradually, Tina calms down. "How about you?" she asks. "How's it going?"

"Fine," Carly says. There's no way she's going to tell Tina about Mark, though it's tempting. "How's Graham?" she asks instead. She regrets it the moment the words are out of her mouth. Why does she do this to herself? What is she trying to prove? It's bad enough thinking about him, but saying his name out loud drives a million daggers into her heart. It's not as if Tina notices or cares.

"I haven't seen him for a while," she replies. Carly can

almost see her shrug.

There's nothing much to say after that. Having extracted the right amount of attention from Carly, Tina seems mollified, although Carly knows she'll probably call all her other friends (the ones she hasn't already called) to get the same reassurance.

There's another text from Mark at ten o'clock. *"Night, night,"* It reads. *"Sweet dreams xx."*

She decides to reply to this one.

"xx"

She sends. Just enough to keep him in line. It's all a game. This time she wants to be the winner.

Three

It was February when Carly met Mark. Cold, dark days; freezing nights. She'd been grateful for her small, warm flat where she could creep home and hibernate. The house she and Graham had shared in Reading was old, and the cold crept in through the window frames and under the doors. In the winter, she used to wake up in the morning with a cold nose. Graham hadn't felt the cold. He was still in a t-shirt when she sat huddled in layers of jumpers and cardigans. In the summer, he'd have all the windows open, and she'd go around closing them again.

Now March bursts in on them with blue skies and warm sunshine. Mark's been texting every day, just a few words so she knows he's thinking of her. They've been back to the Cross Keys for lunch and had a drink one evening in the Rumwell Inn. They can't hold hands or anything, but she feels his attraction: it's in his eyes, in the odd brush of his hand as he passes her something, the soft touch of his arm on her back as he guides her through the door. In the car, they kiss but it's furtive, fleeting. She knows it won't be long before something more happens though.

Today, he's suggested a picnic lunch. *"It's too nice to be indoors,"* he texts. And she knows he can't risk being seen with her in a pub garden. At least inside, they can hide in a corner, somewhere out of view.

He picks her up at the usual place and they drive out of

Taunton, up a long winding hill. He pulls in at a lay-by and the whole of Taunton Vale is spread out below them.

"I thought you'd like the view," he says.

He spreads a rug on the ground by the car. "I've got French bread and pâté, grapes, wine. I brought rosé as I thought it would be more summery."

It's actually quite cool up on the hillside in the shade of a large tree, but he's tried so hard and she doesn't want to spoil the occasion, so she keeps on the fleece she brought with her and joins him on the ground. She wonders idly how he managed to smuggle all this food into the car under the watchful eye of his wife. Maybe he picked it up in a delicatessen somewhere in town. But it's in the sort of insulated cool box that families take on picnics, and she pictures him secreting it into the boot of his car from the back of the garage when no one is around.

She has to admit it's very romantic here in the dappled shade. As they tear the French bread and spread the pâté with little plastic knives, Mark keeps up a steady banter, telling her a funny story about one of the boys in his class who fancied himself as a bit of a boffin, and how he had to bring him down a peg or two.

"It doesn't seem long since I was teaching you," he finishes wistfully.

They're sitting close together. He leans towards her. The kiss starts gently but soon becomes more passionate. He tastes of garlic and wine. His tongue is in her mouth, he's clawing at the front of her shirt, undoing buttons, sliding his hand inside. She moans.

"Let's go back to the car," he breathes in her ear. He bundles the picnic stuff away with none of the ceremony with which he had carefully laid it out. She helps him pack it into the boot. The air is heavy with tension. She's hardly sat down when he's kissing her again, reclining the seat, climbing on top of her.

"Not here…" she manages to say. "Not now…"

"We must go to bed," he groans. "I want you…"

"Yes..."

It shouldn't be too difficult to organise. She has her own flat and they're consenting adults. But he's married. There are excuses to be made. It's another week before he can come over. She buys steak, salad, and red wine because she knows it's his favourite, and a dessert that she intends not to have much of.

She's on tenterhooks all day. She can't stop thinking about him. She rushes home from work, heads straight into the shower, and then changes into the new underwear she's bought: midnight blue satin and lace, worn with a casual top and leggings so it doesn't look like she's trying too hard.

She jumps like she's been scalded when the buzzer sounds. Seven o'clock—he's early. She's only just laid the minuscule table in the corner of the sitting room.

"On the first floor," she tells the fuzzy image on the video phone. "There's a lift..."

He arrives a bit breathless. "I took the stairs," he says, handing her a bottle of red wine and a cellophane-wrapped bunch of flowers, obviously picked up at a petrol station or supermarket.

"All I could get, sorry," he apologises as he hands them to her.

She hurries him in, wary of the old ladies either side who, with nothing else to occupy their minds, will be dying to ask who her visitor was. He's dressed more casually than usual, in jeans and a checked shirt. Her stomach clenches at the sight of the dark hair curling just above the opening at the neck.

"Oh, it's lovely here," he says. It's been another sunny day, and the evening sun is setting. The bare branches of the trees stand out blackly against the pearly sky. The garden below looks lovely, the old wall lit up with a golden glow. "It was beautiful coming up the drive," he continues. "I had no idea. It's so peaceful. No wonder people come here."

He crosses over to the window, and she stands next to him. "And you've got a balcony," he says. "It'll be lovely out there in the summer."

"It used to be a rose garden," she says, gesturing to the garden below, which is now mostly lawn with borders of shrubs. A stone fountain sits in the centre: the statue of a semi-nude woman pouring water from a shell. "They have the fountain going from around May, apparently."

They're standing close. He turns and they kiss. She forgets about the drink she was going to offer him, the flowers that should be put in water, the steaks she was going to start soon because presumably, he can't stay long.

The bedroom is scarcely more than twenty paces away. She draws the blinds. For a brief moment, she's shy. It's been a long time. But desire quickly overcomes shyness.

He's brought a condom, "I hate these," he says, "but…?"

"Yes." She's no longer on the Pill but she would have insisted he wear one anyway. She hasn't forgotten he was hoping to meet someone else the evening they met. God knows how many other lovers he's had since he's been married to Paula.

It's over quickly. "Are you okay?" he asks. She moves his hand downwards. She comes quickly too. They lie together, naked, pulling the duvet around themselves. They both doze.

"There's steak…" she says after a while.

"Um-hum…" he says. He doesn't seem to be in any hurry, but his stomach rumbles and she giggles.

"How long have you got?" she goes on. How many other men or women are asking their lovers the same thing?

"I'm out for drinks with the lads," he says. "Eleven, maybe?"

She knows even before she reaches her hand down that he's hard again.

She showers first, then leaves it for him while she does the things she was going to do earlier: open the wine, put the flowers in a vase, the salad on the table.

They talk over dinner. He tells her where he's travelled,

and the idea he had once of emigrating to Australia, "Paula wasn't keen though. Then we found out she was pregnant. She'd been wanting a baby for ages…" He doesn't say he did as well, but somehow she knows. In her experience, men seldom admit to wanting a family. They discuss music (he likes classical, like she does, so she puts on a little quiet Mozart as background). Also, films and books; they differ on some, agree on others. Of course he's on his best behaviour, they both are, but he's good company and she's been on her own too much.

Soon he's looking at his watch in that way she knows so well, and it's time to go. They linger in the tiny front hallway of her flat like two teenagers, crammed together between the three doors to the living room, bathroom and bedroom.

"I'll be in touch," he says, with a final kiss and a squeeze of her arm.

Left with the detritus of the evening—the dirty plates and glasses, the damp towels in the bathroom, the rumpled bed— she feels alone and deflated. No one else has been to her flat. She's made friends with a few women at Pilates, called Michaela and Kristin, but Michaela's married and Kristin has a boyfriend. They haven't invited her out in the evening, suggested meeting up for coffee or shopping, or any of the things she used to do with Kelly and Ruth back in Reading. And she has the complication of not being able to tell them she's seeing someone. Taunton isn't a big town. For all she knows, they might know Paula, or know someone who knows her. How has she managed to spin this web of secrecy around herself? It was supposed to be a new beginning— complication and worry free—but now she has to watch every step. It's the same with Mark. She has to remember carefully what she has told him and what she hasn't, which version of the past is Caroline's and which is hers.

"Why did you move to Reading?" he asks one day.

"To be with my sister." She's pleased with the way this makes them sound close even though it's not the truth. She only went there because Mum and Dad put so much pressure on her.

"I thought she lived in Manchester," he says.

"Yes, of course," she says quickly. "But she was living in Reading then."

"What does she do?"

"Well, now she looks after the children. Dan and Eva." Where did those names come from? They just seemed to fly into her mind. "But she used to work in a hospital. She started as a healthcare assistant but now she's a diabetic retinopathy screener." She says this with genuine pride. Tina might grumble about the stress of her job, the responsibility, her colleagues, the hospital system—everything really—but she's done well to get where she is. "She's going to go back to work," she decides for the fictional Emma, dedicated to her family, "when the children are older."

Of course, it's only a matter of time before they talk about ex-lovers. She could gloss over it, say she doesn't want to talk about it. But part of her does. It hurts to say his name but she wants to tell someone, someone other than Tina, who only repeats various versions of "I told you so."

"He was my supervisor in my pre-registration year. I was…" She searches for the right word, "Overawed, I suppose. He seemed to know everything. He was older, confident. We were together such a lot as we went over patient records. It was a close relationship. There was no place for me there once I qualified, but we kept in touch. I used to ring him to ask for advice." She stops, wondering how much more to tell him. "Then his place closed down. There was a vacancy where I was working and it was like it was meant to be…" She goes on. "You'd have thought it would have kept us together, wouldn't you? Having the same profession, being able to talk about work, understanding each other's problems. But it didn't." Her voice breaks slightly but she's not going to cry in front of him.

"It's so easy in the beginning, isn't it?" he says. "But once you're together all the time, things change." He says it lightly but that familiar tight look comes over his face. "I met Paula at a party. She was so confident, self-possessed, and strong. It took me a while to realise she's none of those things..."

It turns out Paula has "issues": bouts of depression and anxiety, hysteria even. She has tried everything over the years, from anti-depressants to every type of counselling and complementary and holistic therapies. Carly can't help wondering how she copes with twins, a full-time job, staff and payroll to manage, and sales targets to achieve, but Mark says she's better when she's working.

"It was a nightmare when the twins were little," he tells her. "I'd come home and find her still in her dressing gown, the breakfast stuff still on the table, and the twins crawling around in the chaos. Working gives her something to focus on other than herself. Better to pay people to look after the children and the house than to have her at home all day, worrying about herself..."

Mark can't keep making excuses to come over to her flat in the evenings, but they meet for lunch at least once a week. Sometimes they go to a pub, sometimes they drive up the hill to the lay-by.

The sunny spring has given way to a cold wet May, and he picks her up one lunchtime from work as usual.

"I was thinking of a picnic," he says. "But we can't in this weather..." He pauses. "Paula's away at a conference. We could go to my place..."

She hesitates. "What about the children?"

"They won't be back." He insists. "They're at college."

She's still unsure. What if they skived off? Were taken ill? Went back home for something?

"What about the neighbours?" she asks.

"They're all out at work." He laughs. "Anyway, the house is on the market. If anyone asks, I'll say you're a prospective buyer."

The experienced adulterer with his ready excuse. But the idea is exciting: swift illicit sex with a married man in a double bed on a rainy lunch hour. Also, part of her is curious to see where he lives.

The Sherford estate is a ten-minute drive from the centre of town. Identical white stucco and redbrick houses line the road either side. He draws up outside one of them. She's still nervously aware they might be watched but he walks next to her into the house, a confident smile on his face. Inside, she has a quick glimpse of an untidy front hallway: coats, scarves and gloves hanging on hooks opposite the stairs; shoes and trainers littering the floor; a guitar leaning against one wall, a tennis racquet next to it. He's all over her the moment he's closed the front door, untucking her shirt, pulling it from her shoulders.

"Let's go upstairs," he says urgently.

She follows him up. She can't shake off the feeling that Paula will walk in at any minute. "Are you sure it's okay?" she asks.

"The conference is in Bournemouth, Even if she comes back early, she won't be back for hours."

"But…"

"Neither will they," he says firmly. "Anyway, I've double-locked all the doors."

By now, they're on the top landing. Four doors are ahead of her: the two children's ones slightly ajar. Shoes litter these floors too, along with clothes and school books. She can see posters on the walls, toiletries on the desk in the pink room; a laptop in the one painted dark grey.

Mark is hurrying her through the other door. The bedroom is strewn with clothes—they're on the backs of chairs, hanging on hangers on the front of the wardrobe, lying on the floor. The linen basket in the corner is overflowing with sheets and towels, the lid balanced precariously on the top. The bed hasn't been made, the duvet just thrown over any-old-how. Either Paula was away last night as well or she doesn't bother to make the bed in the mornings. Mark pulls the duvet back, pushes her down on the bed. He's on top of her, her skirt is rucked up, his hand is in her knickers.

"Wait..." she says breathlessly. "Let's..."

"Yes," he says, standing up and stripping off his shirt and tie, undoing his belt, taking off his trousers. She undresses quickly, slides under the duvet, and tries to forget it's Paula's bed, yet at the same time wonders which side is hers. Probably the one with the earplugs, glass of water and spectacle case on it. The other side has an alarm clock and a book. She will have taken hers with her.

"For God's sake, stop thinking about her!" she tells herself, but it's impossible. She can smell Paula's perfume or face cream on the sheets, see mascara stains on the pillow next to her head. Maybe Mark likes the idea of sex in the bed he shares with his wife. Maybe it adds spice. Maybe he's brought other women here. Maybe this is what turns him on. He climbs on top of her again and thrusts into her quickly; he's desperate, almost rough. She forgets about Paula, about the other women, as she wraps her legs around his back, grinds her hips into his, claws at his back, taking care not to dig her fingernails too deeply.

It's over very quickly. He ties the condom at the top like a balloon and wraps a tissue around it, presumably to dispose of it in a bin later, like the practiced philanderer he is. They both glance surreptitiously at the clock and their watches as they dress quickly. Then they go back down the stairs and get into the car. Anyone watching, anyone wondering if Mark Exton of 63 Sherford Park (the one with the For Sale sign outside) is bringing someone home for a quick session in his lunch hour, would never believe there had been enough time. But neither would there have been time for a prospective buyer to view the house. As he reverses out, she recognises the Hardy's logo on the For Sale sign and wonders idly if Paula is allowed to handle her own house sale.

"Where are you moving to?" she asks. It suddenly strikes her with a jolt that he might say "Penzance" or "Manchester".

She's surprised at the relief that floods through her when he says, "Oh, it'll never happen. It's another one of Paula's pipe dreams. This is the problem with her being an estate agent. She's got the details of a house out near Wiveliscombe. A big rambling old place that needs loads of work on it. She hasn't thought it through. The twins won't want to live all the way out there. All their friends are here. They can walk to most, cycle to others. Out there, they'll be miles from anywhere. Also, we're not the sort to do up a house. She had this idea about moving to Italy once, buying a *trullo* in Puglia—you know, one of those little roundhouses. Then she realised she hadn't thought about the children's schooling. I just go along with it, leave her to get it out of her system…"

She likes to hear him complaining about Paula. While he had been in the loo, she had opened Paula's wardrobe and seen the business suits and shirts hanging there, along with the long dresses, and the jeans and trousers. This woman who shares Mark's life, this woman who is the mother of his children, this woman she doesn't know. She doesn't consider her a rival—why should she? She doesn't love Mark, she doesn't want to love him or for him to love her, and she certainly doesn't want a future with him or anyone else. She's done that once already. It only ends in tears. And she has enough friends who've found the same. Oh, there are the odd one or two who are married *"till death us do part"*, but even they have times when they seem to hate each other; years even, when they were going along on parallel lines, bickering at each other, staying together only because the alternative was too much upheaval. So she doesn't look to the future, to their relationship lasting much longer than the summer. But it doesn't stop her wondering about what Mark does when he isn't with her, what he says to Paula, the excuses he makes to her, to his children, to his friends who were expecting to meet him when he's meeting Carly instead. The friends she doesn't know and never will, any more than he can ever know hers. Not that she has many yet, but nevertheless, they will have to be kept in a separate compartment from him.

She didn't deliberately choose Mark, of course. He just parachuted into her life as though it was destined. But sometimes she thinks she shouldn't have started such a complicated relationship. She should have waited, made other friends first; friends who would have known unattached men, men with no baggage, no areas of their life that she couldn't be part of. She could end it now, of course, give herself a chance to meet this mythical single male friend of one of her new friends. She can hear herself telling Mark he should "give his marriage a chance". However, she knows she won't do it. The sex is good. He's a considerate lover; he makes her feel good, cherished, and special. And they get on: they have the same sense of humour and like many of the same things. There are things they disagree on, but it's good to have some differences, something to discuss. Most of all, she just likes being with him. It's not doing anyone any harm, she tells herself. He's obviously done it before and will do it again. And what Paula doesn't know won't hurt her. Sometimes she sees him glance at his phone, frown, and then type a reply. Maybe it's Paula, asking where he is. Carly wonders how he keeps their messages and calls private—the ones Paula mustn't see at any cost. Maybe there's no way she'd ever look at his phone. Even so, he must delete every single one the moment he sends or receives it. A small part of Carly feels guilty about the loyal wife at home, waiting unsuspectingly for her husband to return. But maybe Paula's doing the same; in a conference hotel last night or today, between those boring repetitive training sessions.

That evening, Carly looks for Paula on Facebook. She's not hard to find: *Paula Exton, Hardy's Estate Agents.* She has her own business page as well as a personal profile, her privacy level set sensibly high to avoid the two being confused. The business page has the logo of Hardy's but there's a photo of her on her personal profile: a thin-faced, thin-lipped woman, her dark hair cut professionally short. She's wearing one of those crisp designer shirts Carly had seen hanging in the wardrobe.

Carly may not be jealous but Mark, illogically, is. With no one to be jealous of in her present life, he's jealous of anyone in her past.

"Is this your grandmother's wedding ring?" he asks one evening, idly twisting the plain gold band on her right ring finger. She could lie, but why should she?

"No," she says. "It's mine."

She couldn't bear to take it off, couldn't bear to think of one of her last links with Graham shoved at the back of a drawer somewhere, never to see the light of day again. Anyway, she argued to herself, her marriage might be over but it was still a part of her life. Why should she be ashamed of it? So, with the aid of a bar of soap, she had forced it over the bigger knuckle on her right hand. Now she can't get it off again. She even wears her engagement ring with it sometimes–the antique diamond solitaire she and Graham had bought in a little shop in the Cotswolds. It was always a bit big and she's glad now that she never had it re-sized. No one else has noticed, and she's surprised Mark has. But he's noticed a lot of things lately: the new top she bought, the inch she had cut off her hair, the new perfume she's started wearing. They're lying in bed naked as he twists the ring on her finger, in that quiet and sated time that follows sex. Carly is on her side, Mark curled around her back. She can't see his face, but she can tell from his silence when she tells him it's her own wedding ring that he's not pleased. She knows that if she turns to look at him, his face will have that stern unsmiling look he has when he's talking about Paula.

"What about before?" he asks suddenly.

"Before what?" she says, confused.

"Before you were married. You must have had other boyfriends. That boy at college—Greg what's-his-name—did you sleep with him?"

She almost laughs. It seems so absurd to be jealous of a boy he taught at college. "No,'" she answers. She can't imagine Caroline would ever have slept with Greg, not while they were both at home anyway. And obviously they split up after that.

"What about at uni then?" he asks.

"Oh, you know…" she says vaguely.

"I want to know," he says. "Tell me."

"Mark, it doesn't matter. It was a long time ago…"

"Please."

Graham had been the same, badgering her until she told him everything. She could make something up: she'd told enough lies already, a few more wouldn't make any difference. But she doesn't.

"You know what it's like at uni," she says. "There were a couple of mistakes…"

She feels him nod his head against her shoulder.

"Then there was Will. We met in the second year. He was doing Sociology but he never took it seriously. We were quite different. By the third year, we were already drifting apart. I worked hard: there were evening clinics, not to mention course work and revision. He liked to party. In fact, I never saw him do any work at all. Somehow he scraped through with a third-class degree. We talked about living together in London, but then I got the job in Reading, and he didn't want to live there. Which was probably just as well because he had no job and was back living with his parents. I went to stay there a few times. They were … well, they weren't like my parents. God, I sound like such a snob. They thought I was stuck up. We began to seem poles apart. He came to stay with me, but he had no money and I did; I had a good job, good prospects … it was hopeless. Some of my friends had the same problem. It was one of those relationships that worked fine at uni, when we were on a level playing field, but didn't work out in the real world."

He says nothing for a while. In fact, he's so quiet, she wonders if he's fallen asleep. Then he suddenly says. "I don't make a habit of this sort of thing."

"What?" she says. She'd been thinking about Will;

remembering his voice, his laugh, the first time they made love, how good it was at uni, how bad it was at his parents' house in Tooting.

"Having affairs," he says. "I don't have affairs."

Every instinct tells her not to believe him but she says nothing.

"There've been…" He pauses. "You know … casual things. At conferences, when you know you won't see them again…" He stops again. "That night I met you," he goes on, "I was meeting someone else. I think you knew."

"You said, I think, or at least you implied…"

"Yes, well, she didn't turn up. Thank God…" He gives a shaky laugh. "Otherwise I wouldn't have met you."

She turns over to him. Their lips meet. Their bodies slot together.

She assumes that's it, and that they don't need to talk about it again. However, a week or so later, he suddenly says, "How long were you married?"

They're sitting on the balcony of her flat. The wet day has given way to a cloudy but dry evening. It's beginning to get dark, the branches of the trees standing out blackly against the pale grey sky. She's just made coffee for both of them.

"Ten years," she says, setting the tray with the coffee down on the low table between them.

"That's a long time," he says. "I'm surprised you didn't make it work. Most people have got used to each other by then." He spoons two sugars into his coffee. "Did you love him?"

"Of course I did," she says slightly impatiently. "I wouldn't have married him otherwise."

"And you got on? You liked the same things?"

"Yes."

"So why did you split up?"

"Lots of things. You know, you're married, you know what it's like…"

"Yes, but…"

"Look, can we talk about something else? It's in the past.

It doesn't matter. What matters is here and now." She reaches out and puts her hand on his arm, waiting for him to look at her and smile, but he has a stubborn sulky look on his face.

"Did he meet someone else?" he persists. "Or did you?"

"No, nothing like that. He just… I don't think he loved me anymore."

"But you still loved him. You love him now?"

"For God's sake, Mark!" she explodes. "Are you like this with all the women you sleep with? I don't ask you about them or about Paula! It's got nothing to do with you. It's over. In the past. Can't we just enjoy what we've got now?"

It's the nearest they've got to an argument. He gets up quickly, almost spilling the coffee, and goes back into the sitting room. She hears the rattle of his keys as he grabs them from the table, swoops up his mobile phone, and picks his jacket up from the back of the chair. If it were Graham, she'd be running after him, begging him to stay, but she's done all that. She swore she'd never do it again.

She feels a pang though as she washes up the coffee cups. She's not sure if it's just the thought of the loneliness ahead of her, if it's the fact she's got to start all over again with someone else, or if she's genuinely becoming fond of Mark. She knows they should stop now, before the arguments start; the misunderstanding, the sniping, the bickering. *"It was fun,"* she should say, *"but let's call it a day."*

She should do it now before he does it to her. She puts the cups and saucers away, pours herself a glass of wine, then reaches for her phone. Her heart sinks when she sees she has a message from him. He's beaten her to it. But no: *"I'm sorry,"* it reads. *"I was stupid. Please forgive me. M xx"*

She sits with the phone in her hand for a while. She should still finish it, of course. She even starts the message. But she can't bring herself to send it. The thought of being on her own again is just too much.

"Of course." She types instead. *"Let's just forget it."*

So they're back where they were.

The cold wet May gives way to a warm fine June. Her

flat, closed up all day, is stifling in the evenings. In any case, it seems a crime to be indoors on the glorious balmy evenings. Mark picks her up from work, and they drive up onto the hills, or down to the coast if there's time. Time is something they never seem to have enough of as Mark's always looking at his watch. Carly has no idea what he says to Paula. Maybe she doesn't mind what he does. Maybe they lead quite separate lives. She knows some couples do. She worked with a woman once whose husband arranged his weekends without any thought to what she might be doing.

She looks forward to these long light evenings. Mark might work in a classroom all day but at least he has open windows that allow him to look outside. He can even go outside in his lunch hour, no doubt eying up the pretty sixteen-year-olds as they hitch up their skirts and roll down their tops to sunbathe in the school grounds. But Carly is stuck in a dark room all day. She can only draw the curtains back briefly between patients, and the hour she has for lunch is not enough to make the most of the warm sunny weather.

Carly brings shorts and a t-shirt to work to change into; Mark has to make do with taking off his jacket and tie. As she gets into the car next to him, she sees him run an appreciative eye over her slim bare legs and arms. Mark is the sort of man who admires women openly. She's noticed the type he likes: tall and willowy. Since they've been together, she's been even more careful about what she eats: with enormous willpower, she refuses the cakes and biscuits Madison and Hannah wolf down mid-morning. It's also easier because she lives on her own, meaning there's no one to tempt her to eat calorie-laden desserts. Pilates classes have stopped for the summer, but she does some of the exercises every day. She also walks down to the village and back most evenings, and swims in the outdoor pool when it's warm enough.

"You'll be going over to your parents sometime soon, I suppose?" Mark asks one day.

"Not this year," she says, desperately thinking of a reason

why she wouldn't go. Then it strikes her. "I can't really afford it, with the move and everything."

He raises his eyebrows but says nothing. Perhaps he'd been assuming she'd had a good divorce settlement, or that she was paid well. Neither is true: there was very little left once the solicitors' fees were paid, and she took a huge drop in salary when she moved back down here from the more affluent commuter belt. But he doesn't pursue it. She already knows he's taking the family to a villa in Umbria for two weeks in July.

"I shall miss you, Caro," he had said when he'd told her.

"Me too," she'd said. Not just because he expected it but because she knows she will. Seeing Mark gives her something to look forward to and she likes being special to someone, even if it's only temporary. She hasn't stopped him calling her Caro. She doesn't want this emotional intimacy but it's happening anyway. He knows what she likes to eat and drink, the places she'll want to go, he puts the music on in the car that she likes. They don't need to be always talking, sometimes they sit in silence—then when one of them speaks, they find they were thinking the same thing. They don't need to be having sex all the time either. These summer evenings are about companionship, togetherness. After a day cooped up inside, it's liberating to be driving along in the evening sunshine, walking along the beach or the clifftop, stopping at a pub for a drink outside. They're risky though. Mark and Carly aren't the only townies to escape to the coast on a summer's evening. He doesn't put his arm around her or hold her hand in public, waiting for the path they're walking on to be empty or a sheltered part of the beach before he reaches out and kisses her. If they stop for a drink or something to eat, she sees him scan the pub car park to see if there's a car he recognises. Inside, his eyes travel around the room nervously before they sit down.

Though she looks forward to seeing Mark, she still thinks about Graham. Not a day goes by when he doesn't come into her mind unexpectedly. When her mind is idle: drifting off to sleep at night, dozing for those few extra minutes in the morning, driving, or during a routine eye exam. She finds herself calling his name in her mind, thinking about the good times they had, pushing the bad times to the back of her thoughts. She wishes she could turn back the clock, do things differently. She'll never forget the bewildered, disappointed look on Graham's face.

"I can't understand what you were thinking of," he said.

"I was thinking of *you*," she said. "I just wanted to make things easier for you."

She has to remind herself that things were going wrong long before then. She'd already made plans to leave. But she never wanted to go like that. Not with Graham hating her. She had seen them having a civilised, amicable break-up; they wouldn't wrangle over money or what belonged to whom. They would stay friends, live near each other maybe, go around with the same crowd of people. Like they did before they were married. He'd look over at her. She'd see regret in his eyes that he'd been so foolish, so bad-tempered and over-bearing; that he'd allowed her to slip away from him.

She's schooled herself not to ask about him whenever Tina rings. Luckily, Tina doesn't seem keen to talk about him either. She still says she doesn't see much of him, but Carly knows it's unlikely. It would be nice to think that Tina's trying not to hurt Carly's feelings, but it's probably her own feelings she's protecting.

Tina has been asking for ages when she can come and stay.

"I haven't got a spare room," Carly prevaricates.

Part of her wants to see Tina again—she is her sister, after all. She's the only one who knows her, knows all about her, knows what she's been through. And she wants to show her flat off to her, show her that she's managing fine without Graham. But why can't she come and stay when it suits Carly, not when it suits *her*?

"I don't mind," Tina says. "I can sleep on the sofa."

"It's a sofa bed," Carly is forced to concede. She had realised when she furnished the flat that in the future, she might have friends that wanted to stay. "But it's a tiny flat. There's not much privacy for you."

"I don't mind that either. And you said you've got a pool? It sounds lovely. Just what I need, a break from everything."

She tries to persuade her to come in the last two weeks of July, when Mark is away with his family. However, it doesn't work that way. "Everyone else wants July," Tina complains. "I can only get August."

"Late August then," Carly suggests. "It'll be cooler. Less crowded maybe." Though that was unlikely, as Mark had told her the traffic was a nightmare all through the summer holidays. "Better still, September," she says hopefully. "When the schools go back."

But no, it has to be the beginning of August.

"I'm not sure I can get time off," Carly says doubtfully. "It's quite short notice." But Tina sounds so upset and disappointed that her conscience pricks her. It's too longstanding, the habit of looking after Tina, of pandering to her every whim. "Don't worry," she says quickly, "I'm sure it won't be a problem."

And it isn't. No one wants school holidays. Bob and Lesley are still squabbling over a week in late September.

"But *you* had *that* week last year." Carly hears Bob saying like a spoilt child. "Clare wants to go to Portugal. It's cooler at that time of year, and the golf courses are less busy."

"I don't see why you can't go in October," Lesley rallies. "It's cooler still then…"

The first week in August is, of course, the week that Mark is due back from Italy. Luckily, Tina can only have a week's holiday, but that will still make it three weeks before Carly and Mark can see each other.

The two weeks Mark's in Italy drag by with nothing to look forward to. Not even his usual daily texts. He does manage one on the day he arrives, making her heart leap and colour flood to her face as his name appears on her phone.

"I miss you," it says, but it's enough.

She saves it to look at when she's feeling lonely. And she has to make do with it because, after that, there's nothing. There may be no signal where he is now, she excuses him in her mind, and the villa may not have Wi-Fi. Or his wife and children are with him all the time and he doesn't get a chance to message her.

"Or they're all getting on so well, he hasn't given you a thought," a small voice says.

She pictures them all sitting-around the pool in the sunshine, Paula getting a beautiful tan that Mark will find irresistible. They'll visit little Italian towns with cobbled streets. The children, separated from their iPhones and iPads, will find a new interest in their surroundings. They'll walk along together, the perfect family, indulging in the silly in-jokes that all families have. Laughing and talking. In the evenings, they'll sit around the dinner table, eating pasta and salad that one of the kids has cooked. Afterwards, they'll play games. In this renewed family atmosphere, influenced by the romance of the Italian countryside and culture, Mark will fall back in love with Paula. They'll make love every night. How can he resist this new, beautifully tanned, relaxed version of his wife—the wife he'd forgotten he had? Appreciating her and his family anew, he will text the day he gets back.

"I feel I should give my marriage a chance," he'll say. *"For the sake of the children."*

Jealousy surges through her, a feeling she knows only too well from being with Graham. But this is different. She's not jealous of Paula like she was of Graham's lovers. Graham *chose* those other women over her, chose to spend his time with them rather than her. She recognises Paula has priority over her. She's Mark's wife. It's not exactly jealousy of Paula or the children, they have a right to have time with Mark. But it's time *she* wants.

She comforts herself by remembering how Mark had said he was dreading the holiday, how the children always argued and that however hard he tried to get things right, Paula grumbled about everything: the flight, the villa, the heat, the food.

The week before Tina arrives, Carly hurls herself into a flurry of activity: vacuuming the flat throughout, bleaching the sinks, buying food she knows Tina likes. She gets a bunch of lilies for the sitting-room table. She even removes some of the china from the cupboard in the sitting room in case Tina wants to put any clothes in there, squashing it into the kitchen cupboard next to the tins and boxes of cereals. Then she makes space in her wardrobe for anything she may want to hang up. She's pleased with the result. The flat has the all-important wow-factor, including that lovely distant blue view of the Blackdown Hills, with the tall outline of the Wellington monument just visible on the horizon. How could Tina not be impressed?

Two days before she's due to arrive, Carly goes down with a cold. Struggling into work, sneezing and croaky-voiced, she almost rings to put Tina off. But she knows Tina will make such a fuss and anyway, she may be better in a few days.

Tina arrives with the usual drama.

"Nightmare journey!" she grumbles the moment she walks through the door, wheeling her suitcase into the centre of the flat and leaving it there, carefully ensuring she doesn't notice when Carly moves it out of sight behind the sofa, where she's left enough room for Tina to unpack if she needs to.

"You need to know I'm not that well..." Carly begins.

Tina would have had to be really dim not to notice her still-slightly croaky voice, her blocked up nose, and the way she constantly searches for a tissue to wipe it.

"Yes," she says impatiently. "Well, we can talk about that later." Then she launches into a description of her journey.

She doesn't seem to notice the vase of lilies, the tray of tea and biscuits set out for her, or the windows open onto the balcony, where chairs are set out for them. She breaks off suddenly. "You've lost weight."

"No, it's just that you've put it on," Carly wants to say. But she doesn't want to start squabbling with Tina the moment she arrives. Although they will no doubt fall out before the week is up.

"I don't think so," she says instead. "Just toned up, that's all. Pilates, swimming, walking. And I'm careful what I eat…"

It's still hot and Tina has worn a strappy top and shorts for the drive down. She's always been bigger than Carly but no one could call her fat: a womanly figure, curvaceous, the sort many men (though not Mark) seem to find attractive. She was a plump baby, a chubby toddler. At fourteen, when Carly suddenly shot up, Tina stayed at the height she'd reached as a twelve-year-old, developing a generous bust and wide hips that the flat-chested Carly envied. Now, at thirty-six, the thin straps of the t-shirt cuts into the rounded flesh of her white shoulders, and the tops of her arms jiggle when she moves. Her thighs bulge through the sensible knee-length shorts and her calves and ankles are rounded. She had beautiful long white-blonde hair when they were little; it fell in soft waves down her back. Carly with her long, dead straight dark hair, used to be so envious. But years of daily washing and straightening have taken its toll on Tina's lovely hair, turning it dull and brittle. She wears it shoulder-length but it's so fine that it looks much shorter. There's no denying though that Tina is pretty: she has a lovely face; soft, round, girlish with pale blue eyes, a little upturned nose, a curving mouth, and a dimple in her left cheek that comes and goes when she smiles.

"I thought we could go to Dunster tomorrow," Carly says. Her cold is definitely a lot better and she feels she should make an effort, particularly since Tina doesn't even seem to have noticed. "It's not far, and there's a castle and a pretty little village..."

"Oh, I don't know..." Tina whines. "Can't we just stay here and relax? I've been in the car all day today..."

"I can drive," Carly says.

As far as Carly's concerned, it's settled. She sets her alarm for eight o'clock and is showered and dressed, make-up on and ready by eight-thirty. There's no sound from the sitting room and she opens the door cautiously. She knows Tina works long hours—maybe she's being unreasonable to expect her to get up early on her holiday. Carly creeps past the sleeping shape in the sofa bed, almost falling over the suitcase that's once more in the middle of the room, but open now, its contents spewing all over the floor. Tina's clothes, including a capacious bra and a G-string that would go around Carly twice, are hanging on the back of one of the dining chairs that Tina has moved next to her as a bedside table. A glass of water, a book and her spectacles sit on it.

The sound of the kettle boiling wakes Tina up. "I'd love coffee if you're making it!" she calls through.

"It's not a hotel!" Carly calls back, but she keeps her voice light. Their mother used to say that to them when they asked what was for lunch or dinner. It's one of those silly family jokes.

She searches for the cafetiere that she'd pushed to the back of one of the cramped cupboards when Mark went away (she only drinks coffee when he's here), wishing she'd remembered Tina likes coffee in the mornings and not tea.

Tina is under the covers again, just the top of her blonde head visible, so Carly puts the coffee and her own mug of tea on the table and pulls back the curtains.

"Oh God, do you *have to?*" Tina groans as sunlight floods the room.

"Sorry, have you got a headache or something?"

"No, it's just... What time is it?" Tina reaches for her glasses to look at her phone.

"Quarter to nine," Carly supplies.

"I'm on holiday," Tina groans. "I thought I'd have a lie-in."

"We should get going soon. So the traffic's not too bad. And the parking…"

"Can't we go tomorrow?"

"I thought we'd go to Bath tomorrow. The weather's due to break. We could go shopping…"

"Oh, okay…"

But by eleven, she's only just showered, and is still wandering around the flat in leggings and a loose top that presumably she isn't considering wearing to go out for the day, her hair wrapped up in a towel on top of her head.

"I can't find my contact lenses," she mutters, throwing yet more things out of the open suitcase.

Tina is quite short-sighted. Without her contact lenses and with no make-up on, her hair hidden under the turban-towel accentuating her rounded face, her eyes look small and piggy. These are the times when Carly doesn't feel jealous of her pretty, oh-so-feminine, helpless little sister, with that ability from the day she was born to wind people around her little finger. Instead, she has the same sudden almost-uncontrollable urge that she used to get when they were teenagers: she wants to grab her by the shoulders, shake her and scream, "For God's sake, get a move on, you selfish cow! Can't you ever think of anyone but yourself?"

In desperation, she walks out onto the balcony, sits down on one of the chairs, and takes out her phone. She was going to open Facebook and have a scroll through other people's posts to see how they're spending this sunny day, but she sees she has a text. Without even opening it, she knows it's from Mark. Her heart leaps.

"Just back." It reads. *"Can't wait to see you. When can we meet?"*

"My sister's here, remember?" she texts back. He can't possibly have forgotten but his eagerness is flattering.

"Can't you make some excuse?" he texts back instantly.

"She's only just got here." She adds a smiley face. *"We'll have to wait till next week."*

"You have no idea how much I want to see you," he replies.

She puts her phone in her pocket and goes back into the room with a smile on her face. "Did you find them?" she asks Tina. "Look, let's forget Dunster. I don't really feel up to it. And it'll be hot and crowded with screaming kids anyway. Where's your bikini?" She joins Tina, who is surrounded by the detritus of her suitcase. "Let's go to the pool instead."

The health farm is a nineteenth-century house converted into a hotel and spa, with an indoor pool, a Jacuzzi and treatment rooms, a gym, a bar, and a dining room. The grounds retain the atmosphere of a once-monied estate, with a landscaped garden, fountain and ornamental lakes. The outdoor pool, with its sun loungers and parasols, is surrounded by an old red-brick wall that once enclosed the vegetable garden.

The weather that had been forecast to break—with thunderstorms and rain—remains stubbornly hot and dry. The itinerary Carly had drawn up in her mind is quickly shelved, as every day follows the same pattern of lazy lie-ins and days by the pool. Doing nothing has certainly helped her cold improve and while it's not at all what she had in mind, Carly has to admit it's more like being on holiday. The apartment itself, despite, or maybe because of Tina's possessions strewn all over the place, feels like a holiday home. She's given up trying to tidy up after her, it just makes finding everything more difficult. Tina seems to have some sort of logic in her messiness and knows where everything is.

"God knows how she manages at home," Carly thinks.

But then, there's usually a man around to organise things for her, get her breakfast, make sure she gets to work on time. Not at the moment though. Alan left six months ago and Tina has declared she'll stay single, at least for a while.

They go to the pool every day, lying side by side, their eyes closed. Tina has one of those bodies that looks better with fewer clothes on: her firm, generous breasts perch pertly above her bikini top, her waist looks slimmer without anything around it. Her hips are full and rounded. Lying down, her bulging tummy disappears into nothingness. Her hair is twisted up into a clip, a few fine strands falling around her face. She looks stunning. There are very few men at the health farm, but the odd one or two who have been coaxed into going by their wife or girlfriend cast covert glances at her. Women look too, envying her curves, her pretty face, and her almost-film star confidence.

Carly comforts herself that her stomach is flatter, her thighs and the tops of her arms are firmer, and her hair is longer and thicker. Compared to Tina though, she feels flat-chested, big-boned and ugly.

The physical proximity yet inability to look at each other lends an intimacy that reminds Carly of their childhood bedtime talks back home in Haydon Road, Tiverton; snatched whispered conversations punctuated by stifled giggles when one of their parents would call up, "Settle down and go to sleep!"

When they were younger, there were silly guessing games in the bedroom blackness, graduating as they got older to conversations about boys and periods. Here on the sun loungers, they're joined by visitors to the health farm: their talk is of the treatments they've had, the service in the health farm (which never seems very good despite its popularity), and the usual domestic problems that women talk about.

To the background of this chatter and the occasional gentle splash and restrained shriek of surprise as someone enters the cold water, Tina relates a litany of work problems. As usual, this leaves Carly mystified as to how she ever made it to such a position, let alone held it down. Yet she sails through every work appraisal, so she can't be as overwhelmed by everything as she makes out. Carly would love to be a fly on the wall when Tina's at work: maybe then she'd see the real Tina: the competent, confident, professional she must be as opposed to the helpless little girl she portrays to everyone else.

It's not a coincidence that they have both ended up

dealing with eyes. When Tina saw the position of Diabetic Retinopathy Screener advertised, she asked Carly what it would entail. Carly explained that diabetic retinopathy is a complication of diabetes that affects the back of the eye. The screener's job is to photograph and grade the images for the consultant to look at. It's a very responsible job with a lot of kudos and a corresponding increase in salary. Tina has done well. When Carly does an eye examination, she examines the back of the eye and often sees cases of diabetic retinopathy: this gives them something in common. It gives Tina something in common with Graham too and before long, they're talking about him.

"He's back with Lucy," Tina says. "I didn't want to tell you, but..."

"No, it's okay." Carly somehow manages to keep her voice steady, but she's grateful for the dark glasses that hide the tears that have sprung to her eyes. "Let's face it, he never really split up from her, we both know that. Ten years of marriage to me, and he's still joined to her at the hip."

"Well, there's Edward, isn't there? Graham will always have to go on seeing her..."

"She had him deliberately, just to keep Graham. He's so blind he just can't see it." The usual bitterness has crept into her voice, the bitterness that Graham hated. *"You don't need to say that,"* he used to say. *"You've got me now. I'll never leave you..."*

Obviously, he said the same thing to Lucy. And to Tina. And to a whole host of other women that she'll never probably know about.

"I don't know why I ever married him..." she says. "I must've been mad."

"I thought you'd nailed it," Tina says, a note of wistfulness in her voice. "You seemed so happy."

"You didn't exactly help," Carly thinks, but she knows it wasn't all Tina's fault. Graham was hard to resist once he set his mind on someone. "It would never have worked," she says out loud. "He hasn't got the staying power."

"Oh, I don't know. I reckon it might've been okay if you hadn't…"

"I know, I know," Carly says quickly. "Please. I don't want to talk about it…"

"Okay," Tina says lightly. She says nothing for a while, then suddenly she rolls onto her side to face Carly, props herself up on her elbow, and nudges her.

"What?" Carly says, opening her eyes. This is usually Tina's cue to bitch about someone wearing a bikini who really shouldn't, or someone with a weird swimming style or a hideous pool-side outfit. Her fair hair, lit by the sunshine, shines like a halo around her face

"So, you seeing anyone else yet?" she asks.

"No," Carly says firmly.

"Oh, come on…" For a moment, Tina looks the image of Mum; that same look she used to give her when she didn't believe her.

"I'm not!" Carly lies. It's none of Tina's business.

"You're constantly looking at your phone," Tina says confidently. "With a soppy secret smile on your face. I'm not stupid. And there's that super-sexy underwear in your drawer…"

Trust Tina to go rifling through her things. And trust her not to care about admitting it. "You shouldn't be snooping!" Carly says.

"I was looking for tissues."

"Yeah, yeah…"

"So who's the mystery man? Am I going to meet him?"

"No," Carly shakes her head. "It's early days yet."

"Not another optician, I hope?"

Carly laughs. "If you saw the opticians I worked with, you wouldn't even ask." The thought of Bob Gray even considering having sex is hilarious to her, but obviously he has had his moments of passion, otherwise he wouldn't have the two children he's so proud of.

Trailing back from the pool every day, smelling of chlorine and carrying damp towels, sunglasses and books,

Carly has to turn her mind to something to eat. She bought enough food for breakfast, assuming they would eat out the rest of the time. But they spend as long as possible in the warm evening sunshine, staving off the time they have to return to the stuffy flat and by the time they've both showered and dried their hair, it's getting too late to go out for a meal. It seems easier just to put something in the oven; something simple she can just serve with a salad. Even this, of course, involves Carly in preparation, and she has to drive down to the village a couple of times for supplies. If only Tina might think to do it for her sometimes. But after her shower, she sits around in nothing but a loose t-shirt, watching television or reading, whilst waiting for Carly's "It's ready!" before she makes a move.

After dinner, Tina collapses onto the sofa, leaving Carly to carry everything out and then calling out half-heartedly, "Can I help?"

When Carly replies on the first occasion, "It's okay. There's not much room out here and I know where everything goes," she takes that to mean she doesn't need to ask again. So night after night, Carly washes up, dries up, and puts everything away to the background sound of the television or Tina talking on her mobile to one of her friends.

Two days before Tina is due to go back, Carly plucks up the courage to ask the question she should have asked the moment Tina arrived. It's not the sort of thing she can ask down by the pool with other people around. She's not sure what Tina's reaction might be. She might burst into tears, become hysterical. Carly can't bear the idea of a scene in public. She waits until after dinner one evening. They're sitting on the balcony. It's just beginning to get dark. They can hear the occasional trickle of water as the neighbour in the ground floor flat below them waters her tubs of geraniums. She's hung a string of solar lights from the wisteria that climbs up the wall on her patio, and they suddenly burst into a pattern of starry white lights.

Carly clears her throat nervously, swallows drily. "Do you want to go to Tiverton while you're down here?" she asks in what she hopes is a casual voice.

"No," Tina shakes her head. "It's too soon."

"It's six years," Carly wants to say. But of course, Tina knows that. "We should," she says instead, more firmly this time. "We should go and see Auntie Louise and Auntie Sharon. They'd like to see us."

But Tina just shakes her head. "I can't," she says.

Carly doesn't want to look at her. She doesn't want to see if she's crying. Her own face is burning. Tears prick her eyes. They don't talk about it again.

The next day brings the promised rain, following a night of rumbling thunder and flashes of lightning. The gloomy grey day is depressing after the long hot days of blue skies and sunshine. The apartment no longer looks like a carefree holiday let. It just looks a mess: Tina's clothes and possessions on every single surface; her dirty coffee mug from the night before, and her glass of water on the chair by the un-made sofa bed; the stylish tall lilies Carly had been so pleased with are now turning brownish yellow, dropping petals and little blobs of pollen onto the surface of the table.

"What would you like to do today?" Carly asks.

"Oh, I don't know," Tina says. "It's too wet to go out. And I think I'm getting your cold." She speaks in what Carly knows by now to be a deliberately croaky way, designed to get attention.

"We could go shopping," Carly says jauntily, as though suggesting a treat to a child. "To Cribbs Causeway. It's all undercover."

"Oh, I don't know..." Tina says again in that pathetic voice.

But they go anyway and it's not a bad day. Tina buys a top and Carly gets a pair of jeans. She doesn't need them but she feels she should buy something. They're late leaving, and make do with coffee and muffins in a café instead of lunch.

Tina offers to buy dinner in a pub on the way home as a thank you for having her to stay. In fact, the whole holiday has made Carly realise what it must be like to have a sister who's also a friend. They've managed a week without arguing, something they've scarcely ever done before. And while it's true they've skirted around some issues, directly avoided others, they have also talked about some things they don't often talk about. By the end of the week though, she knows it's enough sister-time together. Tina can scarcely begin a sentence without mentioning herself—"I think... I feel... I find..."—and although she has asked about Carly, she still manages to bring everything back to herself and her own perceived issues. She leaves with the same drama as she arrived— packing at the last moment, and leaving Carly's sitting room in chaos.

Carly is stripping the sofa bed when her phone rings. She knows without looking that it's Mark. He has messaged every day since he's been back.

"Are you having a good time?' he had asked generously. *"Can you send me a pic of your sister? I'd love to see her. Bet she's not as pretty as you."*

"I can't take a photo of her just like that," she had messaged back. Luckily, he didn't pursue it.

He's on school holidays, of course. *"I've got a list of chores,"* he messages. From Paula, obviously, though he discreetly doesn't say so. *"The twins are in bed till midday. They don't know what mornings are."*

"It's good to hear your voice again," he says as she answers the phone. "I've missed you, Caro." This, in a low gentle voice that sends a thrill through her.

"I've missed you too," she says, knowing that it's the truth. The three weeks apart seem like an age, and the furtive texts since he's been back have only heightened their separation.

"I can't wait to see you," he says. "How about tomorrow?"

"I'm not sure which lunch hour I'll have. I'll text you…"

"I can do any time. I just want to see you. Even for five minutes…"

News awaits Carly when she walks back into work: Madison has upped and left without giving notice, leaving them all in the lurch.

"She's gone to work for EyesRight," Hannah whispers to her. "Much better pay—good for her! I'd go too if I could…"

"I wouldn't be so sure," Carly says. "I've worked in a multiple. It's all targets and appraisals… She should have given notice though."

"They needed her straight away, and she needed the money. She's moving in with Rob and wants to buy some new stuff for the kitchen. You know what men are like. And things for the lounge—cushions and things…."

The few minutes' muted chatter is cut short by the door opening and the phone ringing at the same time. Carly reaches for the phone and Hannah pastes on her smile of welcome.

Bob and Lesley are in a state. Drafted in to do reception work at lunchtimes and in busy periods, they're like fish out of water. Every optometrist starts on the reception desk. As such, they can answer the phone, make appointments, and fit a pair of spectacle frames just as competently as any ancillary staff. But once they're qualified, they prefer the sanctuary and peace and quiet of their testing room to the hurly-burly of the reception desk.

Carly, however, doesn't mind working on reception as she started at an independent opticians. Hudson Opticians hadn't been established long when Carly applied for the pre-registration position in her final year at uni. Graham was the only optometrist and they had become really busy. A newly qualified optometrist may be slower at first but, by the end of the year, they are pretty much up to speed. And they didn't have to pay her a high salary. However, there was no position for her once she qualified. She had enjoyed her year there, not only because she was working with Graham, but because of the variety. She liked the very fact that she could be called to work on reception, do a repair, or adjustment to someone's glasses. She missed it when she moved to a multiple and became nothing more than an automaton that examined people's eyes, her half-hour examination time cut to twenty minutes to squeeze the maximum amount of work out of her.

There were advantages of working in a multiple of course: no one expected you to clean your own examination room, change the light bulbs or batteries in your equipment, or empty the bins; you knew you would finish dead on five-thirty, when the lights would go off and the store would close. No waiting for your last patient to make their mind up about which letters are clearer on the chart or which frame they like best. But in a multiple, as she'd told Hannah, there are targets and appraisals and salaries. The pressure is enormous. If you don't perform, you have to explain yourself. These things are important in an independent, of course: business is business. But in Hudson Opticians, like in Pender and Brown, the figures took a back seat behind professionalism and patient care. Here the store is called a practice and the customer is a patient; someone treated with deference, not someone to be persuaded into buying the most expensive frames and lenses. This is why she chose an independent this time—although she was so desperate, she would have taken work in another multiple, or even a locum agency if necessary. They would have been more particular about references though. She was so lucky that Pender and Brown were just as desperate to have her as she was to be there. They didn't question why she gave references from her pre-registration year at Hudson Opticians and Specs Express, where she had done her summer work experience placement the year before, and not from her present employer, even though she'd had the ready-prepared excuse that she didn't want Optimum Vision to know she was thinking of leaving yet.

With Madison gone, the reception desk is a nightmare.

Telephones ring, patients queue up, paperwork is behind, NHS forms wait to be processed, and patients' records can't be found. Rachel hares around, a harassed look on her face, arriving long before the practice opens, eschewing lunch hours and staying on late. Bob and Lesley flap around on reception, doing little more than answering the phone; they hand it over to Rachel or Hannah, or making the odd appointment—something even they can remember how to do. It is their business though, and even they do without a full lunch hour and stay on after hours. In between patients, Carly jumps happily on to the reception desk. She quite enjoys escaping from her testing room and the monotony of eye exams to the challenge of adjusting someone's glasses or helping them choose a frame.

Bereft of Madison and thrown constantly into contact with her, Hannah is more friendly with Carly than she has been before, throwing her grateful glances when she rushes out to answer the phone or comes out to take her own patient through.

With none of them taking full lunch hours until Madison's replacement can be found, Carly has no choice but to text Mark,

"I can't see you today. Chaos at work. Madison has left."

"What difference does that make?" he texts back. *"You're not a receptionist. You're entitled to your lunch hour. Take it."*

She sighs inwardly. *"I can't,"* she texts back. *"No one else is. I've got to help out."*

He doesn't reply. She checks her phone several times during the afternoon, but it remains silent. A heavy lead weight sits in her chest. She'd been looking forward to seeing Mark far more than she realised. She stays on late, double-checking the till that Hannah hasn't managed to get to balance. Like totting up the NHS forms, this was another one of Madison's jobs, and although Hannah should be perfectly able to do it, she had just left it to her so she could do the jobs she preferred: adjusting people's spectacle frames and straightening and repairing their glasses.

"You don't have to do that," Rachel says when she sees Carly counting out the coins. "Go if you like. I can do it."

"No, it's fine," Carly says. "I've got nothing to rush home for."

She regrets the words the moment they're out of her mouth. It makes her sound like some sort of sad old spinster.

As she tips each pile of coins back into the till, she hears Bob and Lesley talking in the office.

"This one sounds fine," Bob is saying. "I think we should have someone the same age as Hannah. For team fit."

"You don't think they'll just leave again?" Leslie says. "Like Madison did…?"

They've been overwhelmed by applicants since Rachel put the advert in the paper. But working in an opticians is quite different from most reception work, especially in a small business. Here, they don't just answer the phone, make appointments and welcome people through the door. They need some knowledge of optics: people come in with a whole host of queries, from questions about contact lenses to a sudden loss of vision that might require hospital treatment. They help people choose frames, straighten and repair spectacles, complete NHS paperwork and of course, cash up the tills. For someone with no optical experience at all, it can be daunting. Finding and training the right person to fit in with a small team will be a long job.

Carly can't help glancing around every so often as she walks back to her car. She half-expects Mark's car to draw up behind her, to see his welcoming smile as he leans over to open the door for her. *"I'd love to see you any time,"* he'd said, *"even for five minutes."* She'd love to have those five minutes now.

She spends the evening still clearing up after Tina's visit. There's a text from Tina, saying how busy it is at work; one from her old uni friend Jan, that says they must get together soon; and surprisingly, one from Rachel:

"Thanks for helping out today. Much appreciated." And

a smiley face.

But nothing from Mark. Several times she composes some sort of apology, but she stops before typing it. Why should she apologise for something she knows is the right thing to do?

She's taken her make-up off and is just going to get into bed when her phone pings.

"Any chance of tomorrow?" She reads. No *'Hi'*, no *'How did it go?'*

"I can't," she texts back. *"It'll be the same for a while, until we get a replacement. Can't you come over one evening?"*

She waits ten minutes, but there's no reply. She knows he's sulking. Clearly he thinks she prefers her work to him.

She's walking back to her car the next day when his reply finally comes through.

"I'll be there at seven. Can't stay long. xx"

She quickens her pace. It's nearly six o'clock. The traffic in Taunton will have eased off by now, but it's a ten-minute walk to the car park and a good twenty-minute drive home. Not much time to get ready.

Back home, she slides the patio windows open and looks around the usually-pristine flat in despair. There's still washing hanging on the airer, and her breakfast cereal bowl and mug are on the draining board. If it was anyone else, she'd rush around and put everything away. However, Mark's a man, he may notice but he won't care. She'd rather spend the time having a shower and putting on make-up than tidying the flat.

She's only just finished drying her hair when she hears the buzzer go. Two minutes to the door and they're in each other's arms before she knows what's happening. His mouth is hard on hers, his hands everywhere at once. They're both moaning and panting.

"Oh God, Caro… You have no idea…" he groans.

She closes the door, he pushes her against the wall. They

stumble into the bedroom. All that trouble she's taken with her clothes, her make-up, her hair, and he hasn't even looked at her. He's on her and in her, his trousers and pants down at his knees, his shirt undone but still around his shoulders. It's over very quickly, and they lie on top of the duvet in a tangled mess of sweat and undone clothes.

"I've missed you," he says.

"I noticed!" She laughs.

"I can't stay long."

"I know. It doesn't matter." She pauses. "About work..." She feels him tense. "I'm sorry..." she says, then stops. She wasn't going to apologise. *He* should be apologising for not understanding. "Sorry I let you down," she goes on. This much is true. "But I *have* to help out. It's just the way it is in a small business. And I need the job." This is true too. The thought of starting all over again, probably somewhere like EyesRight, with all their rules and regulations, is more than she can bear. "It's just for a few weeks, till they find someone else. I'm working Saturday next week though. So I've got Tuesday off."

His face brightens. "Tuesday? That's fine. We can go out somewhere."

He picks her up just after nine on Tuesday and they drive up to North Devon. They've missed the main rush hour, and they glide easily along the sweeping roads, up onto Exmoor, which looks oh-so-beautiful in the late summer sunshine; the hills painted purple by the heather, the yellow gorse bushes waving against the blue and white sky. Carly feels that same holiday feeling she had with Tina by the pool—like a kid let out of school. She glances over at Mark: his eyes are hidden by dark sunglasses but she can tell he's feeling the same. He feels her eyes on him and takes his left hand off the steering wheel, reaching for hers and holding it tightly.

Carly knows this isn't real life. This is a version of reality they've dreamed up for themselves: a reality where she is Caroline with the perfect family background, and Paula and the twins don't exist. There's no place in this perfect world for the arguments and misunderstandings of a real relationship. They're on their best behaviour all the time. It's never like this in real life. In real life, Mark would grumble about the traffic like Graham always did; there'd be nowhere to park; and then they'd argue about where to go and what to do, before driving home in moody silence.

Mark, however, demurs to her every wish. "We could stop in Lynmouth for coffee if you like? Or go on up to Lynton? There's a lovely hotel up there that overlooks the sea. Whichever you prefer."

"I don't mind," she hears herself saying. The perfect easy-going companion he wants.

And when they stop in Lynmouth, he comes with her into each little shop full of trashy knick-knacks, professing interest in everything she picks up, even offering to buy one of the necklaces she sees in a glass-fronted cabinet. These are the other things that disappear after years of familiarity: Graham might have started the same, but later on, he would wait outside each shop with a sullen, impatient look on his face until she felt obliged to go and join him. He would miraculously cheer up until she stopped at the next shop, when the same thing would happen.

Lynmouth is still busy with families on school holidays; they dodge prams and pushchairs, whining children, and harassed parents.

Lynton, in comparison, is quieter: high up on the cliffs, there's no beach to tempt the families here, only cliff paths and more of those little shops; these ones specialising in art, antiques, and home decorating, rather than seaside gifts. Graham would have hated it. The nearest he got to anything antique or artistic was a classic car.

"Isn't it beautiful?" He would enthuse. "Look at these lines…"

She remembers a week they'd had in the Lake District. She thought they had gone to look at the lakes and mountains, but instead, he took her to a car show and dragged her around a motor museum.

Coffee was in a cafe in a shady street in Lynmouth—a big cafetière with hot milk and handmade shortbread biscuits—before they wandered around the village. Lunch is in the hotel in Lynton that Mark had talked about, along a narrow winding lane that opens out onto a view-to-die-for over the bay.

The warm weather, the clear blue skies and water below, and the steep cliffs dropping sheer into the blue sea, all remind Carly of the lakes and mountains in Austria, where she and Graham holidayed one year. The feeling is reinforced by the décor inside the hotel: strangely bohemian and Teutonic, with heavy dark furniture, stuffed animals in glass cabinets, and sideboards and tables laden with old-fashioned ornate cutlery and china. She only just stops herself saying this to Mark: he would only get jealous like he has before, probably asking her again and again whether she was happy with Graham and why they split up, and she doesn't want to spoil the day.

They eat outside under a parasol, overlooking the bay. Carly had seen Mark's eyes scanning the car park for anyone he might know (fellow teachers on holiday, maybe?), but there's only one other couple there: a dishevelled bearded young chap with his lissome-limbed long-haired girlfriend, who are so wrapped up in each other, they don't even glance their way.

The waiter is like someone out of the Bates Motel, his dark eyes ranging creepily over Carly's body.

"D'you think he keeps his dead mother in the attic?" she asks Mark with a laugh when he glides off to get their order.

You need to know about this place to bring someone here. Most people eat in the restaurants and cafes that line the streets up in the town. Mark must have brought Paula here. Many times. Maybe when they were first together. She can picture them here in the days before home and work and kids got in their way. Young and in love, like the couple kissing openly at the next table. Something she and Mark can't do.

Too soon after lunch, she sees him looking at his watch.

"Sorry." He shrugs apologetically.

"It's okay. It's been…"

"Yes," he says, "I know…"

They're quiet on the way home, but it's a pleasant companionable silence. The countryside sweeps by; the sea, cliffs, and moors giving way to the roads through Simonsbath and Exford.

He stops the car in a lay-by on the way home. She doesn't need to ask why. They haven't been able to touch all day. She aches to kiss him, to feel his hands on her body. They're all over each other like teenagers, desperate for release. It's quick, urgent, furtive, and desperately exciting. They're on the road again almost before she's had time to pull up her shorts and run a brush through her hair.

"I'm glad you had a good time with your sister," he says as they drive past the swimming pool at the back of the health farm. Carly had been thinking about Tina too; she had told Mark how they had spent every day there. Oh, if only she could tell him the truth. *"She's a pain in the neck."* She can hear herself saying. *"She only talks about herself."* Well, that's not quite true, of course. She *did* ask about Carly. But only briefly. Mark might even understand. From what he's told her, Tina's not a million miles away from Paula. No one else has ever understood, not even her old school friends who've known her for ages. And as for Graham, well, he always took Tina's side. *"I think you're being a bit harsh,"* he used to say. *"She doesn't mean it like that."*

But Mark thinks she has the perfect sister in Emma, her best friend and confidante.

"It was great," she says as wistfully as she can.

"I expect her family were glad to have her back though," he says.

Just for a moment, she's thrown, as the thought of Tina with a husband and children is so totally alien. One of Emma's Facebook pictures flashes into her mind: the perfect nuclear family, two dark-haired children smiling broadly, a parent either side. "Yes," she says. "She rang them every day."

She tries desperately to remember the names she had chosen for them, then equally desperately to think of any children's names, but Mark's a man, he isn't interested.

"That'll change when they're older." He laughs cynically. "They can't wait to get away from you then."

These are the little comments she likes to hear. To know that Mark doesn't have the perfect family, the perfect marriage, and that he's happy with her. And on days like today, she knows it isn't all about sex. It's about companionship and getting on. In a perfect relationship, she'd be able to talk to Mark about everything: the painful stuff about her parents and Graham, how she really feels about Tina, all the things that bother her—but all this is out of bounds. It isn't a perfect relationship, she knows that, but it works for both of them. And she doesn't want to change it.

"Do you want to come in?" she asks as he parks the car in the car park.

For proper sex. She means. *In bed, however quick it has to be.*

"I can't," he says as he turns to her. This time, it's she who glances around. Her neighbours are gossipy old ladies. They must know about Mark but she doesn't want to be seen kissing in the car park.

Madison's replacement at work starts the following Monday, but it doesn't make life any easier. The new lady has never worked in an opticians before and there's a lot to learn. The bulk of the training falls on Rachel and Hannah: even the simple task of making an appointment takes twice as long, and patients tut impatiently as the queue lengthens and the telephone rings incessantly.

From the long list of applicants, Carly is surprised to see that Rachel has chosen one of the oldest. Maybe she thinks there won't be so much girlish chatter or that she'll be more reliable. But it's a small business, they all have to get on, and

one look at Valerie—a stern, bosomy, pushy-looking lady—
is enough for Carly to know that Hannah will hate her.

"She thinks she knows it all already," she mutters to
Carly after the first hour.

Carly says nothing, but inwardly she agrees.

"Oh no, Mrs. Ridgeway," Valerie is saying officiously.
"I'm sure your doctor didn't mean you to come here. We're
an opticians. We can't do that…"

Carly intervenes swiftly. "It's all right, Valerie," she tells
her. "Mrs. Ridgeway is quite right, I can take a look at her
eye. Let me find the form we need. I'll explain it to you
later." She looks at the bewildered patient. "It's Valerie's
first day. She still has a lot to learn…"

Valerie's face reddens. She turns away, clearly offended.

It's left to Rachel to calm the waters and steer the team
back to some sort of pleasant working environment. She likes
Valerie. "She'll be a good asset to the practice once she finds
her feet," she tells Carly.

With no other friend at work, Hannah turns more and
more to Carly, popping into her room at lunchtime, bringing
her sandwiches and cups of tea while Carly writes referral
letters.

"D'you fancy a drink after work?" she asks one evening.

Carly hesitates. The occasional lunchtime chat is one
thing, but Hannah is a good ten years younger than her. What
will they talk about over a drink?

"Oh, go on," Hannah urges. "I'm meeting Madison at The
Perkin. It'll be fun."

"Okay," she says. It will be easier with them both there.

Hannah and Madison run shrieking into each other's arms
when they see each other, hugging and kissing as though
they've been separated for months. Carly squirms with
embarrassment but no one else seems to notice. The bar is
crowded with after-work men in suit trousers and open-
necked shirts, and women in work skirts and blouses or smart
dresses. Some, like Hannah and Madison, have changed into

high-heeled sandals or flip-flops, but many are still in their flat work shoes.

The atmosphere reminds Carly of the after-work bars in Reading. There's even a crowded outside terrace with chairs and tables. The three of them head for it, clutching their drinks as people jostle past.

As they make their way to a table, Carly's heart nearly stops: the man sitting with his back to them looks just like Graham from behind, with the same brown wavy hair, the slim shoulders. He even sits forward in his chair in exactly the same way, his whole attention on the person opposite him. She has the sudden crazy idea that Tina must have told Graham where she is and that he's followed her down here. It's ridiculous, of course. This man obviously knows the people sitting at his table, and Graham knows no one here.

Madison has seen her looking. "Not your Mystery Man, is it?" she asks.

Funny she should use the same phrase as Tina.

"No," Carly manages to laugh. "I thought it was someone I used to know."

"D'you still see him? Your Mystery Man, I mean? Hey, we can't keep calling him that. What's his name?"

"No," Carly says quickly. "I mean…" She can't tell them Mark's name. Okay, so there's a lot of Marks, but the next questions will be "What does he do, where does he live?" They might know him, Paula, or someone connected to them. "Not the same one…" she prevaricates. God, that makes her sound like she's sleeping around.

"Ah…" Madison says knowingly. "Internet dating. That's what we thought. We used to have bets on whether you were seeing someone that day. If you wore a skirt and perfume, we knew you were."

Carly manages to laugh with them and, later, when she says goodbye, leaving them happily nursing their free second jug of Blue Lagoon cocktail, she hopes they'll ask her again.

She's almost out of the door when she hears someone call her name. For a moment, she thinks it must be a patient who recognises her, but then she sees it's Kristin from Pilates. She doesn't recognise her at first: she's used to seeing her in leggings and a tight top, not the clinical-looking tunic and trousers that she's wearing now. Carly suddenly remembers she works in a dentist's. Her fair hair, usually up in a clip, is down around her shoulders. She waves Carly over. They kiss briefly, scarcely touching each other's cheeks; they've never been this friendly before. Then Kristin introduces her to her boyfriend, Mike, a big-built tattooed builder-type with a nose stud who doesn't even get up from his stool. He looks at Carly as though she's mad when she holds out her hand to shake his. Kristin pulls over another barstool and gestures to it.

"I can't stay," Carly says, even though she can. She's had the one glass of wine she allows herself when she's driving, but she could always have an orange juice or something.

"Another time then," Kristin says easily. "We're always here. At least I am—Mike's usually working. Give me your number and we can meet up. Maybe at lunchtime, if it's easier…"

Driving home through the now-almost-empty town and then down the long main road out to Bishops Lydeard, Carly feels a new sense of contentment, achievement almost: the tree-lined road, the distant blue Quantock Hills, even the slow combine harvester that holds her up for miles, all seem new, different and exciting. Maybe it's that one glass of wine that's causing this rosy glow, but this is the sort of life she had seen for herself when she was back in Reading, desperate to escape. She sees herself meeting up with Kristin, far more her type than Hannah and Madison, despite the surly boyfriend—maybe he'll improve on knowing. And there's Michaela from Pilates too. They could go for dinner or to the cinema. They'll invite her to their houses, they can come to her flat. Here, the picture begins to fade: Kristin has Mike, Michaela is married to …James is it? She can't remember his name. They'll expect her to have someone to bring along. She can't take Mark. Maybe she should take up Madison's suggestion and join an internet dating site.

She still hasn't been able to meet Mark at lunchtimes, and they're back to hourly messages and daily calls when the twins are out or still in bed. She only works one Saturday in three, so she doesn't have another weekday off until September, and Mark is back at school then. Evenings have always been difficult. Presumably there's a limit to the number of times he can say he's at a meeting, especially in the school holidays, or that he's going for a drink with a friend. A trapped feeling descends on Carly: how did she find herself in this position? She doesn't want things to change, yet she's unhappy with always coming second in Mark's life.

"Maybe we can go away somewhere sometime," he says one evening.

"Where? When?" she asks miserably. "And how would you do it? It doesn't matter, Mark," she adds quickly, reassuringly. "I don't mind…"

"But I do," he says. "I'll think of something."

They're on her balcony. The late summer sun is turning everything golden. Although it's not yet September—not for a few days anyway—there's that September feel to the air. The mornings are cooler, fresher; it's darker earlier in the evenings. Wasps crawl lazily over the back of chairs. Soon the leaves will start turning and it will be autumn. It's a season Carly used to love: the colours and smells, slightly damp and wood-smoky; that feeling of nostalgia at the end of a lovely summer; the fresh cool air that means back to school, back to normal. Now, though, it brings back too many memories of that awful November, and even the smell of a bonfire turns her stomach.

Mark drains his coffee cup. This is his cue to look at his watch or check his phone. His time to leave. As if reading her mind, he shifts in his chair, turns to face her full on, and leans forward. His face is serious. Even before he speaks, she knows what he's going to say. *"Don't."* She wants to say. *"Don't say it. Please. Let's stay as we are."* But she doesn't, and he speaks.

"I love you, Caro," he says. "I think I always have, ever since you were sixteen and I saw you on that first day... I've just been waiting for you to come back to me. "

This is where she should say she loves him too. And she thinks maybe she does, she really does. She still thinks of Graham, but this is so different. With Graham, it was more of a hero-worship. Now she can see more clearly what he's like, she can see it would never have worked out.

The name Caro, however, is like a bucket of cold water. He doesn't love *her,* he loves someone else, someone he thinks she is, an idea of a person that he dreamt up, someone who doesn't exist. If he knew what she was really like, he wouldn't want to see her again.

Four

Carly can't remember a time when she wasn't jealous of Tina. Her earliest memory is sitting next to her in the double buggy as their mother manoeuvred it out through the garden gate. Tina was grizzling, and their mother put a rusk into her fat little hand. When Carly put her hand up for one too, her mother said, "No. Not between meals."

"But Tina's got one!" she wailed.

"She's teething," her mother said sternly. "Now stop that noise."

So she did. Tina always came first. She was such a nervy, nervous little girl: afraid of insects, wasps, birds, even harmless flies. She was a dreadful hypochondriac: the streaky pains in her chest were a heart attack; the pains in her stomach an ulcer or cancer; the headaches a brain tumour; earache meant she was going deaf. Whatever it was, she was a hundred times worse than anyone else. Carly would sometimes wake up in the middle of the night to the sound of Tina crying. Soon she'd call out to Mum and Dad, who would come in and fuss over her for a while. Phone calls to the doctor or the out-of-hours service would follow. It was never anything serious but Tina just loved the attention.

When she was little, Tina loved fairy stories: princesses with golden tresses in turreted towers; handsome princes; wicked witches; fairy godmothers.

"You're not really my sister," Tina used to taunt Carly.

"You're a changeling. My real sister was taken away and you were left instead. Brought by the bad fairies."

"Don't be stupid!" Carly would snap. "I'm the oldest. *You're* the changeling."

"But *look* at you." Tina would argue back. "You've got dark hair. Everyone knows princesses are fair." She shook her long blonde hair. "You're a changeling... *Changeling! Changeling!*" she'd chant, running around the house until their parents stopped her.

It was true, of course, they were so different it was hard to believe they were sisters.

"You're from Dad's side of the family," Mum used to say. "Look at Auntie Louise. You're just like her."

Her father's sister, Auntie Louise, was a tall gaunt woman with brown hair and dark eyes. Her skin was sallow. Carly didn't think she was anything like her.

When Tina was in a bad mood the whole household knew about it. Mum was a bit more objective, but Dad always took Tina's side in whatever dispute it was. She was a daddy's girl through and through. Tina was Mum's favourite too and Carly always knew that, even though she'd try to make up for it.

"You were my first baby girl," she'd whisper to Carly. "Before you were born, I had a dream: a baby was drowning in a lake. I jumped in, swam over, but I couldn't help her. She drifted away from me. 'Don't worry darling,' I called to her. 'I'll come back for you.' And when you were born, you looked just like that baby. And I knew I'd saved you."

Carly lapped this story up, trying to reassure herself she mattered as well. But everything always revolved around Tina.

When Tina was about thirteen, she fell in with a bad crowd: she started smoking, hanging around in town with them, not bothering with any school work.

"You're at school with her all day," Mum and Dad said. "You must keep an eye on her."

But Carly had her own friends. The last thing she wanted to do was check up on Tina. And Tina certainly didn't want it. The only reason she acknowledged Carly at all at school was because the two year age gap meant that the boys in Carly's class were the right age for her.

"Your sister's a bit of a looker." She'd hear when Tina waved and smiled at her in the corridor. She hated it. Tina with her long blonde hair, her oh-so-sexy figure, and her confident air.

It was around this time that Tina first ran away from home. It was a silly row that started it. She had been late back from her friend Anna's house one evening. The following weekend, a crowd of them had arranged to go to the cinema, but Mum and Dad told her she couldn't go.

"If you can't be trusted to get back on time, you can't go out at all."

They didn't mean "ever", but Tina took it that way. She tried everything: screaming and shouting, crying, sulking, refusing to eat, and finally, threatening.

"I'll run away. *Then* you'll be sorry!"

No one took it seriously.

When she didn't get back from school on time the next day, they weren't particularly worried: she often went around to her friend Anna's house afterwards, but she was always back by dinner time. They rang Anna's mum, who said she hadn't seen her. Next, they tried some friends that Anna suggested.

At ten o'clock, Dad called the police. They questioned Carly but she only knew the friends they'd already asked. They left to check with them again, and to tour the town looking for her.

She turned up of course. At eleven o'clock, someone's mother rang to say Tina was at her house. "She says she doesn't want to come home," she said apologetically. "But I told her I had to tell you. You must be so worried…"

Welcomed home like the prodigal son, Tina was suitably contrite: tears and cuddles and apologies all around. From then on, Mum and Dad were too scared to refuse her anything.

Tina was fifteen when Carly started her A-level course at East Devon College. Here, Carly made new friends: friends like Danielle and Lisa, who she still keeps in touch with on Facebook. And there were boys of course—boyfriends she brought home, only to find their eyes sweeping appreciatively over her prettier younger sister. Just occasionally, it might work the other way around: someone would go out with Tina, then find they preferred her. But mostly Tina was the one they wanted.

It wasn't long though before even eighteen-year-old boys lost their appeal for Tina and she moved on to older men.

There was one in particular, he must have been easily in his late twenties. Carly saw her with him in a café one day. He was sitting hunched over across the table from her. She was leaning forward too, twiddling her hair in her fingertips, gazing over at him in a little-girl adoring way. They weren't touching but anyone could see it wasn't a casual friendship. He wasn't even attractive: thin, bald, with a slightly beaky nose. He was wearing a suit, his shirt open at the neck, a heavy gold chain nestling in the chest hair that was visible at his throat. Carly shuddered.

Later on, she had challenged Tina. "Do Mum and Dad know?" she'd asked.

"Don't be ridiculous!" Tina had looked at her as though *she* was the older one, the one who knew more about life.

"How old is he?"

"I haven't asked," Tina had sounded bored now.

They were sitting in the kitchen. Tina had just come home from school and was unpacking her school bag, putting her lunchbox and thermos flask on the side for Mum to wash. In her uniform and without any make-up, she looked more like her real age. Carly wondered how the man would feel if he saw her now. Or maybe that was part of the appeal. Years of being told to look after Tina made her say:

"Tina, you've got to stop. He'll expect... I mean, he's a *man,* not a boy..."

Tina had whirled around, the thermos flask in her hand. *"Leave me alone!"* she'd said viciously, and with a quick thrust, she hit Carly with the metal flask, catching her fairly and squarely on her forehead. The pain was intense, causing tears to spring to her eyes. Carly was so shocked, she didn't know what to do. Mum was in the next room and if they'd been younger, she'd have called her, told on Tina. But Mum would want to know what this was all about. Loyalty— misplaced though it might have been—silenced her. The tears that had sprung to her eyes trickled down her face. She sniffed, and rubbed them away with her hand. Tina, beyond caring whether Mum might come in or not, banged the flask noisily down on the work surface, clattered the plastic lunchbox next to it and stormed out of the kitchen, slamming the door behind her. Carly waited for Mum to come in and ask what was going on, why she had upset Tina, but she didn't.

However, she did ask about the big bruised egg-shaped lump on Carly's forehead. So did Dad.

"I bumped it on a cupboard." Carly lied. Tina didn't even blush.

Carly and Tina still shared the same bedroom, but they managed to occupy different spaces. It had been around now that Tina started creeping out at night.

Carly had woken up one night. She knew something had disturbed her and she sat up in bed. The room felt empty. She tiptoed across the room, gently feeling for the outline of Tina's body in the next bed. Any moment, she expected to hear Tina's outraged voice. *"What the hell d'you think you're doing?"* But the pillow was flat, the bed smooth. She must have gone to the loo, she told herself. She waited for the usual creaks and muffled bumps that told her she'd come back. Waited and waited. She dozed for a while, woke again, and crept back over to the bed. Empty. Then she realised: the noise she had heard earlier was the patio door opening and closing. Tina had gone out. Had Mum or Dad heard? No, she could hear Dad snoring—he could sleep through anything, even thunderstorms—and Mum wore earplugs to deaden the noise, though she always complained she could still hear him.

There used to be a time when they had talked about who they fancied, especially if it was someone in Carly's year. Carly wasn't sure if it was that older man that Tina was creeping out to see, or someone else. She longed to ask her, to ask if she was "being careful", but she was too scared. *"Leave me alone!"* Tina had said, and Carly's hand flew to her forehead, remembering the hurt, both physical and emotional.

However, Tiverton was a small town. People saw her. Once their parents found out, Carly assumed they would put a stop to it, but Tina said: "I told them I can't give him up. I love him. They want to meet him."

Once they had vetted him, Tina's dates with Paul were strictly monitored. He would turn up on certain nights of the week—the nights Mum and Dad had decided she didn't have too much homework—dressed immaculately in jacket and trousers, and he and Tina would go off in his car together. This was ostensibly to the cinema or a restaurant; but more likely to the pub, or the flat he shared above a shop in Gold Street.

Looking back on it now, Carly can see that Paul was still young, even though he seemed positively ancient at the time. He just wanted a bit of fun. Despite the fact that Tina was still sneaking out at night, he hated the strictures placed on him by Mum and Dad. By making their relationship official, serious even, they had placed a tacit trust on him not to sleep with her. It must have been hard for him to know that Tina was breaking that trust all the time.

By the time Tina had reached her sixteenth birthday, she and Paul had broken up. Carly had to endure night after night of listening to Tina sobbing. When she wasn't crying, she was railing against Mum and Dad for splitting them up. For months, the whole household was held to ransom by her hysterical outbursts. It was like treading on eggshells, waiting for the next one to blow up.

Gradually, however, Tina settled down. She took her GCSEs, and went to the rash of parties that came at the end of secondary school. She even worked out which A-levels she was going to do at East Devon College. She still cherished the dream that Paul would change his mind though, and turn up on the doorstep with a diamond solitaire and the promise of a future together.

Carly was leaving college by then. She'd had her name down for ages to go to City University to study Optometry. It was a decision she'd made entirely on her own. Like birth control and relationships and anything really important in life, her parents never discussed further education or careers. They were surprisingly uninterested in hers or Tina's future. Neither of them had gone to university and they didn't think it was important. Maybe it was because they didn't consider a university qualification necessary to get a good job. But Carly wanted more. The idea of optometry first came to her at a careers' evening at Tiverton High School. The young female optometrist had obviously been chosen by the multiple in Exeter she represented (EyesRight probably— they had the market share of the optical business) to encourage youngsters to work for them when they qualified.

"It's a great job," she enthused. "Slightly medical and you're helping people. Steady hours, and you can take career breaks, work part-time if you want to have children...You can go to City University, London," she said, pushing a brochure towards Carly. "Or Birmingham, or Cardiff."

London. The bright lights. There was no choice and Carly could see no downside. She took a sharp intake of breath at the average salary. There and then, she knew she wanted to be her—this smart-suited, sleek-haired lady sitting at the desk in front of her, with her important job, her money, her freedom and opportunity.

She knew a bit about opticians, even then. When Tina started secondary school, she began to complain about not being able to see in the distance. Both girls were taken to the local optician in Tiverton, where Tina was told she was short-sighted while Carly had perfect vision. When she went to university and knew more about how the eye worked, it surprised Carly that Tina was the only one who was short-sighted. Myopia tended to run in families. None of their relatives needed glasses for distance. At the time, however, all she remembered was looking on jealously while Tina took ages to choose the most expensive spectacle frame in the shop. By the time she had reached thirteen, Tina needed her glasses all the time. Far too vain to wear them, she persuaded Mum and Dad to let her have disposable contact lenses. This meant lots of trips to the opticians, followed by tantrums—complete with the stamping foot that she'd never grown out of—once she brought the contact lenses home and couldn't get the things in or out. Carly watched in fascination as Tina eventually learned how to slide these pieces of plastic into her eyes and then miraculously, she could see again, her eyes no longer small and piggy behind the thick lenses

The whole procedure of having her eyes examined enthralled her: how on earth did they work out what glasses you needed just by asking that silly question: 'Is it better with lens one or lens two?' Then there were the ranks of gleaming instruments with their eerie green or white lights; the way the optometrist had to peer closely into your eyes with what she now knows is an ophthalmoscope, murmuring in a gentle, almost seductive voice, "Look up... Look down... To your left... To your right...." Carly, like many of her own patients nowadays, used to panic, looking right instead of left, down instead of up. It was never a problem. Never a problem either when she couldn't decide whether the letters were clearer on the red background or the green.

The two years that Tina spent dreaming of weddings and houses and children, Carly concentrated on getting the grades she needed to get to City University.

The end of the summer term at East Devon College brought leaving parties and get-togethers. This was the last opportunity to be with the friends that Carly had made over the years, before they all went off to universities or colleges. It was the end of an era. After this, they would split up. It would never be the same again. There was excitement: they were all longing to get away from home, to start their new lives away from their parents. But there was apprehension too: it was a big change, away from all the things they were used to.

Carly was over eighteen now, legally allowed in pubs. Tina was often out too, sometimes with one of the boys in Carly's year, sometimes with other friends. In her make-up and high heels, with her confident attitude, she had no problem passing for eighteen. Sometimes Carly would glimpse her from across the bar, sometimes they'd find themselves in the same crowd of people, drinking together. Occasionally Tina acknowledged her, was friendly with her even; other times she ignored her, pretending she didn't exist. She had far more freedom at sixteen than Carly had ever had. Mum and Dad often mistakenly assumed they'd be together and that as her big sister, she would keep an eye on her. Maybe Tina allowed them to think that. The truth was, Carly had absolutely no control over Tina. Watching her across a crowded bar or room, laughing, drinking, basking in the attention that always came her way, Carly often felt like Tina was the older one and she was the immature, naïve, younger one.

In July that year, the College Amateur Dramatics Society put on an open-air production of King Lear. It wasn't the sort of thing Carly usually went to, but her friend Danielle was doing A-level Art and had designed some of the costumes for her coursework. She couldn't get out of going.

As she and Danielle queued to show their tickets, Carly was surprised to see Tina in front of them. At first, Carly assumed she was with Scott, a boy from Carly's year who she'd been hanging around with for a while. Carly knew he did drama—he must have cajoled her into coming. Like Carly, she'd never dream of it otherwise. Neither of them had ever had any real interest in plays and things. When they sat down, however, she saw Tina lean her head against the shoulder of an older-looking boy with longish fair hair and a sort of hippy, student-ish look about him.

She didn't think Tina had even noticed her, but she was just heading off for a drink with Danielle and a group of friends after the play, when she felt a tug on her arm.

"I'm going back with Joe," Tina said, as if Carly would know exactly who Joe was and where she meant she was going. "I shouldn't be too late."

Carly glanced at the boy standing next to her, his arm proprietorially around Tina's shoulders. Close up, she could see he was older than she'd thought.

"Okay," she said. "What time are you s'posed to be back?"

Tina flushed, clearly embarrassed that she might be thought young enough to have to get back at a certain time. "Oh, you know…" she said with a shrug.

Looking back on it, Carly can see she should have said: "No, I don't know. What time did you tell Mum and Dad you'd be back? Make sure you *are* back. And where exactly are you going?" If Tina had been a different kind of younger sister, the sort she had wanted, the sort she could be protective of like Mum and Dad expected, she would have. But Tina was standing there, a look of defiance on her face. Carly didn't want to let her down, to make her feel foolish in front of this new boy she was so besotted with.

"Okay," she said.

It was just after eleven when Carly got home. Her parents were in bed and she crept upstairs as quietly as she could.

She'd had a few drinks, and she was woozy and tired. The room spun when she closed her eyes. She opened them again to let it settle down, then closed them and was asleep almost immediately.

She was woken suddenly by Mum shaking her. "Tina's

not back," she said. "Where is she?"

Woken from a deep sleep, still under the influence of the drinks she'd had in the pub, Carly was confused. She looked at the empty bed next to her for confirmation that Tina wasn't there. She was very good at creeping in and getting ready for bed without disturbing Carly. Even better at creeping out again, even though she hadn't done that since she and Paul had split up.

Vague memories of the evening before drifted to her mind. *"I'm going back with Joe,"* Tina had said. But who *was* Joe? And where was she going?

"I don't know…" she said.

"Did you see her this evening?

"Yes… No… Not really. I saw her at the play … and after … but only for a moment…"

"Who was she with?"

"I don't know." It was only half a lie. She *didn't* know Joe.

This might be enough to satisfy Mum and Dad, but it wasn't enough for the policemen who interviewed her.

"Now, Carly, take me through the evening bit by bit. What time did you first see your sister?"

Memories of Tina running away two years ago came back to her. She had sat then, as she was sitting now, in the living room, Mum next to her, with two burly policemen questioning her. But that was different: it was after a blazing row, she was only gone a few hours and it was a gesture really, to get Mum and Dad's attention. It was 3 a.m. now and she'd gone off with a boy. A boy none of them knew.

"I saw her in the queue," Carly said. "Around seven, I suppose…"

Of course, it all came out. After she'd described what Tina was wearing, she had to describe Joe. It was so hard. She'd only seen him for a few moments. She'd had no idea anyone was going to ask her for a description. She couldn't even remember what he was wearing, let alone the colour of his eyes.

"He had fair hair," she said. "Sort of straggly…"

"And you have no idea where she was going?"

"No," she shook her head.

They didn't say anything but everyone obviously thought she should have asked her, the little sister, only sixteen, going God knows where with someone neither Carly nor her parents knew.

Someone knew though: Anna probably. She must have been sworn to secrecy but faced with the police, even she had to give way. And she did.

"You could try Joe Peterson," she said.

Joe was a medical student at Exeter University. Tina had met him when he was working behind the bar at the White Ball during the holiday. The police found her in bed with him. "I fell asleep." She shrugged, as if that explained everything.

Mum and Dad were so shocked. They had no idea what Tina was like. Mum marched her off to their family doctor to be put on the Pill. She was due to start it the following month. But her next period was late and when she realised she was pregnant, she ran away for the second time. This time it took longer to find her but she was finally tracked down to a flat in Exeter. A friend of Joe's had let her stay there. She had told him some story about her father mistreating her. He had no idea how old she was or what was going on.

Tina was persuaded to have an abortion. Of course it was the right thing to do. She was sixteen. The idea of her becoming a mother was ludicrous. She couldn't possibly live with Joe—the last thing he wanted was a wife and baby while he was struggling to make his medical career. And even if Mum and Dad had done the unthinkable and let her keep the baby, Tina would never, ever have coped. But Tina didn't see it that way.

Carly remembers the day Mum and Dad brought her home from the hospital, white-faced and shaky, and sent her straight to bed. She stayed there for days, too ill to get up.

Carly heard her crying every night. If she'd been a good sister, the sort of sister she wished she was, she would have crossed the few feet that separated their beds, put her arm around her, and comforted her. It might have made them closer. But it was already too late for that. It was another barrier that separated her from Tina, a secret they shared but never spoke about. There were to be others later—worse ones. Thoughts, words and feelings festering under the surface, never spoken aloud.

The small family closed around their secret. They never spoke about it to close friends or relatives, but especially not to each other.

When she found she'd failed most of her GCSEs, Tina announced she was going to re-sit them so she could go on and do her A-levels.

"I want to be a nurse, she said. "Then I can work with Joe when he graduates."

Mum and Dad didn't say that it wasn't as simple as that. They were just so relieved that she seemed to have pulled herself together and had some enthusiasm for life again.

With all the fuss and worry about Tina, no one took much notice of Carly's three grade A's, even though they were better than she expected or needed to get to City University to study Optometry.

It was so hard being away from home for the first time. Like everyone, she felt lonely, bereft, unsettled. But for her, at least there was a certain relief from the tension at home. It was the first time in her life she'd been free to do what she liked.

She made a few mistakes. One drunken night, she ended up in bed with someone she wouldn't usually have looked at. Luckily for her, he was too drunk to do anything, but it scared her enough to make her go down to the medical centre the next day, where the doctor gave her a prescription for the Pill without a question.

As she only went home for the occasional weekends, she

had less and less to do with Tina. Even though they shared the same bedroom, they got up and came back at different times. Tina didn't ask her how she was doing at uni; Carly didn't ask Tina about college, about how she got on with her re-takes, or about Joe. Caught up in their own separate lives, it was the most distant they had ever been.

Like all students, Carly's first year was about settling down, finding her feet, making friends. In the turmoil of the first few weeks, the rush to meet people and make friends meant that the friends she did make, turned out to be ones she didn't really get on with. It was in her second year that she fell in with Jan and Amber, who were both doing the same course as her. It was in her second year too that she met Will, the first boyfriend who really meant something to her, and the only one that Tina never got her claws into. Everyone else, even Graham, was Tina's, either before or afterwards. She never brought Will home, just to make sure.

Carly had done her six-week summer placement in Specs Express in Croydon. She had liked it there and was hoping to do her pre-registration year with them.

"Why don't you see if you can get a job there?" she said to Will. They were already sharing a flat in Upper Street with another couple. It seemed to her to be the obvious thing to do.

"Croydon?" he said. "It's a dump."

"But we have to live somewhere."

"I dunno," he shrugged. "I might just go back home for a while. See what happens..."

He wouldn't be drawn on it so she gave up.

One evening, Mum rang. "Tina's gone," she said.

"Gone? Where? Why?" Carly was shocked. In the two years since Carly had been away, Tina seemed to have settled down. She re-took her GCSE's, gaining passable grades in the ones she needed, and was due to sit her A-levels the following summer.

But Joe had graduated in July and had a place as a Junior House Officer in the Royal Berkshire in Reading. Although she saw him at weekends and in the holidays, Tina couldn't bear the idea of being that far away from him. She had moved to Reading.

"But she must have known it would happen," Carly said.

"We tried to tell her. There are her A-levels. University..."

It was the first time Carly had known Mum or Dad to be interested in either of their future careers. It seemed more likely that they were just trying to split Tina and Joe up.

But Tina was eighteen. They knew where she was. They couldn't force her to come back.

Carly had to go home that weekend. It was strange in the house without Tina, in the bedroom they had always shared. Tina had left her side of the room in the usual chaos, but Mum wouldn't touch it. She was sure she would come home again before long.

But Tina showed no signs of coming home yet. She'd found two part-time jobs: one in a bar, the other in a pizza restaurant. She and Joe were sharing a flat near the hospital with some other doctors and nurses.

Without her there, the dynamics of the family changed. At mealtimes in particular, there was only Carly to talk to. In the past, Tina had dominated everything, even with her silence.

Carly found herself telling them she'd applied for her pre-registration year.

"Do they have a branch in Reading?" Mum asked.

"I'm not going to Reading to babysit Tina!" she snapped.

"But she's your sister," Mum said. "And she's only eighteen.

"*I* was only eighteen when I left home. I didn't have anyone to look after *me!*"

"But you could come home if you needed to."

"So can she!"

"But she doesn't..." Mum's face crumpled and she reached for the tissue in her sleeve.

"For God's sake!" Carly said heavily. "She's only been gone a few weeks!"

On the train back, Carly knew she'd have to give way. It was so unfair. She'd been looking forward to going back to Specs Express. It was one of the top multiple practices: well-equipped, well-managed, with a good supportive pre-registration programme.

There was a branch of Specs Express in Reading but someone had already been given the pre-registration position. The only other place available was in a small independent opticians.

Tina was furious when she found out Carly was coming to Reading. "They've sent you here to spy on me!" she yelled at Carly on the phone. "I'm not having it! You can tell Mum and Dad I won't see you!"

She had calmed down by the time Carly went for her interview, and agreed to meet her in the town centre for lunch afterwards.

Hudson Opticians, in Shinfield Road, right on the outskirts of Reading, was a far cry from the smart practice Carly had hoped it might be. The shopfront had been recently painted but it was a small, one-windowed store, sandwiched between a betting shop and a Chinese takeaway. Inside had also been recently refurbished with a gleaming reception desk and rows of well-lit spectacle frames on stands, but with the waiting area made up of a row of four chairs crammed up along one wall, it seemed small and poky after the large store she had worked in last summer. She reminded herself that it was the professionalism of the practice that mattered, but she couldn't help thinking there would be none of the up-to-date equipment that she had longed to be able to try out.

She was shown around the practice and had a brief chat with Sandra, one of the optical advisors who were in that day. She only saw Graham briefly: he was fully booked and it was the manager, Andy, who would decide to employ her or not. She fancied Graham instantly, but she had reminded herself that he would be her supervisor and it would be ridiculous to have some sort of schoolgirl crush on him. Except for Kath, the other receptionist, there was no other staff. Andy was a Dispensing Optician as well as managing the store. He explained that Graham worked in their Newbury store once a week. "Tuesdays," he said. "That will be your day off."

As she waited for the taxi Sandra had insisted on calling for her, Carly knew she wanted to work there. The brief look she'd had in the examination room that would be hers had confirmed there was none of the brand new equipment that Specs Express could afford, but she liked Andy and she liked Sandra. Once she had seen past its size and overheard them all dealing with the "patients" (not "customers"), she could tell they were all professional and caring. They had made her a cup of tea, shown her where the loo was, asked about her family and where she was from. It had taken weeks at Specs Express before anyone had asked her anything. There was far more staff at Specs Express of course: three Optical Advisors, a Dispensing Optician, the manager (who wasn't qualified), two full-time optometrists, and two glazing staff. They were encouraged to think of themselves as a "team". At Hudson Opticians, they were more like a family.

Tina was already waiting for her in the restaurant when she arrived. She looked older, more confident. She'd had her hair cut into a sleek bob and was wearing more make-up. Carly couldn't help noticing though that the top she wore was one she'd had for years, and her shoes were scruffy. Money was obviously tight.

Carly would have made do with a sandwich but Tina wanted a hot meal, so she ended up joining her in the Shepherd's Pie with peas which was Dish of the Day. When they came to the till, Tina didn't even take out her purse.

Keen to show Carly she didn't need looking after, Tina talked about her various jobs and how well they paid (which Carly didn't believe for one moment), and about the flat she and Joe were hoping to get once they'd saved enough to move out of their present one.

When Tina stopped talking about herself long enough, Carly told her about the job.

"Graham?" Tina said incredulously. "Graham Anderson? But I know him…"

Carly's heart sank. Whatever she did, wherever she went, Tina had always got there first.

"He's seeing my friend Lucy. She works at the hospital. She's…" She lowers her voice as if someone might be listening. "She's just found out she's pregnant."

Remembering the way Graham had looked at her, the answering gleam in his pale blue eyes that told her he was attracted to her, Carly was amazed.

"They're not married or anything," Tina said, as if she'd read her mind. "They don't even live together. But she wants to keep the baby. And I suppose they'll get married. Or something." She shrugged.

With her pre-registration position organised, Carly settled down to her final year at uni. She worked hard for her 2:1 degree, unlike Will, who scraped through with a 3rd. She held a forlorn hope that he might move to Reading with her, but as far as he was concerned, Reading was even worse than Croydon.

Her parents came up for Graduation Day, calling in on the way to collect Tina, who turned up in a flouncy yellow dress and a big hat, looking more like she was going to Royal Ascot than to a Graduation ceremony and drawing glances wherever she went. Carly, who had been so pleased with the navy suit and crisp white blouse she had bought to wear under her graduation robe, now felt plain and dowdy.

They were standing around chatting afterwards, when Tina suddenly cleared her throat and said: "I have some news."

For one awful moment, Carly thought she was going to say she was pregnant. The same thought obviously occurred to Mum, because Carly saw her stumble slightly in her high heels. Dad, of course, was blissfully unaware.

"I've got a job," Tina said. "A proper job, I mean. In the

hospital. Healthcare Assistant."

"A toast," Dad said, raising his glass. "To Tina and her new job."

How did Tina do it? She took the shine off everything Carly did. The champagne they were drinking, the champagne that was supposed to be for celebrating Carly's graduation and the start of her new career, was used instead to celebrate Tina's new job.

"Healthcare assistant," Carly thought. *"When she could have gone to uni and been a proper, qualified nurse."*

Carly had found a room to rent in a house on Cirrus Drive, not far from Hudson Opticians. Her fellow tenants were two girls: one worked in a solicitors' office, the other in a bank.

She turned up ridiculously early on her first day, and stood shivering nervously on the doorstep in her new navy suit and white shirt.

Kath was the first to turn up, a plastic container of milk clutched to her chest. "Wow, you're early!" she laughed. "You must be Carly. I'm Kath. Hang on to this a mo'..." she thrust the milk at Carly, "...and I'll let you in."

Andy was the next to arrive, then Sandra, who greeted her like a long lost friend. Then the door opened and Graham swept in. Carly's heart leapt as he made a beeline straight for her.

"Hi," he said. "You're Tina's sister, aren't you?"

Five

"I love you, Caro. I think I always have."

Carly can't get the words out of her mind.
She knew he was waiting for her to say it too. She saw the disappointment in his eyes. But she can't. Not yet. She's scared. Here, alone and safe in her bedroom, is the only place she can voice her feelings.

"I love you too," she says to the empty room. Tears smart her eyes, trickling down her face and into her ears. She reaches for a tissue, wipes her face, and turns over onto her side. How did she allow this to happen? She promised herself she would never get close to anyone again. Yet, here she is, less than a year in a new town, in a new life, and she's in so deep she can't get out. The thought of losing Mark is unbearable. She practices the words out loud:

"I think we should stop seeing each other. It's not fair to your wife."

Her voice wobbles with tears. The words sound unconvincing and she knows she can't say them. She puts the light on to type them into her phone, but there's a message from Mark waiting for her.

"Goodnight, girl of my dreams. Sleep well."

The tears come in earnest now, and sobs tighten her throat. She's trapped. Trapped by her love for Mark, by the position she's put herself in. The obvious answer, the one staring her in the face, is to leave Taunton. But where would she go? She can't go back to Reading, however tempting it is to be back near her friends. They're Graham's friends too and even if she doesn't actually see him with Lucy and Edward, they'd all know and they're bound to talk about him. But the thought of starting again somewhere else is just too daunting. She likes it here; the flat is beginning to feel like home, and she likes her job. The thoughts go around and around in her mind. Everywhere she looks is a dead end, leading only to the same conclusion: she's in too deep to get out.

Crying and sniffing and reaching for tissue after tissue to wipe her face and dripping nose, she doesn't think she'll sleep at all but finally, she drifts off, only to be woken every so often with a feeling of dread.

It's a real effort to get up the next morning, and her eyes feel heavy and puffy. She doesn't feel at all like going to work. She even considers phoning in sick but she knows how hard it would make it for everyone else: her full clinic to be cancelled; irate patients they haven't been able to get hold of turning up to be squeezed into Bob or Lesley's clinic. She's never done it before and she can't do it now. Too much depends on her. So she rubs concealer into the dark smudges under her eyes, puts her foundation on thicker than usual, and adds extra mascara.

She's glad she made the effort. There's something about being forced to be cheerful to your colleagues, professional to your patients, and the routine of an eye examination that's calming—reassuring even—and by lunchtime, she's feeling much more positive. So Mark loves her. And she loves him. They make each other happy. Isn't that all that matters? It's not as if he's asking for more, saying he'll leave his wife for her. She'll just carry on as usual. Why change anything? There's no point.

"I've been thinking," Mark says the next time she sees him.

Alarm bells sound in Carly's head, but she keeps her voice casual as she says, "Yes?"

"There's a conference at half term," he says. "In October. I wasn't going to go, but I thought maybe you could come too."

"Isn't that a bit risky?"

"Not really. You don't have to stay in the same hotel. We can look for one nearby."

She's quite excited now. "Where is it?"

"Stratford-upon-Avon. It's only a couple of days and I won't get much free time. But *you* could look around... And we'd have the evenings. I don't have to go to all the dinners. I can make some excuse..."

And the nights, she thinks. *A whole night with Mark; two, maybe three. It's enough.* "Yes," she says instantly. "I'd love to. I'll need to check if I can get the time off. What's the date?"

Half-term. It's going to be difficult. Bob's sure to want it to spend time with the kids. However, she's in luck—he doesn't. He's got a week off at Christmas instead.

"Going somewhere nice?" Rachel asks, when Carly asks her about it.

"Stratford-Upon-Avon," she says. "With my sister." She adds on the spur of the moment. "A holiday for both of us. Her husband's going to look after the kids."

"Again? That's good of him."

"Again?" Carly repeats stupidly.

"She's only just been down for a week, hasn't she?"

"Oh. Yes, of course. Yes, he's very good like that."

What a clumsy mistake. But she's stuck with it now.

Mark comes around with a list of hotels in Stratford-upon-Avon to choose from.

"Let me know which you like and I'll book it for you."

"Won't that be a bit risky? I can do it myself," she tells him.

"It's okay," he says. "We have separate bank accounts

and I do all the finances. Paula hasn't a clue where the money goes. She just spends it."

"But I can still do it." Carly insists. "It'd be easier. And you don't have to pay."

"But you said you were short of money. Let me do it."

"Did I?"

"You said you couldn't afford to go over to France to see your parents. With the move and everything."

"Yes," she reddens guiltily. "But it's okay, I can afford a few days in a hotel."

"I'd *like* to pay," he says, and she can see he's getting angry now.

"And I'd like to pay for myself!" she says, angry too.

"For God's sake Paula!" he explodes. "Why're you being so bloody difficult? I'm trying to book a good hotel for you. I don't want you staying in some cheap dump!"

"Carly," she says coldly. "Not Paula. Look, let's just forget the whole thing. I don't want to go. Not if you're going to confuse me with your wife."

"I'm sorry," he says. "It's just…"

She knows the reason. They are arguing. That's what he does with Paula. But it doesn't make it any better.

"Forget it," she says again. "Forget the whole thing. I don't want to go. I'm fed up with the whole bloody thing. You, your wife, everything…" Her voice breaks on the last few words and to her annoyance, she finds she's crying.

"Caro. Carly. Please. Don't. Come here."

She goes dutifully into his arms and he holds her. "I love you," he says. "I want to be with you, I want to do the best for you…"

"I know," she mumbles incoherently. "It's just…" She still hasn't said, *"I love you too."* She knows it's what he's waiting for, but she can't.

"Let's not spoil everything," he says. "Why don't we look at some hotels now, shall we?"

It's quite fun scrolling through the hotels, looking at the reviews. He books her into the White Swan, an old-fashioned romantic-looking Tudor building in the centre of Stratford-upon-Avon. Mark is staying at the more corporate Stratford Hotel, within easy walking distance.

Now it's all booked, she's quite excited. She rifles through her wardrobe, wondering what clothes to take, trying to decide if she can justify buying anything new. Bedtime is a difficult issue. She hates sleeping naked, but she can hardly take one of the old t-shirts she usually wears in bed. She goes around all the lingerie shops and departments in her lunch hour, running her hand through racks of flimsy sexy nightwear, but everything she picks up looks way over the top, as though she's trying too hard. In the end, she buys a cream-coloured satin slip nightie.

The few weeks they have to wait seem to drag by. As the day draws closer, her excitement must show. She wishes she hadn't told Rachel she was going with "Emma", yet it's hardly the sort of place she'd be going on her own, and they're bound to talk to her about it.

"Funny place for a holiday," Hannah says. "Why don't you go abroad somewhere? Your parents have a place in France, haven't they?"

"Emma can't afford it," Carly ad-libs swiftly.

"London then? The bright lights. Shopping. Go to a show..."

"Believe me, the 'bright lights' aren't quite what you think they are!" Carly laughs. "I've lived there! Anyway, Stratford's easier for both of us. I've googled it. There's loads to do..."

"Going to a Shakespeare play?" Lesley asks.

Carly shakes her head. "Too expensive and they'd probably all be booked up by now. But we'll do all the other tourist stuff. Shakespeare's house. Anne Hathaway's cottage. A boat trip..."

She doesn't sleep well the night before they go, visions of motorway pile-ups with mangled bodies and tangled wreckage chasing through her mind. But she's awake and out of bed the moment she hears the alarm. She gets ready in super-quick time and is still checking and double-checking that she has everything packed when she hears the buzzer to the outside door.

Mark's ready smile, his warm kiss, the feel of his arms around her, dispel the nerves.

It's a beautiful crisp late autumn morning, the dew on the grass, the leaves changing colour. The grounds of the health farm have seldom looked lovelier as the car eases gently down the drive.

The town is chock-a-block with early morning work traffic, but soon they're joining at Junction 25, where Carly feels the familiar knot of tension in her stomach—the feeling Tina must have felt too when she came down, but never spoke about. She reminds herself that this is one of the reasons she came back here, to lay that particular ghost to rest.

Mark senses her tension, notices her hands tense against the seat maybe, and then misunderstands the reason.

"It'll be fine," he says, taking his hand off the steering wheel long enough to squeeze hers gently. "We'll have a great time. Nothing will go wrong."

Her eyes are on the road ahead, on cars and lorries streaking past, weaving in and out of the lanes. She's grateful when the hand returns to the steering wheel and his eyes go back to the road ahead.

They pass Bridgwater and the Somerset Levels, then she must have dozed for a while because she wakes to the feel of the car slowing down.

"I thought you might like to stop for breakfast," he says.

"Where are we?"

"Just north of Bristol."

She sees the sign: *"Michaelwood Services."*

Mark puts his arm around her as they queue up for a cooked breakfast that she knows she shouldn't really have. However, she'd been too nervous to eat this morning and now her stomach is rumbling. He reaches for her hand when they've finished, squeezing it gently. "I've been looking forward to this for ages. Time on our own together."

Back in the car, her stomach comfortably full, she's wide awake now. It's a beautiful autumn day, the sun slanting through the copper-coloured trees. They drive through the Vale of Evesham—with its iconic church spire—and by eleven o'clock, they're approaching Stratford-upon-Avon.

The hotel is in the centre, looking just as good in real life as it did in the photos.

Mark drops her off with her suitcase, so she can book in while he parks the car. Then waits in the bar for her. The hotel is old, with sloping floors, and floorboards that creak underfoot as she walks along the narrow corridor to her room.

"Is it okay?" Mark asks her when she comes down to the bar.

"Lovely, thank you," she says, accepting the glass of wine he hands her. The room is overlooking the back of the hotel, so at least it will be quiet. It's furnished in the modern "boutique" style, with crisp white bedlinen and heaps of navy ruched cushions on the big double bed.

"I thought we'd have lunch here, if that's okay with you," Mark says. "I have to register at the Stratford at two o'clock. We could go for a walk down to the river afterwards."

He holds her hand while they wait for their sandwiches to arrive, but he doesn't take it or put his arm around her when they walk outside into the autumn sunshine.

"Will you know anyone here?" she asks.

She sees a frown cross his face. "No," he says, "it's just…"

"It's okay," she says quickly. "I understand."

It's beautiful down by the river. They walk along the back of the Royal Shakespeare Theatre, where crowds of people are feeding the swans and ducks. They stop to look in the theatre shop, then head back to the hotel.

"There's a couple of lectures I'd like to go to this afternoon," Mark says. "Will you be able to find something to do? We can have dinner out somewhere tonight. No one will miss me. But there's a do tomorrow night that I can't get out of. With dancing, you know. I can see you after that though."

"It's fine," Carly says. "Now I've got my bearings, I can look around. Maybe I'll do Shakespeare's House this afternoon."

"Wish I could be with you," he says enviously, "rather than stuck indoors listening to some bore telling me stuff I know already."

She misses Mark as she shuffles around Shakespeare's birthplace with the other tourists. She wonders what he's doing, who he's meeting. Other teachers he already knows, maybe—old flames or new interests.

She's back by early evening and takes her time showering and getting ready, putting on a knee-length black dress and high heels. Mark's face when he sees her in it is worth all the trouble. They've never gone out in the evening before, and she relishes walking by his side, her high heels clicking on the pavement.

They eat in The Vintner, another half-timbered Tudor building, with an upmarket feel and an expensive menu.

Carly's drunk too much wine, and they're weaving their way slowly back through the crowds of people that are making their way home. There's an easy-going, holiday, romantic feel to the air. It's a mild autumn night but there's a chill. Carly shivers and Mark puts his arm around her, holding her close and guiding her along.

Back in her room, he undresses her slowly, gasping as he finds lace-topped hold-up stockings under the demure black dress.

She has fallen asleep in his arms many times but always with the knowledge that pretty soon, he'll be jerking awake and looking at his watch. This time, she knows he'll be staying.

"I love you," he murmurs as he drifts off.

"I love you too." She says it so quietly, she wonders if

he's even heard it. But he pulls her closer, kisses her shoulder, and she knows he has.

The alarm goes off at seven in the morning. For a moment, Carly can't think where she is. She opens her eyes, looks straight into Mark's, and her whole body suffuses with pleasure. She loves him, she wants him, but there's no time for anything other than a brief cuddle. Mark has to get back to his hotel in time for breakfast and the start of the morning's conference lectures.

Carly doesn't hurry. It's Saturday morning. Breakfast is served until 10 a.m., and she has all day and all evening to herself.

The smell of cooked breakfast wafts towards her as she heads for the dining room. It's so tempting to lift the heavy silver covers and help herself to the bacon, sausages, fried bread and eggs that she sees piled high on other people's plates, but there was that fry-up yesterday at the motorway services and a full dinner last night, including pudding. Carly knows Mark likes her slim. He's always commenting on her slim wrists and arms, and her firm flat stomach. She pictures Paula with rolls of fat on her stomach and arms that jiggle when she moves them. So, with great self-control, Carly heads for the section of the restaurant serving bowls of fresh fruit and yoghurt.

She finds a table by the window. The sunshine from yesterday has disappeared behind a veil of grey cloud and light drizzle. A feeling of anti-climax and ennui comes over her. She had been quite looking forward to a day on her own, wandering around the old town, down to the river, a bit of shopping maybe, but now, in this dull weather, and without Mark, the idea is rather depressing. She lingers over breakfast, reading the newspaper she brought down with her, before finally going back to her room.

Room service has just arrived as she gets there, so she darts past the trolley piled high with sprays, cloths, mini soaps and moisturisers, grabs her coat, bag and umbrella, and heads outside.

The rain has worsened to a steady downpour, so instead of heading for the river, she wanders around the shops disconsolately. She ends up in a picture gallery and spends so much time there, the assistant clearly thinks she's made a sale; she gets quite grumpy when Carly finally heads out again.

"I'm not sure about lunch today," Mark had said when he left her. "Lectures are pretty much back-to-back. I may not get time to come over."

She checks her phone constantly, just in case, but at one o'clock his message comes:

"Sorry, only got half an hour free. No time to see you. Will make it up to you later." With a little winking emoji and two kisses.

She orders a sandwich in the hotel bar and then spends the afternoon reading the book she brought with her in the dark oak-panelled foyer of the hotel, where the staff ply her with frequent pots of tea.

Mark texts again later: *"Getting ready for the big do. Have a lovely dinner. Miss you. xx"*

She's dreading the idea of going down to the restaurant alone, but she has to eat something. The hotel does room service but she doesn't want to spend all evening in her room. She showers again, mainly for something to do, and takes her time getting ready like she did last night. The little black dress is probably too smart, so she changes into black leggings and a smart long top. She then walks into the restaurant with as much confidence as she can muster.

"Table for one?" The waiter asks her. "In the window maybe?"

She agrees and takes her seat, then scours the menu for the least calorific meal she can find, opting for steak with salad and no starter. She glances around the room while she's waiting for it to arrive: mainly couples, of course, but she's come down early and there are also some families with teenage children. This isn't the sort of place to bring young children.

She checks her phone again but there's nothing. Mark will have had time to phone Paula, she thinks bitterly, speak to Chloe and Sam even. But no time to speak to her.

It's an odd experience, eating alone, and she hurries through the beautifully-cooked and presented steak, feeling self-conscious, then asks for coffee to be brought to the bar. Here, though, it's worse: the waiters try to make conversation with her and the two men sitting alone glance over at her every so often, presumably to see if she'd "like some company". Wishing she'd brought a book to read, she drinks the scalding coffee far too quickly and goes up to her room. Here she flicks from TV programme to TV programme, ending up watching a repeat of something that she's seen before.

She checks her phone from time to time, hoping for another message from Mark, but still nothing. She tells herself there's no time at a dinner dance. It's rude to text at the table and he can hardly sneak out to phone her, though she wishes he would. She pictures him sitting at the table opposite some pretty teacher who has far more in common with him than Carly has. They'll be flirting, they'll dance together, they'll go to his room, or hers. It's happened before, she knows it has. He won't come over tonight at all.

Dinner must finish about ten, she thinks, so he'll be here by ten-thirty. She waits for the news to finish. She takes out the book she's nearly three-quarters of the way through now, and reads for a while. He won't be long now. At eleven o'clock, she takes off her make-up, changes into the cream nightie that Mark had loved so much, and gets into bed. She tries to read but the words swim before her eyes. Finally, she turns out the light and tries to sleep.

She's woken by a soft tapping on the door. She can see Mark is drunk the moment he stumbles, half-laughing and half-apologising, into the room. Not really drunk, not incoherent, but far more inebriated than she's ever seen him.

"It all went on far longer than I expected," he begins.

"You could've rung me!"

"It was difficult…"

"Or sent a text. For God's sake, Mark, I've been on my own here all day! It's okay for you, wining and dining and having such a good time with all your friends!"

"They're not friends, they're just colleagues… Come on, Caro. I'm tired, let's just go to bed…"

But she's too angry now to think logically. "No!" she spits out.

"What?"

"No. You can go back to your hotel and your friends. I don't want you here. Do you really think I want to be sitting around all day on my own in this godforsaken place, watching crappy TV and waiting for you while you swan off with other women…?"

"Who said anything about other women?" Mark says. "I swear there wasn't a woman there to compare with you…"

"Huh!" Now she's sounding like a jealous wife, but she can't help it. "I *hate* you, Mark," she yells. "Hate what you're doing to me…" To her annoyance, tears are now running down her face.

"Shhh…" he says, glancing at the walls around them.

"I don't *care* what anyone thinks!" she yells. "The whole world can know for all I care! Now get out!" She picks up the nearest thing, which happens to be her phone, and throws it at him. Instantly she regrets it. It hits the side of his head and he stares at her unbelievingly, his hand against his cheek.

"Sorry," she says, overcome with remorse. "Sorry, sorry, sorry…"

Suddenly he's like a little boy. "Why did you do that?" he asks pitifully.

She can't answer. She's crying in earnest now. "I don't know … it's just… I thought… I was so miserable…" None of it makes any sense but it doesn't seem to matter. He puts his arms out and she goes to him.

"I'm sorry," he says. "You're right, I should've called. I just thought you'd be fine. You're so … capable.

Independent."

She half-laughs through her sobs. This is how he described Paula when he first knew her. This is what he wants: someone perfect, someone who won't care if he comes and goes as he likes, someone who won't nag him. She tries to regain her equilibrium to show him she's not a weak, hysterical woman like Paula. But she can't. "I missed you," she says in a weak, pathetic voice. "I was lonely…"

"But you knew I'd have to do this…" he says.

She nods, still crying.

"Come on," he says. "Let's just forget it. Let's go to bed."

She stays awake for ages after he's fallen asleep, prodding him occasionally as he snores. Tears fall down her face and she wipes them away. How did she get herself into this situation? She's trapped and there's no escape. She loves Mark, she knows she does, but this is the life she'll have with him. And she can't be the perfect woman he wants her to be. This won't be the first time she'll crack under the pressure.

Mark groans when the alarm on his phone goes off at 7 a.m. "Oh, God, do I have to go? I've got such a bad head…"

Carly's face feels tight and her eyes are puffy from crying. She stretches, turns over, tries to go back to sleep, but it's impossible with Mark stumbling around the room as he tries to find his clothes in the dim light of the bedside lamp. In the end, she gets out of bed and makes a cup of tea.

"I finish at lunchtime today," he says. She already knows this. "Maybe we could go on a boat trip or something. Most people will be going straight home."

"I'd love to. If you're sure. Or we could stop off somewhere on the way home if you'd rather?" She's trying to be perfect again. But then so is he. And at least they're friends again.

The day starts out cloudy and grey, not the sort of weather for a trip on the river. Carly has an extra-long shower, puts on extra make-up to hide her puffy eyes, is almost the last down to breakfast again, and then packs her stuff. Her phone buzzes several times. It's Mark, making up for not messaging yesterday: little smiley faces, a couple of emoji hearts, and a message that says: *"You have no idea how dull this is."*

Carly is packed and ready to check out by eleven. She leaves her suitcase with the hotel staff, ready to pick it up later.

Stepping out from the dark hotel interior, she's surprised to see that the sun has come out in a watery sort of way, and the clouds are clearing. She wanders down towards the river, half-heartedly peering into shop windows on her way. The gallery she spent so long in yesterday is open, but she daren't show her face in their again. Besides, she looked at every single painting several times—she can't look again. The usual corporate shops are open, the privately-owned ones firmly closed. She ends up down at the Royal Shakespeare Theatre again, wandering around their gift shop, fingering scarves, mugs, jewellery and t-shirts emblazoned with quotes from various Shakespeare plays.

When she goes outside again, the sun has broken through the clouds and swathes of blue sky are appearing. People are swarming along the river banks: families with children running amongst the swans and ducks, throwing crusts and crumbs to them; old people moving along slowly, heading for a bench to sit on; couples hand-in-hand. Carly heads for an empty bench and takes out her phone: no more messages from Mark. It's only just gone twelve, so she takes out her book to read for a while. It isn't easy to concentrate though: other people join her on the bench; a middle-aged couple, who smile apologetically as they sit down but carry on talking to each other. The sun is too bright for reading and the cool wind flutters the pages of the book so she gives up, puts the book away, then tries to sit and relax as she looks at the scene around her. But the couple take this as a cue to talk to her, asking if she's been to Stratford before, and whether she went to the play last night. (Antony and Cleopatra apparently, three whole hours!) Then they ask if she's here all on her own. At this last question, thankfully, her phone buzzes and Mark's name flashes up.

"I'm sorry," Carly says. "Please excuse me. My boyfriend. We're meeting for lunch." This last comment is an excuse. She knows Mark has to stay for lunch, but now she can clamp her phone to her ear and walk away with a clear conscience.

"I thought they were going to adopt me," she laughs to Mark. "Poor little me, all on my own. Next, they'd have been asking me to have lunch with them…"

"We're just going to lunch now," Mark says. "Will you find yourself something somewhere?"

"I'll be fine. I managed yesterday."

"I know, but I feel bad, you know… It isn't quite what you expected, is it?" His voice is low and she can hear the hubbub of conversation in the background. He must be huddled in a corner somewhere, with people streaming past him.

"It's fine, really," she says, though she's lying. She knew of course that he'd be at the conference all the time, but somehow she hadn't realised how alone she would feel. As she talks to him—arranging to meet him back at the hotel at two o'clock to pick up her suitcase, and then deciding how to spend the afternoon—she feels a sudden urge to go to his hotel, to see him from a distance amongst his colleagues.

She ends the call, tries to dismiss the idea from her mind, but the conviction grows and almost without realising it, she finds herself walking up the street towards the Stratford Hotel. She's not exactly sure where it is, but she goes into a charity shop and asks the kindly elderly lady behind the counter, who gives her clear instructions several times over.

At the entrance to the hotel grounds, she almost changes her mind. This is the sort of thing she used to do with Graham. She remembers driving over to Lucy's place one evening after work, to check Graham was going there to see Edward like he said, and that he wasn't with some other woman. She wished she hadn't. Graham was standing on the doorstep talking to Lucy, while Edward bobbed about between the two of them. Lucy was smiling up into Graham's face. He was smiling down at her. It was an image she would never get out of her mind.

This is just as risky. What if she sees Mark with someone else? An attractive colleague? Someone he might meet up with again?

Against her better judgement, she finds herself walking confidently up the drive to the hotel. There's Mark's silver Audi parked in the car park. It's a modern building, the type you'd expect a conference to be held in—nothing like the old timbered White Swan. A receptionist looks up and smiles as she goes in, but Carly has glimpsed the board that shows the conferences and meetings on that day, and walks over to it as though she's going to one of them herself. Her eyes scan down it until she sees the word "Education". It's in The Henley Suite, but she can hardly go to it and march in. And if Mark finds her here, he'll have a fit. She suddenly realises how absurd she's being. The receptionist is still eying her. She pretends to check her watch, then gets out her phone and pretends to ring someone, turning her back on the receptionist and heading back outside.

Here, she puts her phone away and walks swiftly back down the drive, her heart racing and her palms clammy with sweat. She half-expects to hear Mark's surprised voice behind her and she only begins to calm down when she's way out of sight of the building.

She was hungry earlier on, but now her appetite has gone. She walks back down to the White Swan, orders a cup of tea from the bar, then takes out her book and pretends to read.

Mark arrives promptly at two, sweeping through the front door of the hotel with a confident air and plonking himself opposite her with a beaming smile. All her jealousies, insecurities and ridiculous thoughts fly out of her head as he leans across and kisses her.

"Now, what d'you want to do this afternoon?" he asks.

"I don't mind." She smiles back at him. "As long as I'm with you."

They retrieve her case from reception and put it in the boot of his car.

"Okay if I leave my car in your car park for a while?" Mark asks the receptionist, using his most charming smile.

"Of course sir," she replies.

"No one else but you would get away with it." Carly laughs, hanging on to his arm as they leave the hotel.

"Let's go on a boat trip, shall we? " Mark says. "I've been cooped up in a stuffy hotel all morning. It's a shame not to make the most of this weather."

Carly reddens guiltily when he mentions his hotel, but he doesn't notice.

The sun is still shining, it's become surprisingly warm for late October, brown leaves drift gently from the trees. The riverside has that English-Sunday-afternoon-in-the-park feel about it: couples sauntering along arm-in-arm like her and Mark; families with children feeding the swans and ducks; old people with sticks, walking frames or motorised scooters. Mark holds her hand as they queue up to buy tickets, and helps her solicitously onto the boat as though she were a Dresden doll.

"Are you warm enough?" he asks as he cuddles up next to her on the seat.

"Yes." she says, leaning her head against his shoulder as the boat drifts downstream past the Royal Shakespeare Theatre, swans gliding by. This is one of those perfect days, like the one they had in North Devon, which she'd like to capture and bottle. It's not like real life. It's a fairytale. It can't possibly last.

They've reached the end of the trip and are shuffling forward with the other passengers when she feels Mark suddenly freeze next to her.

"Oh God…" he murmurs, dropping his arm from her waist as though he's been burnt.

"What?" Carly asks.

"Someone I know. Look, can you go on ahead. Pretend you don't know me."

He lingers behind as Carly forges forward.

"Hi Steve!" she hears him say in a hearty manner. "Great minds, eh? Such a lovely day…"

"My wife, Holly," she hears the unseen man say. "We thought we'd make a weekend of it…"

Will he think it's strange for a man to be going on a boat trip on his own? Will he wonder why Mark didn't bring *his* wife with him? Or maybe he's already seen them together and is being discreet.

Carly finds she's shaking as she strides purposefully along the path. How long will Mark stay with them? Maybe they'll invite him for a cup of tea? What excuses will Mark make? The perfect afternoon is suddenly spoilt. She knew she was right to think that they shouldn't have stayed on here. They could have gone on to one of those pretty little Cotswold villages where no one would have known them.

Her phone buzzes. She wishes she could ignore it, but of course she can't.

"Hello?"

"It's okay, they've gone back to the hotel," Mark says. He sounds tense, irritable, slightly out of breath. He's obviously walking along the street. She glances around the crowded street to see if she can see him.

"I'll meet you back at the car," he says. "That's probably safest."

The moment she sees him, she knows the day is spoilt. His face is stern and set in a way that reminds her only too forcibly of Graham in one of his bad moods.

He lets her into the car and she turns to him. "It doesn't matter," she says.

"Yes, it does. It's spoilt everything."

"Don't be silly," she touches his arm, wills him to look at her, smile, kiss her. But he doesn't.

"We need to get going anyway," he says.

They don't speak for a while. Carly reminds herself that Mark is concentrating on driving, but it's not just that: she can feel his bad mood. Mile after endless boring mile of motorway drift by. Carly feels her eyes closing, her head lolling. She wakes up with a jolt when she feels the car slowing down.

"Cup of tea?" Mark asks.

"Love one," she answers drowsily.

He parks the car, puts the handbrake on, and then turns to her. "I've had enough of this," he says. For a moment, she thinks he's finishing with her, and her heart gives a painful lurch. But then he says, "Skulking around, hiding from people. I love you. I'm proud of you. I want to show you off. To my friends, my family. To everyone. I want to live with you, Caro, be with you all the time."

Pleasure soars through her: this is what she wants, what she's always wanted—someone prepared to face the world and anything it throws at them to have her with him. It's not like it was with Graham. It'll be different this time. With Mark, everything will be fine.

Then it hits her: *"...to my family."* He doesn't just mean his kids—though that's daunting enough—he means his parents. Then he'll want to meet hers. The parents who live in the Dordogne. And the perfect sister she's invented for herself. What has she done?

Caroline

One

If you were to ask Caroline about Carly Spurway, the chances are she wouldn't remember her. Just because they were both doing maths A-level, just because they both thought the maths teacher was the best looking man around (but a man, not a boy, they knew he'd never even look at them), it didn't mean they had anything to do with each other.

When Caroline thinks back to those days she realises how grown-up she felt at the time, how complicated and important everything seemed, and how simple and unimportant it actually was in comparison with real, grown-up life.

They hung around in groups at college. Well, Caroline's friends did anyway. Some people didn't, they just had best friends—either friends they'd known since primary or secondary school or ones they'd made since they'd been there. Caroline's group had been together since they were about fifteen. There were six of them but the undisputed leaders, the two strongest, were Caroline and Vicky. They were the two everyone looked to, the ones who decided what they did and where they went, the ones whose opinion on any and every subject mattered.

Vicky and Caroline had been friends since their first day at Heathcoat Primary. Caroline would always remember plump, dark, curly-haired Vicky arriving at the school gate holding her daddy's hand, her mummy trailing behind. Vicky had a soft, lispy voice.

"That's my classroom," she had said, pointing to the room Caroline was heading for too. Caroline had envied her: the closeness to her daddy, the way she had hung around his neck, kissing him again and again when he left while her mother looked on fondly. Caroline's father was a doctor. He couldn't take time off. Her mother had taken her, but couldn't stay long as she was working too. Vicky's parents had taken the day off for their only child's special day. They always put her first: they were there for every school event, arriving early to sit in the front row if she was in the school play, even a minor part. Caroline liked acting; she was often chosen for the lead role. But her parents never came to see her.

"You know it's not our sort of thing," they would say.

The friendship that began in primary school, inevitably carried on when they went to Tiverton High School, but strangely, after the first year, Caroline and Vicky drifted apart. For the next two years, Caroline was best friends with another girl although looking back now, she can't imagine what they ever had in common.

Vanessa had fine mousy shoulder-length hair and wore big fashionable glasses. She was a flighty, enthusiastic girl. She fancied herself as a musician and carried a guitar around everywhere with her, though she never actually played it or had guitar lessons. She also carried a sketch pad and here she was genuinely talented, achieving with just a few swift strokes, close likenesses of friends at school or horses. She loved horses and wanted riding lessons but although she, like Vicky, was an only child, her parents wouldn't indulge her. Maybe there wasn't the money. Gradually Caroline realised they had little in common and by the next year, she had somehow teamed up with Kate Best.

Kate was tiny—a skinny, flat-chested girl with short blonde hair. She looked far younger than fourteen. Caroline was flat-chested too and was waiting for the day when she would catch everyone else up, when her boobs would suddenly grow. But they never did. But at least she was slim; she was proud of her willowy figure. And she was tall—taller than her older sister Emma. Everyone always thought she was the older one. Emma hated it.

Caroline was friends with Kate for about a year. Then suddenly Kate started hanging around with a girl called Karen. Karen was a big girl; not just taller than any other girl in their year (she must have been at least 5 ft. 10 in) but big built: wide hips, wide shoulders, not fat but far from slim. She was big-boned and statuesque. She looked far older than fourteen and acted it too. She smoked, drank, went to pubs (no one would take her for fourteen and she was never refused a drink). It was an unlikely-looking friendship: tiny, childlike Kate Best and big, mature-looking Karen, but Kate suddenly took up smoking (they were always disappearing outside for a "fag") and tiny adolescent Kate was popular with the older men Karen hung around with. So, despite the fact that there was no way anyone would think Kate was old enough to go into pubs, she and Karen went everywhere else together and Caroline was dropped. It was Vicky who came to her rescue. She had been friendly with a couple of other girls for some time, and she amalgamated Caroline seamlessly into their clique. Over the next year or so, two more graduated towards them, and by the time they were thinking about A-levels and sixth form college, there was no question of the group splitting up.

Caroline's first day at East Devon College was memorable for all the wrong reasons. She had woken early, a knot of apprehension in her stomach. She told herself it was ridiculous to be so nervous, especially as she knew so many other people who were going. The top she had put out to wear now looked too smart and dressy, like she was trying too hard. The next was way too tight—the boys might think she was deliberately being provocative. The one she settled on in the end was just a long-sleeved t-shirt, stripy so it looked casual and student-y. It was not too tight, so she didn't look like she was trying to be sexy. She was wearing jeans, of course. That was the most exciting bit about sixth form college: no more skirts and blouses. They could wear what they liked.

She was far too early. She paced the house, running up and downstairs, checking and double-checking her bag, comparing the time on the sitting room clock with the time on her watch, driving the whole family mad.

"For God's sake, Caroline!" her sister grumbled, "I was trying to have a lie-in…"

"Can't you just sit down and wait?" her mother said irritably.

"It *is* my first day!" she excused herself.

"Big deal!" Emma groaned sarcastically.

"It'll be a different story when you go to uni next month," Caroline thought to herself, but she didn't want to start the day on an argument and anyway, Emma had lost interest, yawning and taking her cup of tea back up to her bedroom. It was okay for her, she had another whole month to wait before she went away.

Caroline had arranged to meet the others outside the college but she was still early. She thought about walking around a bit but decided she might miss them, so she stood around as boys and girls shuffled on, some getting off buses, some wheeling bicycles, others being dropped off by parents.

Groups of two's and three's formed and re-formed as people found friends they knew and hung around with them. She reminded herself how lucky she was to know so many people already. Most people seemed to be the same, but there were one or two who went in alone. It must be awful not to know anyone at all.

This was her first step to university and freedom. It was okay, of course it was. She knew it would be from the moment she saw Vicky, also looking scared as hell, but trying to hide it behind a casual smile. And when the others turned up it began to feel like an ordinary day at Tiverton High School, except that they had to find their way around a strange building rather than knowing where they were going.

Her crowd were all doing different subjects or in different sets, but they met up for break times, lunch hours, and any spare time between classes.

Caroline was doing Maths, French and Business Studies. She wanted to do Business Studies at uni. Her idea of what she would do afterwards was hazy, but she saw herself in the city, wearing a smart suit, travelling the world, earning a big salary, and making important executive decisions.

Caroline had Maths first. Everyone looked up and silence fell when she opened the door to the room. For a moment she thought she was late, but the hubbub resumed with an almost audible sigh of relief and as she found her way to the only empty desk and unpacked her stuff, the same thing happened as someone else came in. As she made a big deal of searching in her bag for her pencil case and pad, which were actually easy to find, she looked around surreptitiously at the others. A group of boys sat predictably at the back of the room, eying each girl, nudging each other and smirking. As she glanced over, she caught the eye of one boy in particular: he was leaning back ultra-casually in his chair; slim, almost skinny, with brown hair and pale blue eyes. Their eyes met. She looked away quickly, but not before she'd seen in his eyes what she was feeling too. Instant attraction. Like a magnet. She risked another glance. He was looking at her too. She felt herself reddening. *"This is ridiculous,"* she told herself, but it was the same all the way through the class. They seemed to share the same sense of humour, be on the same wavelength about so many things, their eyes meeting in silent amusement, his eyebrows raising quizzically at things that were said.

The girls looked at each other with barely concealed smiles when Mr. Exton came into the room: tall and slim, with dark brown, almost black hair and brown eyes. He was the complete opposite of any teacher any of them had ever had before. He might have been in shirt and tie, smart trousers, and a jacket that he soon took off and slung over the back of his chair, but he clearly hadn't long been out of jeans and a jumper at uni. Equally as aware of this as they were, he didn't smile, didn't relax at all, and just stood there, waiting.

People were still talking, chairs scraped across the floor, some still looked in bags for pens and paper. The lighter voices of the girls died down fairly quickly, but the boys' deeper voices continued, punctuated by the odd laugh. Obviously they thought they could get away with it; he wasn't much older than them, after all. He said nothing, just stood there waiting. Eventually, even the bravest stopped talking.

"Thank you," he said, his voice firm. "Now, let's get on."

"There's someone really nice in my maths class," Caroline said to Vicky later as they were washing their hands in the loos.

"Maths?" Vicky said. "You've got that gorgeous teacher, haven't you? Mr. Exton. Lucky you," she laughed.

The hand driers that had gone off with a blast every time someone had gone past in the queue, now refused to work however much they waved their hands under them.

"Yes," said Caroline, wiping her hands on her jeans. "No. I mean, yes, you're right, he's nice, but there's this chap…"

Greg Foster, she found out later. Whenever she thought of him, a thrill of excitement ran through her. She had never felt like this before. Oh, she'd had boyfriends—quite a few actually. She'd even thought she'd loved them. But nothing compared to this. She only had to think of him and she'd find herself smiling inanely. She blushed when she saw him and it was impossible to hide how she felt. For a week she nursed the secret that everyone, including Greg, must surely have known. She nearly blurted it out to her mum. She used to tell her about all her boyfriends: when she saw them, where they went, sharing her disappointments and heartaches. But her mother seemed to get too involved, taking their sides, getting cross with her when she wanted to finish with them.

"But he's so nice," she'd say. "Saving up his money to take you out. Why don't you want to see him anymore?"

How could she explain that Ryan or Jason or Gary or whoever it was had become so boring, or wanted to go too far, or was always flirting with other girls? Her mother couldn't possibly understand. She was too old. It was different in her day.

This time, Caroline decided, she'd keep it to herself. Well, for as long as possible anyway.

That didn't stop her talking to anyone else about it, of course. Vicky was the main confidante, along with the others in the group of six. She was always finding excuses to mention his name.

It felt like forever at the time, the waiting, but it was a little over a week. He came over to her, they started talking. He didn't understand the homework they'd been set, he said. It was calculus—something Caroline found easy. He sat down. She drew a diagram, he bent towards her to look at it, and their heads nearly touched. She could smell his aftershave, something minty on his breath. Chewing gum maybe. He'd been preparing himself for this.

The first time they held hands, the first time they kissed. It's all indelibly printed on her memory. She knew then as she knows now that he was the love of her life. She was a fool to let it go wrong.

He was the first one to call her Caro. He gave her a silver identity bracelet engraved "Caro" for her seventeenth birthday. She loved that bracelet and wore it all the time. She was so upset when the chain broke and she lost it. It was as though the final link to him had been broken.

All through sixth form college and into the first year or so at uni, the name Caro stuck. Vicky insisted she had started it. She was studying Byron for English Lit and told Caroline it was his pet name for his notorious lover, Lady Caroline Lamb. But Greg was doing English Lit too. He knew all about Byron and his affair with the beautiful, wild and wilful Lady Caroline.

Even Mr. Exton surprised her one day by handing back her work with a smile, saying, "Well done, Caro. You seem to be the only one who's got the hang of this."

Her face burned. She hated being singled out like this.

She knew Greg would tease her later: *"Who's teacher's pet then? He's got the hots for you, Caro. Can't say I blame him…"* She wished Mr. Exton wouldn't do it. He was always holding her up as an example. She can't remember now what it was she'd got the hang of, but Maths came easily to her. Greg struggled. Not just with calculus—he got the hang of that eventually, thanks to her—but with pure maths: statistics and decision maths. Caroline spent hours talking him through it, explaining it again and again. These sessions would start innocently, Caroline patiently going over and over the parts he found difficult, but before long, she would find herself watching his hands close to hers: he had long artistic fingers and slim wrists. She thought of those hands on her body, those fingers exploring her. Sensing her attraction, he would wind his hand around hers, lean his forehead on hers; she would lift her face and they would kiss. She couldn't get enough of him.

Why did she find him so attractive? He wasn't conventionally handsome. Not the sort that other girls talked about. He was tall and slim; almost skinny. When he lay on top of her, his bony hips dug in to her painfully. He had a long thin face, a straight nose, grey eyes, fine brown hair that he was always pushing away from his face. He was far from handsome. But he had something: a winning smile, an enthusiasm for life, a readiness always to have a good time. He found it hard to be serious for long. He liked to make fun of things and find the amusing side of any situation. It was only when they were alone that those laughing grey eyes would become more solemn. He would gaze at her. Right at her. As though he knew her completely, as if he had always known her. She felt like they were meant to be together. She couldn't imagine life without him. When she thought of him, her whole body suffused with heat. She loved him in a way she had never loved before or since.

Of course, her parents had to meet him.

"What does his father do?" Her father had been asking her the same question about every friend she brought home since she was five. As the local doctor, Dad was incredibly conscious of his position in society, and all their friends were vetted carefully to make sure they were from the right social strata. Dad always seemed old, stuck in his ways. Mum liked to look after herself but Dad said he didn't have time. And it was true, he was always busy. His prematurely bald head, his slight stoop, and the roll of extra fat around his middle, made him look a lot older than he was. The next question he would ask Greg would be what his favourite subject at school was, and what he wanted to do when he left. But she was safe here. Greg's father was a financial consultant. Greg loved Geography. He had always known he wanted to be a teacher.

When she thinks of Greg—which she does more and more nowadays—she thinks of long hot summers. They were always looking for places to be alone in those days: a barn, a cricket pavilion, the floor of a golfers' changing room, where she was worried someone might look in through the windows. They would walk along the canal or in the park, holding hands or with their arms around each other; they would go along lanes, where they would climb over gates and into fields of long grass, flattening it down to make a hidden nest. They would kiss and mess around, pretend to fight each other. Then it would become more serious: he would roll her over onto her back, climb on top of her, grind his bony hips into her; she would reach down and touch him, he would slide his long fingers inside her bra or knickers. They would pant and groan with the frustrations of young teenagers, knowing the dangers of going too far, stopping before it was too late. They were heady days, laden with secrecy, daring and passion.

Obviously, there were cold rainy days, days they had to stay inside. Their parents were both too strict to allow them into each other's bedrooms, and they had to wait for the odd moments alone on sitting room sofas to kiss passionately and thrust their hands under each other's clothes.

His parents lived out of town and on their first Valentine's Day, he drove all the way over to her house on his L-plated motorbike that he was so proud of (he was one of the few who had his own transport), a huge Valentine's card strapped to his back. For their first Christmas together, he bought her an expensive bottle of perfume. The next year, a red satin nightie that she had to wrap inside a t-shirt and stuff at the back of a drawer so Mum didn't find it.

Mum never liked him. She made it clear from the start, like she always did with Caroline's friends.

"I don't know what you see in Lauren," she'd say, although sometimes it would be Melissa and Amy who were in the firing line. "She's so loud and pushy. I should stick to Vicky, if I were you." She'd always liked Vicky. Vicky with her perfect parents who were almost the same age as Mum and Dad, her father something high up in Devon County Hall, her mother working part-time in a building society in Exeter. Caroline's mum worked part-time too. She was a physiotherapist. Caroline was proud of her in some ways. Other people's mums were plump and old-looking. Her mum was tall and slim, her dark hair in a long bob that she put up for work. She ate the right things, did the right sort of exercise. She had been friends with Vicky's mum, Linda, since they had waited by the school gates to collect both girls from primary school. They met for coffee and tea, went together to Pilates, Yoga, or whatever class was currently in vogue.

Their mums being so close made it hard for Caroline to use Vicky as an excuse if she was out somewhere that she shouldn't be. She could hardly say she was with Vicky, only for Vicky's mum to say she hadn't seen her all evening. So she fell back on one of the others. Mum quite liked Melissa, but she lumped the others as being inexplicably just "not quite the right sort" for her to be friendly with.

It had been the same with Caroline's boyfriends. She had quite liked the odd one or two, and was really upset when they stopped coming to the house. But she took against Greg right from the start. It couldn't have been his background, there was nothing to fault there. And Dad certainly liked him.

Mum was polite enough to his face but she took every opportunity to run him down behind his back. Snide little comments that Caroline did her best to ignore. She never understood what she had against him. Maybe she just thought it was all too serious. Maybe she was right.

One night, Caroline told Greg that she had overheard one of the girls in her French class say that she was "unofficially engaged". When he left, togging himself up in all the gear he needed on the motorbike, and turning back to kiss her again and again like they always did, he said, "Oh, and you can consider *yourself* unofficially engaged." He said it with a flippant grin and an almost-casual throw-away gesture, but she knew he meant it. Her face burned but she said nothing. She was so happy. She told no one, hugging her secret close to her chest.

It was her eighteenth birthday a month later and he bought her a ring. Her heart had leapt when he gave her the small square box wrapped in dark red paper. It wasn't an engagement ring, of course. It wasn't even the sort of ring she would have chosen for herself. It was big and clumsy, silver with a large black oval stone—more the sort of ring a man would wear than a woman.

"Do you like it?" he asked, studying her face anxiously. But Greg had chosen it. He had gone into a shop and bought her a ring because he loved her. A ring to show the world she was his. Of course she liked it.

"I love it," she said. She wouldn't have dared wear it on her engagement finger, but in any case, it was far too big. The only finger it fitted was the index finger of her right hand. She slipped it on, held out her hand for him to admire.

Greg's eighteenth was two months later. She really wanted to buy him a ring too, even though she could scarcely afford it out of the money she made from her Saturday job. She wanted him to have something to wear when he went to uni, so that other girls would know he wasn't available. She scoured the jewellers in Tiverton, looking at signet rings and plain gold wedding rings. In the end, she settled for a plain silver band that wasn't too expensive and would go with the silver St Christopher medallion she had bought him the Christmas before, to keep him safe on the motorbike. Like him, she had no idea what size ring to buy, and it turned out to be too small for any finger except the little finger of his left hand. She knew he liked it though, and they both knew that the rings meant that they were secretly engaged, like in some sort of Shakespeare play.

It was a supreme irony that her relationship with Greg that gave her so much happiness led to her falling out with Vicky and the others. It wasn't that Vicky was jealous—after all, she'd been going out with Jason nearly as long as Caroline had been with Greg—but in the way these things work when gangs of people hang around together, Melissa's boyfriend was a friend of Jason's. So was Lauren's. Amy fancied another guy in their crowd. And Heather was happy just to hang around and flirt with whoever else was around. From being one of the leaders of the gang, Caroline now found herself an outsider. She would come out of a class at break or lunchtime to find them all in a great crowd. She couldn't barge in on her own. She was usually meeting Greg, but even when he was with her, they weren't part of Jason's set. Greg had his own friends, though he saw them less and less. He was happy just with her and she was happy with him, but she missed the peculiar female camaraderie; the chat, the gossip, the bitchiness even. She still saw them all, either individually or in their original six-some; they were friendly enough to her, but there was a distance, a sense of not-quite-belonging as they laughed and talked and joked about things that had happened with the boys, places they'd been to together, people she scarcely knew.

Things came to a head that last summer, the year they all turned eighteen. There were loads of eighteenth birthday parties, some shared with friends to help them spread the cost for their parents, who were inevitably paying for everything. Some didn't bother, just going out for a meal with their parents and maybe a best friend. Caroline's birthday was in

March, Greg's in May. They would have loved a joint party, but she knew her mum wouldn't like the idea, and she dreaded the thought of her parents and Greg's parents getting together to discuss arrangements. In the old days, she would have asked Vicky and the others what they were doing. They'd had a big joint party for their sixteenth birthdays, organised and financed by their parents, but this year they had already gone to several parties without her and she didn't like to bring it up. Instead, she dutifully went out for a meal in an expensive restaurant with her parents and Emma, who came down from Sheffield for the weekend.

Vicky's birthday was two days before Greg's. "What're you two doing to celebrate?" Vicky asked her.

It was weeks away and Caroline hadn't really given it much thought. "We haven't talked about it yet," she said. "But I expect he's going out with his family."

Greg's grandparents were younger than hers. More importantly, unlike hers, they were fit and mobile. The family were all quite close. Greg had two older brothers and there seemed to be numerous cousins, aunts and uncles who liked any excuse to get together and have a party.

She couldn't believe it when Greg said: "Mum and Dad have asked if you can come too."

"What?" Of course, she'd met them loads of times. She liked them. His Dad was a mild, avuncular sort of man with receding hair, and glasses. He was always reading a book or the paper; or in his home office, where he wasn't to be disturbed, the soft drone of his voice as he spoke on the telephone audible from outside. Greg's mum also worked from home—some sort of accounting or book-keeping or something—and when she wasn't cooking, cleaning or ironing, she would be closeted in her own office (one of her son's old bedrooms, with a computer on the desk where he used to do his homework). She was a small, dumpy, motherly woman, always dashing about and tutting as she picked up books, papers, shoes or jumpers that Greg or his father had left lying around. She had the same fine, floppy brown hair as Greg; the same habit of pushing it impatiently back from her face. It was the only similarity though. Otherwise, Greg was just like his father: the same tall, slight build; the same grey eyes; the same easy-going, fun-loving manner. It wasn't difficult to see what Greg would be like in thirty years' time.

She couldn't wait to get to college the next day and tell everyone she'd been invited to Greg's eighteenth. It meant something, didn't it, when you were invited by your boyfriend's parents to meet the whole family? It meant they knew he was serious. They were accepting her as "The One". She couldn't tell anyone about the rings, about the secret engagement, but she *could* tell them his family wanted to meet her.

It was only later that she realised the significance of the look that passed between them when she burst out with it.

"*When* did you say it was exactly?" Vicky asked ever-so-casually.

"Saturday. The 19th. Three days after his birthday. God, I haven't a clue what to wear…"

"We can help you choose an outfit," Lauren said quickly.

"Yeah," Amy said excitedly. "We can all go shopping together. Get some new make-up. Shoes. Everything…"

But the shopping trip together never happened. Whenever she suggested a date, they were all doing something else. In fact, Vicky and the others seemed to be avoiding her. As she made her way to the canteen with Greg, she'd hear Lauren's distinctive laugh, Amy's loud voice disappearing into the distance. The odd times she did catch up with them, she noticed a lull in conversation as she approached. Friends in other classes seemed uncomfortable around her. It was several weeks before she found out what was happening. She was telling one of the girls in her French class about the new top she had bought to go out with Greg, and the girl said: "So you're not going to Vicky's party?"

"What?" Caroline said.

"Vicky and the others. Your lot. The party. On the 19th. They've been talking about it for ages…" Her voice trailed off as she saw Caroline's reaction. "Sorry," she mumbled. "I thought you knew…" Embarrassed, she moved away.

Caroline's eyes filled with tears. They began to run down her cheeks and she brushed them impatiently away. Her face burned. The hurt cut like a knife deep in her chest. Hurt and betrayal, humiliation and embarrassment. The class was due to start. There was that lull as people arranged their books and papers just before the teacher swept in. She had never skived off in her life. But she couldn't stay. She grabbed her stuff and rushed out of the room, wiping at her wet face with the back of her hand and drying her mascara-stained fingers on the front of her jeans. Her throat had closed over. A great sob rose deep inside her, followed by another. She couldn't have spoken if she'd tried. Luckily, no one stopped her. She pushed past people in the corridor, her head bent down. She ran to the loo, bolted herself inside a cubicle, bent double, hugged her arms around herself, and willed the sobs to stop. The last thing she wanted was for someone to hear, bang on the door, ask her what was the matter, and offer sympathy. How could they do it? They were supposed to be her friends. The last time she had asked Vicky about her birthday, she had said she was going out with her parents. Maybe Caroline hadn't been interested enough. Had she been too wrapped up in herself and Greg's family dinner? But none of it excused what they'd done. They'd deliberately chosen the day they knew she couldn't go.

Greg was the only one she could tell. She couldn't possibly say anything to the few odd friends she had outside her own close clique as they all assumed she knew, that she had chosen to go out with Greg rather than go to the joint party. The party they were holding to celebrate their eighteenth birthdays—all five of them. Not her. At one time she would have been the main mover, the one to decide where and when they were going, and who would be lucky enough to be invited. Now she wasn't invited herself. Even to this day, she can feel the hurt.

She couldn't hide the fact that something was wrong, but

she certainly couldn't tell Mum. She wouldn't understand. She'd take Vicky's side, say she hadn't been a good friend to her. So she let her think she'd fallen out with Greg. It was easier than telling the truth.

Greg didn't understand either. "But you're coming out with me. I don't see what the problem is. You can't go anyway."

"But they did it deliberately," she sobbed. "Without me…"

"You don't know that. Maybe it was the only date they could have. You know what these places are like. Mum had to book the restaurant a long time ago. They get booked up."

"No. You weren't there. I was. They asked me the date. *Then* they organised it so I couldn't go…"

He let her cry, comforted her as much as he could, but she could tell he thought she was making a fuss. It was the first time he hadn't supported her. But she couldn't allow it to come between them. Greg was the only true friend she had.

She didn't confront Vicky and the others. She couldn't bear the idea of a scene. She saw them a few days before the party, huddled in a little group, their heads together. Vicky looked up and caught Caroline's eye, then looked away quickly, but not before Caroline had seen the discomfort on her face.

She tried to put it to the back of her mind. She still had Greg. She'd rather be with him than with friends who could ditch her so easily. It still hurt when she saw them together though. Sometimes they called her over, but she didn't go. She just smiled and waved.

"I'm meeting Greg," she'd call over, even if she wasn't. She became closer to other people in her classes, people she'd only been casual friends with before.

The night of Greg's dinner came. She was nervous and excited. She washed her hair, did her nails, took ages with her make-up, and put on her new top.

"You look lovely tonight," Greg whispered when he kissed her hello.

He didn't leave her side, escorting her around proudly, introducing her to everyone—names she couldn't remember, faces that became a jumble in her mind. Greg's brothers, Tom and Nathan, had both brought their girlfriends too. Tom and his girlfriend Gayle had recently got engaged: Greg caught Caroline's eye and winked as Gayle held out her hand for everyone to see the ring. As Greg's Dad proposed a toast "To Greg. On his eighteenth…" Caroline saw his mum's eye travel around the room, taking in Tom and Gayle, Nathan and Jane, Greg and Caroline. This is what she had wanted. To be accepted as the one Greg had chosen. She had never been so happy.

It was warm for May. The restaurant was in a big country house hotel. Later on, she and Greg walked outside into the grounds. He pulled her down onto a bench, kissed her, and slid his hand under her top. Caroline looked around. They were hidden from view by a group of trees and there was no one around. She could just make out the outline of the big hotel behind them, see the lights of the restaurant, and hear the distant chatter of voices and the clink of glasses. She moved her hand inside the waistband of his jeans. He moved back, undid the top button and the zip. She reached inside.

"We shouldn't," she moaned as his hand moved under her skirt, inside her knickers. "Not here…"

But she didn't stop him as he pulled her knickers down. It was a warm evening, she wasn't wearing tights. She stood up, wriggled out of her knickers and rolled them into a ball, and shoved them on top of her bag on the bench. Then she climbed on top of him. She could feel him hard against her, the end of his cock wet. She was wet too. How easy it would be to push him inside her. She wanted it so much. To be truly his. It would be the first time for both of them. She knew she should go on the Pill, as she was risking too much. It only took the one time. There were girls who got caught out—they were always the same type: the good girls with long-term boyfriends, never the easy ones who slept around. Those ones were too clever.

It was Greg who stopped first, pulling away from her quickly, groaning as the sticky cum spurted onto his stomach. He was the one with the self-control. He had a favourite cousin, Megan, who had got pregnant at seventeen. Her A-levels, her university education—all gone in a flash. Now, Greg told her, she was shackled to her resentful husband, living in a god-awful run-down rented house with a bawling baby. Greg was always talking about her:

"She never complains," he said. "She's so positive about everything. She's going to do an Open University degree when Tom goes to school…"

She sounded like a saint and Caroline was quite jealous of her. She and Greg had grown up together and had a special bond. She'd met her tonight: a tired, wan-looking girl, obviously relieved to be out without her child for the evening. She was with her equally tired, grumpy-looking husband, who was always reaching for another drink. They both looked too young to be married, too young for the huge responsibilities. Greg was right. They couldn't risk this as their future.

Along with the eighteenth birthday parties came the A-levels, the long wait for the results, the celebrations and commiserations where necessary, and the packing up to go to university. Caroline was going to Aston in Birmingham. It was the best place for a degree in Business Studies. Greg was going to Oxford Brookes to do Geography, followed by a PGCE so he could teach. They would only see each other at weekends. The thought of the separation was unbearable.

By the time they were all due to leave Tiverton, the situation with Vicky and the others had blown over. They were so young. They'd been falling out and making friends again since they were in primary school.

"We thought you wouldn't want to come," Vicky excused herself years later. "You scarcely knew most of the people going, and you just wanted to be with Greg all the time."

And so the time came for Caroline to part from Greg. Caroline was going first. She wanted to be up there early, unpacked, her room organised, ready to find out where everything was before lectures started. It turned out she was lucky. Greg's best friend Aaron, who he'd known since primary school, was going up to Aston too. It hadn't been his first choice, but his results were better than he expected and he switched at the last minute.

"Aaron will look after you," Greg kept saying.

Caroline wasn't so sure: true, it was nice to think she knew someone there already, but Aaron was nothing like Greg and she wasn't even sure he liked her much. He'd had Greg all to himself before she came along. Since then, they'd seen each other less and less. Aaron was nothing like Greg: he was taller, thicker set; a beer-drinking, rugby-playing type with thick dark wavy hair and grey eyes. He was good-looking—better looking than Greg, in fact—and plenty of girls fancied him. He never went out with them for long though. Greg told her Aaron had been very hurt by a girl in the past.

"Rebecca," he said. "Don't for God's sake tell him I told you. He doesn't want to talk about it."

Except to Greg, of course. He was more interested in male company, at home in the bar of a pub or rugby club. Rugby wasn't his only sport. He loved hockey, tennis, cricket, and squash. He looked good in his kit, with his broad shoulders, strong arms and muscular legs. Greg had skinny arms and legs. He hated sport of any kind.

Caroline would never forget the day she left Tiverton. Her parents drove her up, the car crammed with everything she thought she'd need: bedding and towels, books, mugs, cassettes, and clothes.

Aaron did look after her. Miraculously, he was there to meet her, though she didn't remember organising anything with him. He showed her parents where to park, waited in the long queue with her while she was allocated her room, came up with them to her room, and helped them cart everything up in the lift. Mum and Dad thought he was wonderful,

"What a lovely boy," Mum kept saying. "And so good-looking."

Caroline knew she meant compared with Greg.

"What did you say his father did?" Dad asked.

"I don't know, Dad," she said impatiently. "He's got his own business, I think."

Aaron had told her his mother didn't work, though she would have liked to. Aaron had a younger brother and sister. His father thought a wife and mother should be there for her family.

Aaron stuck to her side like glue those first few weeks, escorting her to the various fresher events like a diligent older brother. And she was grateful to him. Torn from her safe group of friends and with no Greg by her side, she felt lost.

"You're like a little girl," he told her one day. "Little Girl" became Aaron's special name for her. All his texts to her began: "Hey, Little Girl".

People began to assume they were together. "He's just a friend," she said again and again.

Then one day, when they were sitting in someone's kitchen, drinking yet another cup of instant coffee and half-working on a piece of course work each, she suddenly became acutely aware of him: his strong arm lay alongside hers on the table, she noticed the way the dark hairs curled on it. Greg's arms were almost hair-free, just a smattering of fair wisps. Aaron's wide hand was close to hers as he held his biro. She could feel his warm breath, smell his musky smell; a mixture of aftershave and fresh sweat. Desire rose in her, swept over her. She felt her face flush. He would have had to be made out of stone not to sense it. His hand covered hers, his fingers closing gently around it. Neither of them spoke. They didn't kiss. They just sat together like that, both reading their separate books, until inevitably someone burst noisily into the room, and he gently took his hand away.

That night in bed, she went over it, remembering with a

wash of guilt the rush of desire, the way she just let him take her hand. What was she thinking of? Was she crazy? She didn't fancy Aaron. She never had. But she couldn't deny there was something about him: an air of mystery; a distant far-away look in his eyes sometimes, especially when he talked about girls.

"One day, I'll find the right one," he would say, sipping his pint and taking a long drag from his cigarette, blowing the smoke out gently and looking sad. She waited for him to tell her about Rebecca, but he never did and she couldn't say she knew. Somehow though, he managed to give the impression he'd been hurt and wasn't willing to try again; an impression that he must have known was attractive to girls. They wanted to be the one to heal his broken heart. She could see them giving all the right signals, but he ignored them. Was it because of her? Had he always secretly fancied her? The idea was flattering but she brushed it away. What would Greg think if he knew what had happened? And how would she feel if it was the other way around? They phoned each other as much as they could, but already the separation was telling on them. She had no idea what he did every day, who he met, where he went, the friends he made. Names and places that meant nothing to her came into his conversations all the time. If he mentioned a girl's name, she'd become convinced he fancied her. Sometimes she'd end up crying on the phone, and she'd hear his exasperated voice as he promised again and again that he loved her.

She needed to see him, feel his arms around her, remind herself and him of what they were missing, and reinforce their relationship. She'd suggest it to Greg when he called that night.

When they'd first talked of going away, they'd planned to come home as often as they could.

"Or I could come and stay with you there," she'd say. But money was tight, there was course work and other things to do at the weekends, and she'd only been home once.

She expected to feel awkward with Aaron when she saw

him next, but he greeted her as though nothing had happened. She was going to lead up to it slowly but the words tumbled out. "I'm going home this weekend."

She saw his face fall then brighten. "I'll come with you, Little Girl. About time I saw the parents again."

"Greg's coming too," she said quickly. "He's meeting me off the train."

"Fine," he shrugged, but she sensed his disappointment.

Two days before he said he'd go, he changed his mind. "I'll come with you to the station though," he said. "See you off safely."

"You really don't need to." In fact, she was glad he had offered. Birmingham New Street was a nightmare and she would have struggled to find the right platform without him.

It was a cold dismal evening. There was no waiting room and they stood in the freezing cold, walking up and down occasionally. Despite the age it had taken to find the right platform, they were still early. Conversation became difficult, as they had run out of things to say. Finally, as the train appeared in the distance, Aaron turned to her.

"I'll miss you, Little Girl," he said softly.

She looked up at him, right into his eyes, saw what she knew already deep down, and felt a pull like a magnet, the same feeling she'd had before. He drew closer, tentatively pulled her into his arms. She tried to turn her face, pretend to them both this was just a friendly hug goodbye. But it was no good. Their bodies fitted together like two pieces of a jigsaw puzzle, his lips finding hers. She felt his tongue in her mouth, tasted the cigarette he'd just had. With anyone else, she would have felt sick. She hated anyone smoking. But she savoured it, savoured the smell of him, the feel of his body against hers. She buried her head in his warm shoulder.

"I have to go," she said.

"I know…" he replied, pulling away.

He helped her with her bag onto the train. They must have said goodbye again, then he stood watching as she waved from the window until she could no longer see him.

"What am I doing?" she asked herself. *"I must be mad."*

She had plenty of time to think about it on the journey home; to replay over and over again what she had done. Her heart leapt at the sight of Greg waiting to meet her off the train. She hurried off, bumping people's legs with her bag, and threw herself into his arms. He felt different, smelled different, seemed different. They had no time alone together: his father had brought him to the station in his car. Greg only had a learner's licence for his 125 cc motorbike and therefore couldn't take passengers, but it made no difference really, as her parents would never have allowed her on the back of a motorbike.

They couldn't sit together in the back, so she made desultory conversation with him and his dad until they dropped her at her house. Even then, they only had time for another quick kiss, as Greg couldn't come in due to his dad waiting in the car.

The rest of the weekend was the same. It was mid-winter—too cold for long walks and intimacy. Although they couldn't keep their hands off each other, there was the constant danger of parents walking in. It was so different from the freedom of university.

In the short time they had been apart, things had changed. When they had been at college, they had seen each other every day, knew what each other did, and knew each other's friends and the people in their various classes. Now neither of them knew the new people and places they each talked about. A huge gulf had opened between them. The only person they could talk about was Aaron.

"He's fine," she said when Greg first asked about him. She kept her voice deliberately light, gave what she hoped was a nonchalant shrug, and Greg didn't seem to notice her face redden. There were lots of things he didn't notice. They were no longer on the same wavelength. And there were things about him that annoyed her whereas nothing had annoyed her in the past. The way he held his knife like a pen; the way he yawned with his mouth wide open so she could see his fillings; the silly way he pulled his jumper or top on and off, holding it at the back of the neck and hauling it up instead of pulling it up by the bottom of the hem. But most of all, the way he was never serious. He was always messing around, making a joke of everything. Why had she never noticed it before? They never talked properly. She found her mind straying to Aaron and the long, in-depth conversations they had about important topics: politics, climate change, religion. Or their companionable silences when they were reading or studying. The way when one or the other of them did speak, they'd usually find they were thinking about the same thing.

She was too young to realise that habits that at one time seemed endearing could become irksome in the long-term. That relationships go through difficult patches—times when nothing seems right. She just wanted everything to be new and exciting and perfect all the time.

On Sunday evening it was her father who offered to drive them to the station, waiting discreetly in the car as Greg went on to the platform with her.

"I love you," Greg said, kissing her hand with the ring on, twiddling it under his fingers.

Their secret engagement flooded back to her. Tears ran down her face as she clung to him. She had wasted their precious time together and now it was too late. He carried her bag on to the train as Aaron had done at Birmingham. She found a seat, waved goodbye, settled down to do some work, closing her eyes now and again as she dozed. Fields, hedges and towns slid by in the dark. She wiped the misty window now and again to see the station names. Passengers got on and off next to her. Thankfully, no one wanted to chat.

As the train pulled in to Birmingham New Street, she was only half-surprised to see Aaron waiting on the platform for her.

Two

Opportunity. That's what Caroline had with Aaron. It was all so easy, out of the sight of parents and everyone she knew.

She'd told herself it wouldn't happen again but the moment he met her at Birmingham station with that special smile on his face, she knew it would.

"I've missed you, Little Girl," he said softly. She took his hand—how could she not?—and interlocked his fingers around hers. Greg always cupped his hand to hold it. Aaron's hands were big and broad, like the rest of him, not narrow, long-fingered and thin. She wondered how they would feel on her body. Aaron was talking, asking her about the weekend. She answered vaguely and he didn't press her on anything. This was the good thing about Aaron: he knew when she didn't want to talk. He didn't feel he had to constantly fill the silence like Greg did.

She didn't see him much over the next few days but although she talked daily to Greg on the phone, told him how much she missed him, ached to be held in his arms, Aaron was on her mind too. She looked forward to seeing him. Maybe he was avoiding her, doing the decent thing. She was his best friend's girlfriend, after all. He should leave her alone. She should respect him for that, but instead, she missed him. Her heart leapt when he arrived one afternoon out of the blue. She couldn't keep the smile of delight off her face. There was no one else there. She busied herself making them both tea while he cleared a space on the kitchen table for his newspaper and a pile of books.

Aaron liked to do the crossword. He enjoyed the challenge of it. He opened the newspaper to the right page and started studying it while she sat down next to him. They'd done this before. She wasn't very good at it but she liked to help him, liked to watch his face as he mulled over every clue, jotting down letters, counting them out in his mind to see if they fit. She enjoyed the intimacy, the meeting of minds. She bent her head to look more closely at the paper. Their faces were inches away. His fingers curled around hers, crushed her hand tightly. Her heart was pounding, her face burning. Desire swept through her. They were kissing almost before she knew it was going to happen, his tongue in her mouth, his hands in her hair. She heard a deep moan and knew it came from her. God knows where it would have ended if they hadn't heard the distant sound of a key in the lock, voices chattering, a sudden burst of laughter.

Caroline shared the flat with three other girls, Crystal, Shabana and Kim, but she hung around mostly with the girls in her Business Studies group—especially Helen and Kirstie. They all knew about Greg of course. They all accepted Aaron. She didn't need to justify herself to any of them. But they could see what was happening. She and Aaron made no attempt to keep it a secret. They held hands, he put his arm around her. But she still talked about Greg all the time. People were confused.

"Have you finished with Greg?" Kirstie asked her.

"No," she said, her face reddening.

Kirstie didn't pursue it, as it was none of her business. This kind of thing happened all the time—very few relationships lasted the separation. Of course, most people were honest enough to finish with one before they started another. Caroline didn't want to lose Greg though, it was just that Aaron was there and Greg wasn't. She felt like it was destined, as though she and Aaron belonged together. What was it about Aaron that attracted her so deeply? At the time, she loved them both. Only now, all these years later, can she see it for what it was: physical desire, curiosity, opportunity. There was something mysterious about Aaron, something she felt only she understood. He needed her. Oh, maybe Greg needed her too but he had become so distant. She had no idea what he did, where he went, who he saw. She wasn't falling out of love with him, she just didn't seem to know him anymore. He was no longer part of her life, nor she of his. But she knew Aaron. She knew what he did, she knew the people he knew. She was a part of his life; more than that, she was an essential part. Aaron worshipped her, he adored her, he put her on a pedestal. It was obvious in everything he did.

A few weeks into this new stage in their relationship, she and Aaron went back to Tiverton together. It was so much better going back with someone than going on her own. They shivered together on the platform, arms around each other, waiting for the train. Then they cuddled up on the seat, reading their books or magazines, talking and laughing. Aaron found something amusing about every other passenger, whispering about them into her ear. "He's a spy. Look at the way he's writing everything down. Now he thinks he's being watched. See the way he looked over here?"

"That's because you're talking about him, silly. What about the woman over there?

"The one with the fur hat? Oh, she's a famous opera singer. She's hoping she won't be recognised..."

If her parents were confused by Caroline being all over Aaron where previously she had been all over Greg, they said nothing about it. Looking back on it, she can see she was still so young. They assumed she wouldn't stick to one boy. And they both liked Aaron. Mum, in particular, made no secret about preferring him to Greg. "He's so polite and well brought up," she said.

"Greg's polite and well brought up too," Caroline wanted to say, but then Mum would start asking when she'd

finished with him and then tell her that she wasn't being fair (which was true), and she didn't want to get into all that.

Aaron had a way with Mum. He'd take his mug or plate out to the kitchen and wash it up without being asked, or help her carry things to the table. She would talk to him, laugh and joke. She was almost flirtatious.

Dad liked the fact that Aaron's father ran his own business. It seemed to rate more highly than Greg's father being a financial adviser. Maybe he thought Aaron would inherit it one day or something. He knew he was doing Business Studies like Caroline, so perhaps he thought they could both run the company together in due course. Whatever the reason, he treated Aaron like a future son-in-law, taking him into his study to show him his music collection (Aaron liked jazz) and offering him a whisky after dinner.

Mum and Dad allowed her far more freedom with Aaron than they had ever allowed her with Greg. Aaron had a car, an old Ford Escort that was always breaking down. It wasn't strictly his, it belonged to his cousin, but they had some sort of arrangement about it. Aaron had learned to drive in the summer holidays before they went to university. He drove her to Exmouth, where they walked in a freezing cold wind on a freezing cold beach with no one else crazy enough to be around. Then they went down to Exeter, where he trailed behind her around the shops, even though she had no money to spend on clothes anyway. They had lunch in a pub and here Aaron was in his element. A true sportsman, a crowded bar was second nature to him. He found her a table in the corner, steered his way expertly through the crowds, laughing when he was jostled and caught the barman's eye with an easy nod. He had no more money than she did, but maybe his mum or dad had lent him some, because he insisted on paying for lunch (pâté and French bread) and refused her offer of anything towards the petrol costs.

There was an intimacy about being cocooned together in the car. Of course, they were often alone together, but here no one could interrupt them: no parents or brothers or sisters outside the door; no friends at uni likely to burst in just for a laugh. Aaron stopped the car in a lay-by. She didn't need to ask why. He turned to her, kissed her. Their hands were everywhere.

Guilt washed over her afterwards as she remembered each intimate moment. The guilt worsened when she talked to Greg, her voice muffled on her mobile in her bedroom, where the signal was so bad she could only call crouched over in one corner.

"I love you, I love you," she said. And she did. She knew she did. The sound of his voice brought him closer, the things he said took him further away.

"What do you want me to say?" he asked her, bewildered. "Do you want me to describe what I do from the moment I get up until I go to bed? It's the same as you do. Just with different people..."

She went to bed crying, woke up knowing she had Aaron. Aaron, who was always there for her, who seemed to understand her every mood.

"It'll be okay," he said on the train back. "Things will sort themselves out."

It was around about this time she found out that Greg was taking drugs. Even at college, she'd known he was fascinated by the idea of being "high", and she knew that although he never smoked cigarettes, he had smoked Hash.

"It's just a different way of seeing the world," he had excused himself. "It takes away your inhibitions. Opens your mind..."

She'd seen him like this and it didn't change him—it was just like he was a bit drunk. Hardly even that really. More like he wasn't quite there. She didn't like it much but she was so in love with him, she let it go. It was like experimenting with booze, which they'd all done; he would stop once he'd done it a few times. And it wasn't as if drugs were freely available in Tiverton. But of course, they were at uni.

She noticed it for the first time when they were on the phone one evening. His voice was slightly slurred and at first, she thought he'd been drinking, but he swore he hadn't. Then he suddenly said: "The room is full of insects. My God, I can see them everywhere…" She could hear him trying to bat them away.

"Have you been smoking pot?" she asked.

"Nah," he said. She could hear the sheepish tone in his voice. "I dropped an acid tab."

She didn't know what to say. The Greg she knew—or at least, the Greg she *thought* she knew—wouldn't do hard drugs. She didn't want to come over all disapproving or prim and proper but nevertheless, he sensed her reaction.

"It's just a bit of fun," he said. "Like having a drink…"

One evening, she and Aaron were invited to a party. By this time, they were accepted as a couple. No one asked about Greg and she'd stopped talking about him. Helen and Kirstie were going too and they came over to her flat so they could all get ready together. Most first-year students lived in the accommodation on campus in the first year: huge tower blocks, each floor divided up into four flats. This party, however, was in a student house, a good twenty-minute walk from the main campus. It was February and although the days were warming up, the nights were still cold. The girls were wearing short skirts and thin tops. Aaron put his arm around her, and she snuggled into his big warm body, noticing how her head fitted perfectly on his shoulder. They could hear the sound of music as they went round the corner. "I bet the neighbours love this!" Kirstie laughed.

Despite the cold, people were smoking in the garden outside and Caroline recognised the distinctive whiff of Hashish. The lighting in the house was turned down low, probably to disguise the dirt and grime. There were people everywhere: crammed into the tiny hallway, sitting on the stairs, in the kitchen, in the sitting room. There was no room to dance but it didn't seem to be that sort of party anyway. People yelled into each other's' ears, laughed and joked and generally messed around. There was plenty of booze: beer, wine, spirits. Aaron grabbed a beer, found a cleanish glass for Caroline, and poured her some of the cheap white wine. As the evening wore on, she lost sight of Helen and Kirstie altogether, but there were plenty of other people they both knew. Aron kept his arm proprietorially draped around her shoulder. He stopped from time to time to kiss her, and kept asking if she was okay, not too tired, if she wanted to go home yet. He looked after her far better than Greg ever had.

Caroline can't remember now how they ended up upstairs in the back bedroom. There were others there already: Tim and George she recognised, then there were some rugby-playing friends of Aaron's, and a couple of girls she didn't know—although she had been told their names—all crammed together on someone's single student bed. She and Aaron sat on the two hard chairs—one by the bed, and one at the desk. Everyone was pretty drunk. Up here, the music was muted, but not much, and they still had to raise their voices to be heard.

"Well, have you got it or not?" Tim said suddenly.

"Yeah, I just wasn't sure..." George gestured with a jerk of his head to Caroline and Aaron.

"She's fine," Aaron said, speaking for Caroline. "We don't, though..."

Caroline had absolutely no idea what they were talking about but she was too drunk to care and whatever it was, she trusted Aaron. He wouldn't let any harm come too her.

George shrugged. "No problem," he said. He reached in his pocket for a small packet. Caroline watched with fascination as he shook the little packet of white powder on to the glass of a photograph he'd picked up from beside the bed, divided it into lines with a credit card, sniffed it up into his nostrils with a rolled-up five-pound note, and then passed it to Tim and the girls to do the same.

"You okay?" Aaron whispered into Caroline's ear.

"Yeah..."

Her mind flew to Greg. Hashish. LSD. Cocaine was the next step, available if you wanted it and knew who to ask.

After that, things got a bit out of hand as Tim and George careered around the room, the cocaine combining with the drink and making them laugh hysterically at everything they said and did. One of the girls seemed to drift off to sleep, the other sat on the bed, watching and laughing. Aaron held out his hand to Caroline and they left quietly. There were two other rooms upstairs: one equally crammed with people, the other miraculously empty. Aaron pulled her into it. Orange light from the streetlight outside filled the room. He kissed her, ran his hands down her body. She would like to say she was too drunk to know what she was doing, but she wasn't. He wedged a chair under the door handle, then came back to her. She didn't stop him as he undressed her slowly, pushed her gently down on the bed. They kissed again. She was moaning. She was wet. She wanted it as much as he did. He pulled off his clothes, threw them in a heap on the floor.

"Little girl..." he said softly. "I want you so much..."

"We mustn't..." She managed to gasp.

She had never been naked with Greg. She'd never been naked with anyone. She gazed in awe at Aaron's body: the wide shoulders, slightly bulging stomach, the dark pubic hair, the thick erect penis.

He saw her looking. "Look at all this," he joked suddenly, rolling his stomach in his hands. "Too much beer..."

Then he was suddenly serious again. He climbed on top of her and the narrow student bed sank under their weight. He was big, heavy, her arms hardly reached around his back. She could feel his erection hard against her pubic bone.

"It's okay," he whispered. "I won't put it into you."

How could she go back to Greg after that? Okay, so she and Aaron didn't have sex but they'd done everything but. She could never look Greg in the eye now and tell him she loved him. It was over, there was no going back.

She rang him the following evening. She was crying even before she started. God knows what she said, she couldn't remember even after she put the phone down. At one point, she can remember saying, "I can't do this," but she knew she had to. Greg didn't say much. He didn't even ask why. He seemed to accept it without a question.

"I still love him," she sobbed to Aaron afterwards.

"It doesn't matter," he said. "I love you enough for both of us."

That changed too. Of course it did. She fell off the pedestal Aaron had put her on. He was nothing like the person she thought he was. But a lot of other things happened first.

After that night at the party, she could hardly expect things to go back to normal. Now that they'd gone that far, Aaron would expect it to happen again and she didn't have the willpower to stop it. They had all the opportunity in the world: they had their own rooms to go to, they could spend the night together. Everyone did it. No one asked questions. When you started a relationship, the next stage was bed. Most of her friends were on the Pill. Caroline knew she should do the same, but still she resisted. Things were getting out of control. Everything was happening too fast.

"I'm so confused," she said to him. "Maybe we should cool things for a while." She saw his face cloud over in a way she would come to recognise with dread. But back then, it quickly brightened again.

"Okay." He shrugged. "You're probably right. I still love you. I always will. Nothing and no one will change that."

She still saw him, of course. They went to the same lectures. He was usually late. She'd see him approach with his distinctive bouncy athlete's walk. Inside the lecture hall, she'd tried to ignore him, but their eyes would meet across the room. He didn't try to hide the look of worship in his. She couldn't help but feel flattered.

He kept to his word, though, leaving straight after the lecture without a backward glance, intentionally or unintentionally making her feel rejected.

She sometimes saw him in the evenings too. He was always drunk. She had always known he was too fond of a drink, but now he was drinking to excess. Drowning his sorrows. Because of her. She felt guilty as she saw him rolling around, talking too loudly, laughing too much, making a fool of himself.

"Come over here, Little Girl!" he yelled across at her one evening. "I love you! Let me show you how much!"

The others with him—the rugby-playing, beer-swilling lot—all laughed, and she turned away, embarrassed. When she turned back, he was talking and laughing with them again and seemed to have forgotten he'd even said it.

Greg chose that particular night to text her.

"I miss you." It said simply.

Her fingers skimmed over the phone without a second thought. *"I miss you too."*

The phone rang immediately. They were both talking. She was crying.

"I'm going home this weekend," he said. "It's Mum's birthday. Please come."

What could she say? She hadn't told him about Aaron, but then she and Aaron weren't together anymore. At least, not for the moment. Neither were she and Greg. She was free. Free to choose.

"My parents think we've split up," she said.

"Don't tell them then." He laughed. "They don't need to know, do they?"

Her stomach fizzed with excitement: a secret just between her and Greg.

She missed Aaron on the station though. Waiting there in the cold on her own, she remembered the feel of his hand around hers, his big heavy arm around her shoulders, his big boisterous laugh. She checked her phone, as she had so many times recently, but true to his word, Aaron hadn't texted her. No *"I love you"* or *"I miss you"*. She would have liked that.

On the train on her own, she couldn't help remembering that last silly carefree journey down together, before sex got in the way and everything became so complicated.

Her father picked her up at the station and they went through the usual questions about her course, her friends, and whether she was eating enough.

"You're getting very thin, Caroline. I see girls like you. Women too. Obsessed about their weight. Wanting to be like the models in magazines. It's not just the physical damage you're doing to your body, you can't learn properly if you're not getting the right nutrition."

She dutifully answered "Yes, Dad" and "No, Dad" in all the right places. Dad was a distant person at the best of times. He didn't ask about Aaron. But of course, Mum did.

"You've left the poor boy behind on his own?" she said. "He could've stayed here if his parents are away or something."

Caroline was tempted to point out that she'd never offered Greg to stay when his parents were called away to the bedside of a dying aunt. He was shunted off to a relative in Bampton, and had to catch the bus to college every day.

"He didn't want to come down," she lied glibly. "He's playing rugby this weekend." This at least was true. And the last thing she wanted was Mum giving her the third degree about what was going on. "I'm going over to Mel's on Sunday," she went on. "I'll be there all day I think. That's okay, isn't it?"

She was going to use Vicky as an excuse, but Mum would probably check with Vicky's mum, so that was no good. She did consider asking Vicky to say they were going out somewhere together, but she didn't want anyone else to know about Greg and Aaron. She felt bad enough about it herself without anyone else knowing, even Vicky.

Greg's father looked a bit surprised to see her when he opened the door on Sunday, making her doubt for a moment if she was expected at all. But then Greg's mum appeared with a big beam on her face, and everything was forgotten about amid the 'Happy Birthdays' and general chaos. Only one of Greg's brothers had managed to get there—the older one, Tom, with his fiancée Gayle. They had all crowded into the front hallway when she arrived, and there was no chance to say a proper hello to Greg. Her heart leapt when she caught sight of him again though and suddenly she thought everything was going to be okay. Here, with Greg's family, accepted as Greg's girlfriend, it all seemed so simple: she would tell Aaron it was over. She had made a mistake. It was Greg she loved.

She had no idea what Greg had told his parents about her. Maybe he'd said nothing and they had no idea they'd ever split up. Looking back now, she can see that at their age, his parents wouldn't have taken it seriously anyway. Yet it felt so important at the time.

Greg held her hand under the table, put his arm around her when he could. They managed a frantic session in the kitchen after lunch while they were supposed to be making coffee but other than that, they had no time alone together. They both had to be on the train back to uni by early evening, and she had to get back to her parents before that.

"How was Mel?" Caroline's mum asked. Caroline was ready for this. The truth, even half the truth, was always the best strategy in the end. Tiverton was a small town and word got around.

"Oh, she wasn't there. I must've made a mistake. I bumped into Greg and it was his mum's birthday, so he asked me in…"

She saw her mother's face tighten, her lips purse. "I thought you'd finished with him. What about Aaron? That poor boy, what will he think?"

"He's not a 'poor boy', for God's sake!" She snapped but her face reddened guiltily. "He's a grown man. I'm not doing anything wrong. I'm not a child. I can do what I like!"

Three

The spring term of her first year at uni found Caroline sort-of-back with Greg and on-the-verge-of-being-back with Aaron. All she had done by seeing Greg again was to make things more complicated. Now Aaron didn't know she was with Greg. And Greg didn't know about Aaron. It was such a muddle.

It was hard to avoid Aaron. He was at every lecture for a start, gazing soulfully across the room at her. He as good as stalked her, turning up in any bar she happened to be in, accidentally walking past lecture halls as she came out, and popping around to her flat on the flimsiest of pretexts. And they had so many mutual friends.

The following term, Aaron somehow managed to get his cousin's car up to uni. She often found herself included as three or four of them would pile into the battered old Fiesta and drive off to a pub if it was chilly, or to a park if it was warm enough.

She's read since that love is inspired by pity, and that's what she felt for Aaron: pity. He liked old-fashioned pop music, particularly Elvis Presley, and she'd hear him crooning untunefully the words *"This time, the girl is here to stay..."* as his sad grey eyes rested on her. How could she resist? She'd go over to him, cradle his head in her arms. He'd cling to her.

Although nothing was really happening, they were

together all the time and everyone assumed they were a couple. It was only a small step to actually being one.

She still wrote to Greg, spoke to him almost daily on the phone, texted him. But he had become distant again. She couldn't picture his world. He wasn't part of hers. They talked about seeing each other: she could go and see him in Oxford or he could come up to Birmingham; but neither of them could afford the train fare, and weekends slipped by without it happening. She missed him, yet he seemed so far away, like a distant memory of something that had happened a long time ago. And Aaron was ever-present. Whatever she felt like, however black and bleak her mood, Aaron was always there for her, like an older brother or a father figure. Her own father had always been a distant figure. Her mother too, but her dad much more so. He had never been the sort of hands-on, rough and tumble dad, playing with his children, cuddling them, walking along arm in arm with them like Vicky's dad did. She had always envied Vicky for that closeness as she watched them cuddling up together, Vicky holding "Daddy's" hand long into her teenage years, even when she had started going out with Jason Fraser at college, even after they'd started sleeping together, even after she'd married him and had Sally and Ethan. She'd always be Daddy's little girl. Caroline was Aaron's little girl.

But it couldn't stay like that—the big brother/father figure who looked out for her, protected her. Aaron wanted more and she couldn't deny she did too. It was different from what she had with Greg: earthier, deeper, more lustful. Here, far from the watchful eye of parents, she had the opportunity to take it further, in their own bed, in their own room, with no one to judge anything they did.

It was ironic then that the first time they had sex was in the car.

It was one afternoon. Neither of them had lectures and Aaron took her out for a pub lunch. Aaron was in his element in a pub: able to get the barman's attention instantly, ordering drinks before he found the menu, looking so at home as he perched opposite her on a stool with a pint in his hand. On the way back, they stopped off at Kings Heath Park. She can't remember now whose idea it was or why they went there. They could hardly have been planning to go for a walk as it was a cold afternoon with drizzly rain. Anyway, whatever the reason, Aaron parked the car at the end of a long road near the park, under the shelter of an overhanging tree. There was a row of houses next to them, net-curtained against the outside world. The street was deserted. He put the handbrake on and turned to her. Afterwards, she could scarcely remember how it had happened. She had no excuse. She hadn't had more to drink than usual and they had been alone together many times before, in each other's rooms and beds. But this time was different. They were in each other's arms in a moment. She felt his hands grope inside her jeans, her own hand was grinding against the bulge in his. In a moment, she felt him unzip her jeans. She lifted her hips so he could pull them down, his fingers sliding inside her as she moaned. The car windows were misting up. She glanced out surreptitiously but it was a Tuesday afternoon, just after lunch, and the road was empty. Although to be honest, she wouldn't have cared if there had been a crowd of onlookers, as she was hot with passion, wet with desire. As Aaron pulled her knickers down, she stared down almost incredulously at the sight of her own flat white stomach, her dark pubic hair exposed to the daylight. With her jeans around her ankles, she couldn't widen her legs enough. She reached down, pulled one leg out, pushed her knickers all the way off, and left them dangling around one ankle with her bunched-up jeans. In a moment he was on top of her. He was heavy, much heavier than Greg. She felt pinned down by the bulk of his weight; he was possessing her, taking her oh-so-willingly. His cock pushed impatiently into her, stretching her.

"Ow...!"

"Am I hurting you?"

"Yes, but..."

He pulled out of her suddenly, a torrent of warm, wet liquid on her stomach, then collapsed on top of her.

"I love you, Little Girl," he said, looking at her with such adoration. "I love you so much. You have no idea…"

"I love you too," she heard herself saying. How could she not after what she had just felt? After what she had done.

So there it was. She loved Aaron now. And she still loved Greg, clung to the memory of their love like Aaron clung to her.

She found blood in her knickers when she got back. She was sore for days afterwards. Aaron didn't need to tell her it was his first time. They used condoms after that, but Aaron hated them.

"I can't feel a thing," he said.

She knew she should go on the Pill but somehow, illogically, she felt like it was an admission she was sleeping with Aaron if she did.

She put off finishing with Greg for as long as she could. But she felt guilty every time she said "I love you" to him, knowing she had only just said it to Aaron. She couldn't love them both and what she was doing was unfair.

Greg must have known something was wrong: she kept breaking down in tears on the phone and she rang him less because it was hard. Aaron was with her practically all the time, including nights. She had to phone Greg sneakily.

It was an impossible situation and she knew it. So one day, she just rang and told him. Not about Aaron of course— she just said there was "someone else". Poor Greg. He'd had no idea. She cried on the phone. She cried for hours afterwards and had to tell Aaron she had a headache and couldn't see him. For weeks, she had to hide her pain from Aaron. "I'm just feeling a bit low," she lied. She longed to tell him the real reason and at one time she could have, would have, and he would have listened to her, understood. But not now. They had crossed a line, a line where friendship stops and love—with all its jealousies, misunderstandings and lies—begins. They could never return to where they were before.

She dreaded going home in the Easter Holidays. Tiverton was a small town and she could so easily bump into Greg when she was with Aaron. But it never happened. The weather remained cold and damp like it had been all spring, and they spent most of their time at her parents' house or his. She'd try to make excuses if Aaron wanted to go to the pub, the one place Greg might easily have been, and if they did go, she spent the evening nervously looking around the crowd and glancing over every time the door opened and someone new came in. She didn't think Aaron had noticed. Propping up the bar, standing in a crowd or perched on a barstool, he was in his natural element.

He *had* noticed though and one evening, he said with studied casualness, "Greg's parents have taken him away on holiday. Lucky sod. A week of beach and sunshine. I could do with that."

She didn't want to ask how he knew. Greg and Aaron had been such good friends at school, always hanging around together. But maybe being at different universities meant it was just too much hassle. She had no idea how much, or even if, they were still in touch. She couldn't imagine losing touch with *her* friends but she knew boys weren't the same.

A week though. It wasn't long. Greg could walk in next time they were in there, all tanned and fit. How would she feel seeing him again? How would *he* feel seeing her with Aaron? She tried to put it to the back of her mind.

They saw other friends, of course: Vicky, still attached at the hip to Jason Fraser—it was easier for them as they'd gone to the same uni in Bristol so they could be together. Heather and Amy were often around town too. Lauren hadn't got the grades she needed for uni and had ended up working in County Hall in Exeter. "She doesn't come here much now," Vicky told her. "She's got more friends in Exeter. She goes out with them." Melissa hadn't gone to uni either. She'd moved up to London to live with her older sister and was working in a shop.

They couldn't afford to go out all the time, and Aaron's mum made Caroline welcome at their house. Aaron had a seventeen-year-old brother, Neal, who was a moody, silent, slimmer version of Aaron; and a fourteen-year-old sister called Zoe, who had long brown hair, Aaron's grey eyes, and a flighty temperament. She was always at loggerheads with her parents for one reason or another. Aaron's Dad, like Caroline's own, was a distant man who liked his own space. He was the old-fashioned type who thought it was the woman's job to bring up the children, and who retreated to the sitting room behind a book or a newspaper if there was a dispute of any kind. Like her own dad, he was balding already. He was big-built and broad, and he went to the gym once a week to try and keep fit.

Aaron was often still in bed when Caroline came around, and Aaron's mum liked to chat with her while she got on with the washing or the ironing or whatever she was doing in the house. She was a big blustery woman with short greying dark hair and dark brown eyes. She treated Caroline like a daughter-in-law, confiding her worries about the younger children to her.

"He'll be fine," Caroline would say vaguely when she moaned about Neal's moodiness. "It's just a phase she's going through," she'd say about Zoe when she rushed out of the kitchen in tears, slamming the door. In truth, she had no idea about any of it. She couldn't remember either her or Emma daring to behave like Neal or Zoe. She was no more than a sounding board to Aaron's mum, but she enjoyed the intimacy, the idea that she was grown up enough to share the confidences of an older woman.

Emma was home from university too. Like Caroline, she had a holiday job a couple of days a week. Emma's was in a supermarket and she worked shifts, sometimes evenings, so they didn't actually see much of each other.

"What happened to Greg?" she asked one day.

Caroline felt a stab of pain at the mention of his name, her eyes filling with tears. But she had committed herself to

Aaron now in every single way, and there was no going back. "Oh, you know…" she said vaguely.

"Yeah…" Emma said, not unkindly.

They had never been close. Emma was like Dad—a very distant, private person. They weren't the sort of sisters who chose each other's company, shared each other's clothes or secrets. They were only two years apart, an age gap that meant nothing later on. But when they were young, Emma considered herself far too grown-up to worry about her little sister. It didn't bother Caroline.

On her last evening around at Aaron's place, his mum suddenly said, "Would you like to come on holiday with us in the summer? We always take the caravan up to the Lake District. We've got a tent for the children. You can sleep in with them, if you like…"

Of course she said yes. It was flattering to be asked and she liked the idea of a camping holiday, something her parents would never have considered.

They drove up in Aaron's cousin's car, listening to the Elvis songs Aaron loved so much and singing along to them together and stopping at motorway service stations for cups of tea and bags of chips.

Aaron's parents had been there for a few days when they arrived. Caroline had expected a proper campsite with shower blocks and loos, but the caravan was parked on its own in a field next to a farm. Aaron's parents, who she was asked to call Jack and Margaret now that she was almost family, were sitting on camp chairs in the shade of the awning even though the sky was grey. Neal and Zoe came haring out of the tent nearby when they heard the car stop.

The tent was divided into three rooms. "Neal can sleep in the awning," Margaret told Caroline. "Oh, and you can shower and use the loo in the van. Just tell us and we'll make ourselves scarce."

It was far more primitive than Caroline had expected. She hated the idea of having to tell everyone each time she needed to go to the loo, a tiny area with every sound audible to the rest of the caravan.

"I usually go in the woods,' Aaron told her cheerfully. "And wash in the stream."

Shivering in her sleeping bag that night, she longed for Aaron to be holding her close to warm her. It was agony knowing he was so close yet out of reach.

The next day dawned clear, and she woke with sunlight beating down on the tent. She could tell from the lack of movement outside and the chirping of the birds that it was still early. She turned over in the narrow sleeping bag, plumped her pillow, and was just dozing off again when she heard the flap of her little compartment lifting. She sat up quickly.

"Shh..." Aaron whispered, gesturing to Zoe's compartment that was so close to them. Tingling with excitement, Caroline unzipped her sleeping bag as Aaron peeled off the jogging bottoms and t-shirt he was wearing and slid in next to her. It was hard not to giggle. There was so little room and she nearly hit Aaron in the face as she pulled her baggy t-shirt over her head. But soon Aaron was on top of her, inside her, and she felt the familiar pressure of his weight, the rhythm of his hips, the response in her body. They stifled their moans; he bit into her shoulder, collapsed on top of her.

Afterwards, they raced down to the stream, shivering in the cold morning air, taking shampoo and soap with them. It was still early, no sound from the caravan, but Caroline wore her bikini anyway, and Aaron wore trunks. They couldn't stay in long as the water was glacial, and they were freezing when they came out.

With their own car, they didn't have to spend much time with Jack and Margaret. Aaron drove her into Coniston, where they wandered around the shops and had coffee in one of the little cafes; they went to visit Brantwood, John Ruskin's house; they went for various walks in the area that

Aaron knew; they went on a boat trip on the lake. They had sex in the car in secluded lanes. At night, after Zoe was safely asleep or in the morning, before she'd woken, Aaron would creep into Caroline's sleeping bag and hold her close.

She and Aaron usually ate out at lunchtime, sometimes in the evening too if they'd been out all day. On evenings when they stayed with his family, Caroline felt honour-bound to help with preparing dinner, and washed up in the minuscule sink afterwards.

"You're good for Aaron," Margaret said one night, shaking out the tea towel she was holding, ready to hang it on the line outside with Caroline's bikini (that she'd noticed Jack's eyes on earlier). "You settle him down."

It was only later, when her effect on Aaron had long since waned, that Caroline realised what she meant.

After dinner, they played games on the table set up in the awning: Monopoly or Cluedo, often ending up in arguments between Neal and Zoe, where Zoe would throw all her cards or money on the table and stomp off to the tent in a huff.

Back home in Tiverton for the rest of the long summer holiday, Caroline worried again that she'd bump into Greg. Or worse still, he'd see her with Aaron. Aaron never mentioned him and she had no idea if they spoke to each other at all. At that time it was a tacitly forbidden subject between them.

They both had holiday jobs. Caroline's was in the local department store, Aaron's was in the same supermarket Emma was working in, though they seldom worked the same shift.

It was a warm summer and if he wasn't working an evening shift, Aaron would drive out into the country and they'd go for a walk, often ending up at a pub. Maybe Aaron was deliberately avoiding the pubs in town where Greg might go. Maybe Greg was avoiding them too. Either way, they never ran into him.

They were in Aaron's garden one warm summer's evening. Neal and Zoe were half-heartedly batting a tennis ball to and fro with tennis racquets. Jack and Margaret were leaning back on sun loungers, reading a newspaper and a book respectively. Caroline and Aaron were sitting on a rug scattered with cushions. Suddenly, Caroline sat up.

"My bracelet," she said, feeling her empty wrist. "It's gone!" It was the one Greg had given her for her seventeenth birthday, engraved "Caro". She never took it off, not even in the bath, but she had a habit of fiddling with it on her wrist. The chain must have come undone or broken. They both sat up, Aaron on one knee opposite her, searching the rug next to her.

"Aaron!" Margaret called over. "Are you proposing to Caroline?"

Quick as a flash Aaron said, "Yes. Caroline, will you marry me?"

"Yes, of course."

It was a joke. Everyone knew it was a joke, surely? Yet Jack rushed out to the kitchen and brought wine and glasses. Zoe and Neal were called over from their game of tennis.

"Caroline and Aaron have just announced their engagement," Margaret said.

"I'm so happy," Aaron whispered to her.

The bracelet was forgotten in the celebrations. Caroline tried to look for it again surreptitiously when they shook the rug out and tidied up the cushions. She looked again the next time she went over but Jack had cut the grass. If it was there, it would have been chewed up by the lawnmower.

In the meantime, everyone, including her parents, accepted she was engaged. Both sets of parents met up; friends were told, relatives. Caroline couldn't believe it was all being taken so seriously. She was only nineteen. Mum even wanted to put it in the paper, but Caroline refused.

"Please," she said. "It's a waste of money."

It was as though everyone had got together, pushing her towards a future she didn't want. And there was no going back.

"It doesn't feel real," she told Aaron one evening.

The next day he gave her a small square navy box. Inside was just the ring she would have chosen herself: a band of sapphires and diamonds in a delicate ornate antique setting. It even fitted perfectly.

"Does it feel real now, Little Girl?" he asked gently as she slid it on, held out her hand to admire it. Then his face grew serious. "The time for joking is over," he said. "If you don't want it, now is the time to say."

She wanted to say it: *"It's too soon. I'm not sure... It was only a joke, let's just tell everyone we've changed our mind."* But how could she? Everyone knew now. What would they say? Her parents, Aaron's parents, all their friends and relatives. It was like a huge tidal wave that she couldn't swim against. Her life was being written out for her and she was powerless to resist.

She could have gone on wearing Greg's ring. It was on her right hand, after all. But the big silver and onyx ring looked clumsy in comparison to the delicate gold engagement ring. So she took it off, put it away. She's moved house since then and she has no idea what happened to it. Maybe she gave it away with other stuff that went to the charity shop. Maybe it just got lost.

Some people thought she was crazy and told her so. Emma for one.

"You're *nineteen,* for God's sake!" she said.

But Caroline, with the ring that she loved on her finger and everyone making such a fuss about it, chose to ignore her. She knew others thought the same. Not just her own friends, but her mum and dad's friends, and the uncles, aunts and godparents who dutifully sent her Congratulations cards, engagement presents even. Vicky was naturally brave enough to speak out. She'd been going out with Jason Fraser for years but she wouldn't have dreamt of getting engaged.

"What on earth for?" she asked. "I don't see the point."

She didn't say anything about Greg. Everyone had stopped talking about him. They all assumed she was in love with Aaron and she told herself she was. Why then, did the thought of Greg bring a pang to her heart? Why did she still dream of him at night, find her thoughts drifting to him during the day, calling his name in her mind?

He wrote her an email when he found out. Two pages long. She deleted it almost immediately but she still remembers some of the words:

"Your 'engagement' to Aaron has broken my heart," he wrote. *"No one will ever come close to me again like you did. I shall make sure of that."* and at the end: *You will always have a place in my heart, if I can ever put it back together again."*

One day, just before they went back to uni, she was laughing and joking with Aaron as they walked through town. Aaron was trying to tickle her and as she dodged away from him, she almost knocked a passing woman off her feet.

"Oh, sorry!" she giggled. Then she flushed scarlet as she realised it was Greg's mum. "Oh, hello Mrs. Foster," she blurted out. Why did she say that? She had always called her Julie.

"Hello," Greg's mum replied icily. "Hello, Aaron." Her pale blue eyes were as glacial as her voice. "We never see you nowadays. But then, I understand congratulations are in order. I hope you'll both be very happy."

Caroline wished she could disappear. What must she think of her? What must she think of Aaron? Deserting his best friend? Stealing his girlfriend from him?

"You realise you've ruined Greg's chances, don't you?" she went on.

"What?" Caroline asked, genuinely bewildered.

"How's he supposed to concentrate on his university work when you've upset him so much?"

An image of Greg, lying in a crumpled heap on his bed, came into Caroline's mind. She felt small. Small and mean. "I…" she began, but her voice broke and she couldn't go on. "I had work too…" she managed.

"But *you* weren't the one who was upset, were you?" His mother went on.

Caroline was crying now, sobbing as Aaron put his arm around her shoulders and led her on.

"Forget it," he said gruffly. "Silly old cow. It's not true. She just wants to make you feel bad."

"But I *do* feel bad," Caroline sobbed. She couldn't get it out of her mind. The thought of Greg staying in his room, too upset to go out and see anyone, too upset to do any work, too upset to go back to uni. Had she—had *they*—wrecked Greg's chances of the career he had set his mind on all these years?

They went back to uni at the end of September. After their first year in the tower block halls of accommodation, they'd had to find somewhere to live in the second year. Last term, everyone had started to look for flatshares. Sometimes a lucky student had a parent who bought a house and rented it out to them and their friends. Otherwise it was just a case of grouping together with friends, looking around, asking around. Aaron and Caroline had already decided to share together. They were in and out of each other's flats all the time as it was. They looked at several places before deciding on a share with another other boy and girl in a house in Minstead Road. They wouldn't share a room of course; they had separate rooms with single beds. They'd still be in one room or the other at night, but they could be separate for studying if they wanted.

It was mid-November when Caroline began to feel sick in the mornings. Rushing out of bed, she'd retch into the basin of the shared bathroom.

"It was that take-away last night," Aaron said the first time. "I'll get you a cup of tea. That always makes you feel better." But the thought of tea made her feel even worse, a feeling which continued all day, even after the nausea wore off. And the smell of certain foods cooking in the kitchen turned her stomach.

She didn't worry too much to begin with when her period didn't come. She had always been irregular. But three weeks later, it still hadn't. Then one morning she came over all hot and cold during a lecture. Her palms were clammy, her heart pounding, and she thought she was going to be sick. Suddenly it struck her she was pregnant. She and Aaron had always been casual about birth control. Aaron hated condoms: the whole procedure of getting them out, rolling them on; it interrupted everything, and he often threw the condom impatiently to one side. "I'll be careful," he said reassuringly, and he would pull out at the last moment, spilling semen stickily on her stomach. She knew she should insist but she trusted Aaron implicitly in everything he did. She was his "Little Girl". He'd always look after her.

Aaron didn't come with her to the doctor's, didn't see her break down in tears when she heard the result, didn't hear the doctor advise an abortion. Clearly, the doctor was used to this.

"I can arrange everything for you," he said.

So here she was, she thought bitterly, in the same position as Greg's cousin Megan. If she'd stayed with Greg, it would never have happened. He would never have risked that. He would have insisted she went on the Pill.

But she couldn't blame Aaron entirely. She had been foolish. She should have gone on the Pill when they first started sleeping together. *Too late, too late.*

Aaron was surprisingly upbeat about it. "It doesn't matter," he said. "We'll get married."

"But what about university? Our careers?"

He shrugged. "Oh, we can do all that later. When the kid's older."

Caroline heard the death knell, saw the writing on the wall. The life of Greg's cousin Megan flashed before her eyes: her wan, tired face; the impatient stressed husband. Another child would follow. They'd live in a tiny rented house, families all around them. A life of cooking, shopping, cleaning, nappies, and the school run. Aaron would resent her: stuck in a dead-end job, struggling to make ends meet. Gone in a flash was Caroline's dream of a glittering career in the city: smart suits and designer heels, an executive office, shiny car, top-class apartment, holidays abroad.

She vowed silently she wouldn't have another child. She'd go on the Pill the moment this one was born. She'd find a way—*any* way—to have the career she'd wanted.

Aaron never suggested an abortion and to her own surprise, she didn't want one either. There were girls back at college, people talked about them, who'd had abortions. They all seemed to have hated it. Other girls got pregnant and kept the baby, lived at home with their parents. But Caroline didn't want to do that. Her parents would never cope with the shame, especially her father—a respected doctor who hadn't made sure his daughter did something about birth control.

They went home the following weekend to tell their parents. Caroline would never forget seeing her father sink his face into his hands, her mother's lips tremble as she searched in her sleeve for her tissue.

Aaron's father rang after dinner. "I think we should get together and discuss this," he said.

Caroline's face reddened as she sat with them all in the sitting room. Emma had been banished upstairs. She had said nothing but the look of wry pity on her face spoke volumes to Caroline.

And as both sets of parents discussed the wedding and planned a date, Caroline had the same feeling she'd had before; as though she was following a script, as though her life was being mapped out for her and she had no choice.

The wedding was booked for December, after the end of the winter term. They talked a lot about guests. Part of Caroline wanted to invite her friends, their parents' friends, their relatives. This was her wedding, it would only happen once and she wanted a big day; a day with champagne and cake and a big party afterwards. But the other part, the more sensible one, had to agree with Aaron.

"Someone has to pay for it," he said. "Your parents? Mine? Both? We've let them down enough already. We'll need their help in the future. And everyone will know, you know…" He gestured to her stomach.

"They'll have to know anyway." She pointed out.

Once she had got used to the idea, Mum seemed to enjoy telling the friends and family, the ones who had sent the engagement cards and presents. "It's just a bit sooner than we expected," she chirped. "And we're expecting the happy event in July."

For Caroline, telling her own friends, it was quite different. Most couldn't understand why she didn't just have an abortion.

"Kim had one," Helen said. "When she was eighteen. She told me…"

"Do you have to tell everyone?" Aaron asked. "Can't you just say we're leaving uni…?"

But Aaron was a man. He had very few friends. It wasn't the sort of thing he would talk about to his beer-swilling, rugby-playing mates.

"I'm not ashamed of it," Caroline said. Though, in truth, she was. But she still had to tell them.

Vicky cried when she told her, clutched her arm. "Oh no, that's awful. What're you going to do?"

"It'll be fine," Caroline said, more confidently than she felt. "We're getting married."

"What? But what about uni? Your career? Your life…?"

"It doesn't matter…"

Word soon got around, of course, saving her the trouble of telling most people. In Tiverton, her original crowd of six closed around her like a shield, saving her from the harsh critique of others.

Caroline's parents paid for the plain gold wedding ring, even generously paying for one for Aaron because Caroline said she'd like him to have one.

Mum took Caroline into Exeter to buy her a dress (a very plain, knee-length pale pink dress that she thought she could wear out in the evenings afterwards. If she would ever do that once the baby was born). The dress was loose enough to hide the tiny rounded belly she had and in the photos, no one would think she was pregnant. Mum also ordered flowers, buttonholes and corsages for them all, leaving Aaron's parents feeling obliged to pay for lunch afterwards.

After the initial shock, Aaron's mother also seemed to have come around to the idea. "You'll be good for Aaron," she said again. "He needs someone steady like you."

None of them said what they must all have been thinking: what a disappointment it was, what a waste of their education, the careers both sets of parents had looked forward to them having.

She and Aaron had arranged to leave uni at the end of term. Their parents all assumed they'd come home to live. Mum and Dad started posting copies of the Gazette up to them, with adverts for suitable flats and houses to rent ringed around in red biro.

"I don't think I could stand it," Caroline said to Aaron. "Everyone in Tiverton knowing we had to slink back home because I'm pregnant."

Aaron agreed. But if they were to stay in Birmingham, they needed somewhere to live and a job. They could have stayed on in their flat in Minstead Road for another term at least, but it was a student flat, not suitable for a married couple with a baby on the way.

Their university work abandoned, their rooms became littered with newspapers as they searched for flats and jobs. They started off with high ideals, writing to banks, building societies and local businesses, confident they'd find something easily with their knowledge of business studies. But when the rejection letters flooded in, they started looking for anything that would pay money. Caroline found a part-time temporary job in a clothes shop, with the promise of more hours if she wanted them, and Aaron found work on a building site. Caroline hated the idea but Aaron was fit and strong, he'd done construction work before during college holidays, and it was extremely well paid. Both jobs started in January the following year.

Finding somewhere to live was more difficult but in the end, they found a cheap, furnished house to rent in

Edgbaston. It was a tiny terraced house with a paved-over back garden in an estate full of identical houses. There was paint peeling off the mandatory magnolia walls in places, and the beige carpet was stained and threadbare around the edges, but it was no worse than the student accommodation they'd lived in before. They had to borrow the money for the deposit from Aaron's mum and dad because Caroline's parents were still set against them moving away.

"How will you manage?" Mum asked. "All the way up there on your own with a baby? You should be back here with people you know."

"But all my friends are at uni," Caroline countered. Not strictly true. Lauren was still in Tiverton and there were others who hadn't gone to uni. She may not have known them so well but she could have easily met up with them. Mum was right, of course. When Joshua was born, she was on her own and lonely. But at the time she thought she knew better.

Their wedding day dawned grey and miserable, with a steady drizzle falling. Caroline shivered in her strappy dress, wishing she'd thought to ask Mum if she could buy a jacket of some kind to wear with it. The only coat she owned was a parka which she usually wore with jeans. It looked really silly on top of her dress but she needed a hood for the rain. The date, 19th December 1998, stays stubbornly in her mind but looking back now, at a distance of nearly twenty years, she can hardly remember it. Her wedding to Damian— another registry office do—seven years ago, has taken precedence in her mind. But that was so different, with a hairdresser and make-up girl coming to the house, guests filling the room in the registry office, and her long cream dress that made her feel like a proper bride. Bits of her first wedding day do still stay in her mind though. Mum had wanted her to have her hair put up at a hairdressers, but Aaron liked it long and loose, so she washed it in the morning and let it dry naturally. She did her own make-up too and put on the lovely dress that in fact, she never wore again. No one told her she looked beautiful. "Very nice," was the only comment from Mum and Dad, and "I like the dress," was uttered jealously by Emma.

But she remembers Aaron's face when he saw her in it; the love and pride and happiness.

Mostly what she remembers from that day, though, is a feeling of unreality—as though she was watching herself on a film set. It wasn't really her arriving with Mum and Dad at the registry office, not her voice repeating the words of the registrar. It was someone else, surely, with the gold wedding ring on her finger, who would now answer to the one-syllabled surname of Mrs. Lee, instead of the so-much-grander-sounding Miss Westminster.

Caroline's parents were subdued during the ceremony but Aaron's parents made up for it, his father almost falsely jovial.

"You can call me Dad now," he said, putting his arm around her and squeezing her. The top of his bald head glistened under the fluorescent lights in the registry office room. Aaron's mum was beaming too, resplendent in a pale grey suit obviously bought for a previous wedding.

Aaron's parents had booked lunch in the Hartnoll House Hotel just outside Tiverton, where they had also generously paid for Aaron and Caroline to spend their wedding night.

Aaron's parents insisted that Caroline and Aaron's siblings should join them for lunch. Caroline had wanted as little fuss as possible, but all the usual social niceties and topics of conversation had been covered several times while they waited at the registry office, and she was glad the others were there—even if Emma did behave towards her as though she was some silly little girl who'd gotten caught out, and Aaron's sister kept staring in fascination at her stomach as though she thought the baby might pop out at any moment. Aaron's brother just looked pretty bored by the whole thing, but perked up when the food was served.

When they'd all gone home and she and Aaron were alone in their room, Aaron grabbed her in his arms.

"It's only three o'clock!" she giggled, pushing him only half-jokingly away.

"You're my wife now," he said, kissing her neck, her shoulder, sliding his hand under her skirt.

She wasn't really in the mood. She felt full and queasy after the rich food at lunchtime. She could taste champagne and garlic on Aaron's lips and the cigarettes he'd sneaked out for between courses. The smell turned her stomach even more. But she could feel Aaron's erection hard against her stomach, his insistent hands wrenching at her knickers.

"Wait," she said breathlessly. "Let me get this dress off. It cost Mum a small fortune."

"God, you look good..." he said, as she hung the dress on a hanger in the vast mahogany wardrobe and came over to him in her knickers, bra, hold-up stockings and high heels.

They'd never had sex in a double bed. After their tiny student beds it seemed huge, acres of it stretching out either side of them. Aaron's weight on top of her made her stomach heave and she felt bile rise in her throat with every thrust. Combined with the smell of his sweat and his breath, she wasn't sure how she managed not to retch. Luckily he came quickly, rolled off her and almost instantly fell asleep. She moved the heavy arm from across her chest, moved over to the blissfully empty side of the bed, slid between the cool crisp duvet and sheet, and fell asleep too.

She woke to the sound of a bath running and the TV on low volume. Aaron was sitting naked on the edge of the bed, his eyes on the television screen.

"Sorry, did I wake you? I thought you might like a bath..."

They bathed together soapily in the huge bath, washing each other's hair, feeling each other's bodies, having sex again, just because they were married and they could. Caroline ran her fingers over Aaron's wedding ring, glistening newly on his finger. "It feels strange, doesn't it?" she said.

"Yeah ... but good, Mrs. Lee."

"Thank you, Mr. Lee."

They watched television for a while, wrapped in the huge white towelling robes they found hanging on the back of the bathroom door. Then they dressed for dinner, Aaron in his suit again and Caroline in her wedding dress.

They must have looked ridiculously young. Aaron's father had made the booking but the hotel staff knew they were newlyweds. More free champagne arrived before dinner, and red wine with the meal that must have been ordered in advance by Aaron's dad. Caroline naturally couldn't drink any of it but Aaron drank glass after glass. Her queasiness from earlier had disappeared and now she had an appetite, but the smell of the coffee being poured into her cup after dinner turned her stomach again.

She saw the other hotel guests looking over at them as she sipped the glass of water she had asked for instead of coffee. Did they know they were newlyweds too? Or were they wondering how a couple of students could afford a hotel like the Hartnoll? Maybe they were waiting to see if they could pay the bill? They must have been disappointed when Aaron took her arm like a consummate gentleman and escorted her up to their room.

Aaron was very drunk, she could see that the moment they got into the lift. He lent against the lift wall, giggling ludicrously.

"What're you laughing about?" she asked, half-laughing herself.

"Look at us," he slurred, gesturing to the mirror in front of them. "A married couple. How ridiculous."

"But..." she said, stung by his words, "you said you were so proud..." Her voice sounded small, pathetic and whiny.

"Proud, yeah..." His voice was bitter. "Proud I've done the right thing. Made an honest woman of you. Shotgun wedding, that's what it is." He held a finger to his forehead, pretending to shoot.

The tears that had sprung to Caroline's eyes spilled over and down her cheeks as shame trickled through her. She reached for a tissue.

"Oh, for God's sake, don't cry!" Still the same scornful voice, nothing like the gentle Aaron she knew. "Whatever will people think? Making you cry on your wedding night..."

Their room was on the top floor. Aaron was right. She dreaded the thought of the lift stopping, anyone coming in and seeing them like this. She sniffed back the tears, blotting her eyes carefully so no mascara smudges showed, swallowed hard, pulled herself together as best she could.

In the room, things went from bad to worse. Aaron fell sideways onto the bed, fully-clothed, closed his eyes and fell asleep. Caroline went to the huge en suite bathroom to take off her make-up. Then she undressed, sliding the dress on to the hanger again, putting on the pink satin nightdress she had bought especially for her wedding night.

"Aaron..." she said gently. "Wake up. You need to get undressed. Come on..."

But he was dead to the world. She poked and prodded him, tried to ease his clothes off him, tried to move him over, but he was a heavy dead weight that she couldn't budge. The tears that had brimmed up earlier fell easily now. Sobbing and sniffing, wiping her face with the back of her hand, she tried to find a space in the bed to ease herself into but it was impossible. The only other furniture in the room was a pair of semi-circular padded armchairs. She pushed them together, took two pillows from the bed, found a spare blanket at the top of the wardrobe, and made a bed as best she could.

She couldn't get to sleep to begin with, as the pillow kept slipping out of place, her legs were all crooked up and her neck got stiff. But she must have dropped off eventually because she was woken in the early hours by Aaron blundering around the room, cursing as he knocked into bits of furniture. She reached for the lamp on the table next to her.

"What're you doing there, Little Girl?" he asked surprised.

"There was no room..." she began, but he was in the

bathroom by then, peeing loudly, and he didn't seem to hear her.

He came back in, unbuttoned his shirt, and looked for somewhere to sit. She took her legs off the second chair and he sat down opposite her.

"You regret it, don't you?" he asked.

"What?" Though of course, she knew.

"Getting married. It's a mistake. You still love Greg."

"What? Don't be silly. I love *you*. You know I do."

He shook his head. "No. I know you still love him. But it doesn't matter. I love you whatever. I'll have you on any terms."

Her eyes swam with tears again. "Aaron…" she began.

"I love you, Little Girl," he said again. "Come to bed…"

She lay in his arms, wide awake, long after he'd gone to sleep again. It was true. She did still love Greg. A part of her always would. But the decision was made, had been made long ago. There was no going back. She was committed to Aaron, wholly and completely. And she loved him. Just not in the same way. But she had no choice. There was a baby on the way, someone who'd need her totally. She'd have to make the best of it.

Four

After their one night's honeymoon, Caroline and Aaron moved in with her parents until January, when they would normally have gone back to university. It was strange sleeping in the spare room, legally allowed to have sex, but so close to her parents' room on one side and Emma's room on the other that they hardly dared make a sound. Emma stayed out of their way as much as possible. She was working in the same supermarket as before. Caroline and Aaron both had holiday jobs too. Caroline had found a job in a pharmacy and Aaron was in the menswear of the local department store, where he spent most of his time folding jumpers and rolling up ties. Both jobs were tedious but they had no choice, as they needed to save money for the future. Caroline did her best to keep away from everyone she knew. It wasn't too hard as most of her friends worked too, and in the evenings, she was too tired to go out and would just flop down in front of the television with Aaron. She dreaded seeing anyone in town: she knew people were talking about her. Maybe not unkindly but they were bound to gossip. It was only natural. She'd do the same if it was someone else.

She was lucky she didn't actually look pregnant yet. Her tummy only had the slightest bulge and she could hide it in loose jumpers and tops. She was determined not to show for as long as possible. Dad said it was okay to exercise—good for her, in fact—so she walked everywhere, dragging Aaron out every weekend even in the rain and cold. Those were the days when Aaron would do anything for her. He would make sure she had enough warm clothes on, drape his heavy arm across her shoulder as they walked, pull her towards him occasionally, talk confidently about their future together. She felt loved, cherished, looked after. Aaron adored the tiny bulge in her tummy, stroking it gently as though she were made of porcelain.

"Can we call it Rebecca if it's a girl?" he asked.

Jealousy shot through Caroline like a dart. Rebecca was his first love—the one he'd loved and lost. But what could she say? "Yes, of course. I like Jack for a boy."

"We can't have that, it's Dad's name. How about Jonathon?"

"Jon. Jonnie. Yes. Or Joshua?" It was a popular name. She'd heard a mother call out "Josh" to a sweet little boy in town the other day.

"Yeah, I like that," Aaron said.

They'd while away endless empty hours like this, dreaming of their future life, with no solid practical idea of how hard it would actually be.

The only person she still saw at that time was Vicky. Maybe it was because they had known each other for so long but Vicky was the only one who didn't judge her, who knew when she wanted to talk about it and when she didn't. She had already begun drifting away from the others, who were caught up in their own lives of work or uni and boyfriends and relationships of their own. Vicky was the only one from her school days that she was still in touch with.

Mum and Dad liked having Aaron around. Especially Mum. She'd get up early, cook him anything he fancied for breakfast; dinner became an occasion to pile his plate high with his favourite food, and she made cocoa for him at bedtime. Aaron would stand in the kitchen chatting to her while she prepared meals; helped her clear the table and dry the dishes afterwards. Later on, he'd join her again as she made the bedtime drinks and did her last rounds in the kitchen. Caroline often went to bed early and she'd feel quite jealous hearing their voices, their intimate on-the-same-wavelength laughter drifting upstairs to her. Sometimes she thought Mum fancied Aaron more than she did. Emma thought the same. She'd roll her eyes heavenwards, yawning, when Mum leaned across the table to him.

"More potatoes Aaron?" Mum would say. "Come on, you must be hungry after all that work."

"For God's sake, Mum," she snapped once. "It's only a shop."

"But he's a man," Mum said, undeterred, "he needs his food."

Because Aaron worked in the menswear section, he went off every day in a shirt and tie and smart trousers, looking far older now than the scruffy university student he'd so recently been. Caroline felt like a different person too in the clinical white tunic and thick navy trousers supplied by the pharmacy. But these were only temporary jobs, the start of many she and Aaron would have before either of them found any sort of permanent work.

At home with Mum, Dad and Emma those first few weeks of married life, they were sheltered from the world. In fact, Caroline began to wonder if they might have made a mistake insisting they went back to Birmingham. It was so easy there: meals were provided, clothes washed, housework done. After the initial embarrassment of them sleeping together had worn off, they all settled down pretty well. Dad had always liked Aaron and now he began to treat him like the son he'd never had. Although Aaron's first love was rugby, he could talk about any sport. He would sit down and watch the golf on television with Dad after the rest of them had gone to bed.

Emma was the only one who didn't like Aaron.

"Ignore her," Aaron said one night after she'd made yet another snide remark. "She's just jealous."

"What?" Caroline laughed. She knew Emma didn't fancy Aaron. She'd been seeing Robert for years, they were happy together, and anyway, Aaron just wasn't her type.

"Of you getting married first. Having the first grandchild," Aaron said.

It was a bitterly cold January day when they drove back up to Birmingham. Caroline's heart sank at the first sight of the tiny terraced red-brick house. Those last few weeks in her parents' spacious four-bedroom house had made her forget this tiny place: just a lounge-diner and kitchen downstairs, two small bedrooms and a bathroom upstairs. The house had been empty for weeks and was cold and cheerless, the smell of damp and disuse in the air. Aaron, however, was cheerful and optimistic.

"We'll soon have the place warmed up," he said, switching the central heating on. "Cheer up, Little Girl," he went on, seeing her plonk herself down on the sofa and stare around, "we can buy a few bits and bobs to make it look like home."

She knew he was trying and she didn't want to make him feel bad. It wasn't Aaron's fault they were here. But she felt suddenly so alone and helpless, such a long way from home and family and everything she knew, without even the safety net of university to fall back on. Everything was new and daunting and frightening. Despite herself, tears welled up in her eyes.

"Come on," Aaron said gently. He sat down next to her, put his arm around her, and held her close. She leaned her head against his shoulder, allowed the tears to flow. "You're just tired, that's all. What can I get you? A cup of tea?" She shook her head. She hadn't been able to face tea since she'd been pregnant. "A glass of water? Juice? Something to eat? I'll go and unpack the shopping. Or d'you want me to take the stuff upstairs first and make the bed?"

The list of tasks in her mind was overwhelming. She wished for nothing more than to be back in the spare room at Mum and Dad's house, with the electric blanket on the bed, a drink and "something to eat" whenever she wanted it without her having to lift a finger. But she'd made this decision and she couldn't go back on it. She wiped her nose and dried her eyes, though the tears still kept coming.

"I'll make the bed," she said with a monumental effort. "If you can unpack the shopping. Maybe we could have a takeaway tonight...?"

There'd been other first nights: in the halls of residence, in their student house in Minstead Road, in the hotel in Tiverton—but none compared to that first night in Edgbaston. The thin curtains did nothing to keep out the light from the street outside. Cars swooshed by, stopped outside; car doors slammed, then front doors. Dogs barked. People called out to each other as they said goodnight or talked loudly while they walked back from one of the bars down the road. Every time she thought everyone was in bed and she could finally drift off to sleep, she was woken by some other sound. The bed was uncomfortable too: smaller than the one they'd had at Mum and Dad's, and with a mattress so soft that the whole bed moved every time Aaron did.

Exhausted by the long drive, Aaron had fallen asleep instantly. She didn't like to move around too much in case she disturbed him. "I should learn to drive too," she had said on the way up. "Then we could share the driving."

"It's so expensive," Aaron had answered. "Anyway, the old girl won't last much longer with all the miles we're putting on her." He patted the dashboard affectionately. It was true, the car was really on its last legs and except for driving home, they didn't need it. Public transport was excellent in Birmingham and it was a nightmare trying to find somewhere to park: Aaron had already had to double park that evening while they unloaded all their stuff. The car had never really belonged to Aaron anyway, it was his cousin's, and she had no idea if he had to pay some money for it after using it all this time. They didn't talk much about money. Aaron didn't seem keen when she had suggested a joint bank account, so they still had separate ones and just used whichever one had the most money at the time.

Caroline woke first the next morning, with the now-familiar queasy feeling in the pit of her stomach. She edged around the bed in the tiny bedroom to dash to the loo, where she retched violently and brought up yellow bile. She sat shivering on the tiled floor of the bathroom, waiting for the feeling to subside, then crept back to bed to cuddle up to Aaron's back. Neither of them started work for a few days and it was gone eleven before they got out of bed.

Even with their boxes and bags littered around the place and the unpacked groceries on the kitchen surfaces, the house didn't seem quite so bad in the light of day. Aaron still insisted on taking her shopping later on though and she bought cushions and a throw for the sofa. She lingered longingly among the curtains, wishing they had enough money for thicker ones with linings, but a large chunk of the money she had earned in Tiverton had already gone on petrol and food, and she'd also used some money she'd been given for Christmas to buy the cushions.

They spent the rest of the day unpacking boxes and bags and Caroline put the food away in the cupboards, taking pride in arranging them like a proper little housewife. After living in student accommodation, she enjoyed the novelty of knowing they'd still be in the same place when she went to find them again.

Their few days of freedom, of staying up late and getting up late, flew by, and it was Monday and time to start work. Aaron had to be up at five and Caroline was tired the whole time, so they went to bed at ten o'clock. Aaron fell asleep straight away. The novelty of sleeping with him hadn't yet worn off and she listened fondly to his steady breathing. She'd been tired all day, yawning all evening, but now she was in bed, she just couldn't settle as the noises from the street below drifted up to her. It wasn't as though she wasn't used to living in a noisy neighbourhood—the house they'd had in Minstead Road was on a busy estate but that was when she was a student, going to bed at three and not getting up till eleven. Now she wished they were back in Mum and Dad's house in a quiet cul-de-sac. She even toyed with the idea of suggesting to Aaron that they went back home. They could start at Mum and Dad's, save some money, and then buy a house of their own somewhere nice in Tiverton instead of this dump. But that would be admitting defeat, and she was determined to prove they could cope on their own.

She groaned when she heard the alarm going off and the sound of Aaron getting out of bed before he could stop to think about it.

"It's okay," he said, "You go back to sleep. I'll bring you up a cup of tea..."

"No, please," she said weakly, her stomach turning at the very idea. "Juice would be nice. If you've got time."

He disappeared into the bathroom and she heard the sound of the shower, accompanied by sharp intakes of breath as he undressed in the ice-cold bathroom and stood under the lukewarm reluctantly-trickling shower. It seemed only minutes later that he dumped a glass of orange juice on the tiny bedside table.

"I've re-set the alarm so you don't oversleep. Wish I could get back in there with you." He kissed her gently, his mouth tasting of mint toothpaste, and then he was gone. The one sip of orange juice she took turned her stomach again, and she lay as still as possible, waiting for the feeling to subside. It was no good though and a moment later, she tasted the bile in her throat and was rushing to the loo, one hand to her mouth, the other to her stomach. The linoleum floor was icy to her feet and she stood twisting her toes, waiting for the retching to subside. It scarcely seemed worth going back to bed after that and in any case, she was scared she might not hear the alarm if she went back to sleep. So she got up, had the one piece of dry toast her stomach could manage, and read a book until it was time to catch the bus.

The nerves she had been feeling since she woke up increased on the twenty-minute journey into town. Aaron must have been feeling the same, but there had been many first days at new jobs over the past few years and there would be many more. It was just something they had to get used to. Her appearance sparked the usual first-day interest with her colleagues. They were mostly girls of her age, but single, still living at home with boyfriends they saw once a week. They all spoke with strong Birmingham accents and the moment she spoke, she could see she was being dismissed as a posh Southern newcomer. It didn't matter, as she wouldn't be there long enough to make any friends. She saw the swift look of surprise on their faces when she said she was married but she didn't tell anyone, not even the older supervisor who'd interviewed her, that she was pregnant. It might have been advertised as a temporary job, but it could lead to a permanent position and they'd never have taken her on if they'd known she would be needing maternity benefits. So she was careful to hide the waves of nausea, the light-headedness, the desperate need for the loo, and the overwhelming tiredness that increased as the weeks went on.

Aaron was home hours before her, his muddy boots standing tidily in the front hallway, his work clothes in the washing machine and a meal started. However tired and grumpy she was, he would welcome her with a smile, take the bag of shopping from her, unpack it, and run her a bath if she wanted.

This was the best time of their marriage. Despite the squalor of the neighbourhood, the noise and the smell, they were happy at first in that little house. They worked too many hours to get to know the people living either side of them, but Caroline soon began to recognise the regulars waiting at the bus stop with her—well enough to exchange a few pleasantries anyway. And the Indian man who ran the convenience store down the road always smiled and spoke to her, whatever she was buying.

They were too tired to go out in the week, but they still met up with their university friends at weekends; Caroline nursing her one orange juice and lemonade while everyone else, especially Aaron, drank pint after pint. Aaron couldn't play rugby for the university anymore so he joined a club in

Harborne, and Caroline went along, standing with the other wives in the freezing cold and often the driving rain. They watched their husbands play and joined them for drinks afterwards in the clubhouse and for social get-togethers. These friends were all older, they had good jobs, they owned their own homes, their own cars. They'd come over and pick up Aaron so he could get to rugby training on time, or pick both of them up if it was a home match.

Aaron was proud of her in those days. "My wife Caroline," he would introduce her, his heavy arm around her shoulders, his eyes shining as he looked at her. The other wives were all older than Caroline but none of them asked why they had married so young. Maybe they guessed. Certainly, they didn't seem surprised when her bump began to show.

Aaron still lied about why they left uni. "We got fed up with all that learning stuff," she heard him say. "We want to make our own way in the world." The second part was at least true. She and Aaron were a team in those days, determined to show everyone they could cope without any help. Did he tell any of his friends she was pregnant? When he was drunk, maybe, in those intimate, easy, setting-the-world-to-rights hours with his mates? Probably not. Aaron was fiercely loyal at that time. And desperately in love with her. He was always telling her how beautiful she was, stroking her hair, taking her hand, cupping her face in his hands.

It was when her pregnancy began to show that it began to change. He became embarrassed to be seen with her.

"You don't need to come," he'd say as she put on her coat and scarf. "It's raining and you'll be cold. And bored. Why don't you stay at home?"

She tried to tell herself he was thinking of her and the baby. And he was right, she was often bored, standing watching a game she didn't understand, cheering and clapping when the other wives did without a clue as to what was going on. And afterwards, in the bar, listening to those oh-so-tedious conversations about washing powder and the best way to clean the kitchen floor while the men clustered together, joshing each other and guffawing loudly.

The trouble was, it wasn't much better with their uni friends. Happy with his crowd at the rugby club, Aaron wanted to go out with their uni friends less and less, and when she went out on her own with Helen and Kirstie, she had so little to talk to them about. Their lives revolved around university. Inevitably they talked about their course, the lecturers, and other friends who now seemed so distant. They were polite enough, but they weren't interested in her job or the shopping she had to get. She belonged to neither one group nor the other: her old ones at university or the wives at the rugby club. Since Aaron had favoured the rugby club, she had no real choice. But now he didn't even want her to go.

The first time that Aaron went without her, she stood at the doorway and waved him goodbye, with another cheery little wave to Chris and Barbara doing her best to look like the happy, loyal wife. Then she went back inside, listening to the sound of the car driving away, and wondered how she could spend her long, lonely afternoon. She could catch the bus into town and look around the shops, but there was no money to spend so there wasn't much point. She toyed with the idea of ringing Helen or Kirstie and going up to the university, but the memory of the last desultory afternoon they'd had together put her off. Anyway, it was still raining—nothing worse than waiting for the bus in the rain, then sitting next to other people with wet coats and dripping umbrellas, only to have to do it all again on the way home, only this time in the dark. She stood and looked out of the window onto the dingy street outside: the opposite row of net-curtained windows, the battered old cars lining each side of the road, the people hurrying by with hoods up or umbrellas over their heads. She saw a mother with a pram and watched with fascination as the woman manoeuvred it down the kerb and across the road. She still couldn't believe that would be her in a few months' time. She ran her hand over the hard bump below her waist. Aaron had been thrilled when she told him she'd felt it move for the first time. He made her hold his hand against it the next time it happened. She wondered what excuse he'd made to Chris and Barbara about her. "Caroline's a bit tired," he might have said. Or "She's got things to do in the house." That was true, there was always something to do. Her uniform needed a wash and so did Aaron's work clothes, which had to go on a long cycle to get rid of the mud. The sheets needed changing, and the bathroom sink could do with a clean. It was tempting to sit down in front of the television—after all, Aaron was having a good time, why shouldn't she?—but she heaved herself upstairs instead and began to sort out the dirty clothes in the washing bin.

"I won't be late," Aaron had said when he kissed her goodbye. But six o'clock came, then seven. The shepherd's pie she'd cooked began to look dry, her stomach was rumbling and she was beginning to feel faint. She'd just spooned herself out a serving, leaving the rest for Aaron to put in the microwave when he came back, when her phone rang.

"I'm still here," Aaron slurred.

She could hear the sounds of the crowded bar behind him. "Well, obviously," she managed to say chirpily. "But you're on your way now?"

"Not exactly..."

"Why?"

"Bit of a misunderstanding. Chris and Barbara have gone. But it's okay, Bugsy has said he'll give me a lift. Only he's not ready to go yet..."

Bugsy was Rory Malone, a big Irish man, in his thirties maybe, who played in the first row. She heard his distinctive yelp of laughter in the background. This was what she hated about the rugby club. She'd overheard other husbands tell their wives all the same excuses while the wives waited at home with the children. She didn't want to be one of them.

"Aaron..." she began.

"It's okay," he said quickly, "I won't be long."

And he was gone. She could have rung back but she didn't want to be one of those nagging wives. She ate her meal, did the washing up and then sat down to watch television. Usually, she and Aaron quite liked Saturday evening programmes, aimed at families, but without Aaron there to cuddle up to and talk and laugh with, everything seemed dull and lifeless. At ten o'clock, she turned it off. Her phone had made no sound but she checked it anyway in case she'd missed a text. Nothing. Maybe Bugsy's car had broken down. Or they'd been in an accident. She rang his number. It went straight to answerphone.

"Aaron," she said after the mandatory beep, "where are you? It's late. I'm worried." Her voice broke on the last word and she cleared her throat. "Ring me so I know you're okay." She pictured him in the noisy rugby club, like she'd seen other men there, too drunk to check their phone, no idea their wife or girlfriend might be worried.

She was dead tired but it was warm in the little sitting room with the heating on, and she couldn't bear the thought of going upstairs alone to the icy bedroom, only to be woken five minutes later by Aaron coming back. She curled up on the sofa, rested her head on her arm and fell asleep.

She woke an hour later with her mouth dry and her left arm and leg numb. The street outside was full of the usual Saturday evening noises of people returning from the pub. Surely he'd be back soon? Anyway, she couldn't sleep here. She got up, hobbling on her numb leg, and went up to bed. It was worse there, lying in the empty bed, listening to every sound. She started up every time she heard a car draw up in the road outside, the sound of voices. One could be Aaron's. But it never was. In the end, she must have fallen asleep because she didn't hear the key in the latch, didn't hear the door opening. But she did hear the crash as Aaron fell over his work boots in the front hallway. She shot out of bed and down the stairs. He was lying in a crumpled heap, giggling weakly.

"Sorry, Little Girl. Did I wake you up?"

"Aaron, for God's sake. What time is it? Where've you been?"

"You know where I've been, silly!" he slurred. "To rugby…"

"That finished hours ago!" she spat out furiously. "I've been on my own all evening. You could've come home!"

"We won," he said as if that explained everything. "I'm very drunk, Little Girl," he added, rolling over into a ball. For a moment she felt sorry for him, lying there like a little boy, calling her Little Girl. But only for a moment. She'd never seen him as bad as this. She couldn't just leave him there. But she couldn't possibly move him, he was much too big.

"Aaron," she said firmly. "Don't be silly. You can't stay there. Get up and come to bed."

"I can't," he said weakly.

Caroline was angry now. "Well, stay there then. I don't care. I'm going back to bed."

She didn't think she'd settle, but she must have been more tired than she realised because she fell asleep instantly and slept amazingly well. It was just beginning to get light when she felt the mattress next to her sag and smelt Aaron's beery breath next to her.

The next morning, nursing one hell of a hangover, he was contrite. "It was Bugsy's fault," he explained. "He kept buying me whiskies."

She went along next time but standing made her legs ache and her ankles swell. In the end, she had to go and sit in the clubhouse where at least it was warm. There, however, she was in the way of the wives getting the rugby tea. Her offer of help was met with a swift wry glance at her stomach and a "No thanks, dear. You go and sit down. Put your feet up maybe. Those ankles look puffy. You'd be better off at home."

She saw herself suddenly through their eyes: a naïve

young girl who got caught out.

After that, she stopped going. She reminded herself that it wasn't as if Aaron was being unfaithful or something—she knew where he was and it was only a load of men at the rugby club. He enjoyed his rugby and he worked hard, so he deserved a break. And it wasn't as though it was something new: he'd always loved playing rugby. It was just that before there had always been people around her, things she could do. Now there was nothing and no one. She hated that moment when Aaron had just left and the house fell silent. And while it was a chance to get all the housework and washing done, leaving them a free day to spend together on Sundays, it seemed unfair that she should have to do it all herself. They'd only been married a few months. She didn't want to be the sort of wife who nagged and complained. But inevitably, she couldn't stop resentment building up.

Home matches were bad enough. Even if someone like Chris and Barbara were driving, it was usually gone nine by the time he came home and he was always drunk. Away games were worse. She'd go to bed, dreading the sound of the key in the lock, the stumbling steps and curses as he made his way upstairs, his beery breath when he lay down.

It was no good saying anything then. Aaron was too incoherent to listen. The next day, once he had recovered sufficiently from his hangover, she would try various versions of the words she'd rehearsed in her mind as she sat alone in front of the television or waited in bed, unable to sleep.

"D'you think you could get a lift back with someone straight after the match? Or catch the bus or something? It's so lonely here, waiting on my own..."

The old Aaron, the one she fell in love with, the one who would do anything to make her happy would have said. *"Oh, Little Girl, I had no idea. I'm sorry. You're right, it's selfish of me. I'll check the bus times or get a lift back with someone. Come straight home to be with you. I hate the thought of you being lonely."*

But this new Aaron, the stranger who was inhabiting Aaron's body, would snap at her. "For God's sake, it's my only hobby. It's not as if you don't know where I am! I work bloody hard and I deserve a bit of time off. It's not *my* fault you can't find anything to do while I'm gone."

Then he'd retreat into a sulk, a mood that could last for days, while she tiptoed metaphorically around him, doing everything she could to coax him back into a good mood again.

It wasn't just the loneliness, though. There was the money. True, unless he was led on by the notorious Bugsy and his heavy drinking friends, Aaron mostly stuck to beer, which was quite cheap at the Rugby Club. However, week after week of steady drinking and smoking all added up. And there was so much to buy. Once they knew she was pregnant at work, she was provided with a maternity shift. However, she still needed maternity clothes, clothes and bedding for the baby, a pram, and a cot. Even buying secondhand was expensive. Aaron's six-month contract at the building site would finish at the end of June but he'd applied for a job with the Post Office. It would mean getting up at 4 a.m. but the unsociable hours were well paid and Caroline wouldn't be able to work for a while once the baby was born.

The rugby club had an end of season dinner dance in June. Caroline didn't know about it until Barbara rang up to offer them a lift.

"Are you sure you want to go?" Aaron asked.

"Of course," Caroline said. She was big by then and hadn't a clue what she could wear, but all the other wives would be going and she hadn't been to anything special since last year, when she'd gone to the end of year ball at university.

It was a dinner dance. Aaron would wear his only suit. The women would probably wear long dresses, or maybe smart cocktail dresses. She looked longingly at the minuscule size eight dress she'd worn to the university summer ball, hanging at the back of the wardrobe with her wedding dress, loose at the time, but now way too small. She had absolutely nothing to wear. Apart from the maternity smock that work had supplied, she had very few maternity clothes. Most of their money had gone on the essentials for the baby. Even Aaron realised she'd have to buy something new.

They went into town one Saturday morning. Caroline tried on dress after dress, tops and trousers. Every time she came out of the fitting room, she saw Aaron's face fall. "You look so pregnant," he kept saying.

"But I *am,*" she said, trying not to cry. "I can't help that."

It was dreadful to think that Aaron should be ashamed of her.

She ended up buying a pair of black maternity trousers and a dark red maternity tunic. She looked longingly at the matching dark red shoes and bag, but they still didn't have enough money to buy a cot, so she'd have to make do with the black ones she had already.

Chris and Barbara picked them up at seven. Caroline hadn't seen them since April, and she saw Barbara's quick look of surprise as she manoeuvred her huge bump into the back of the car.

"When's the baby due?" she asked.

Caroline hesitated. She hated to lie but Aaron liked to give the impression that it was a "honeymoon" baby.

"Late August," she heard him say into the gap she left. Caroline sensed Barbara's disbelief. With two teenage boys of her own, she must have known the baby was due well before then.

The dinner dance marked the end of the rugby season, but to Caroline's dismay, Aaron announced one day that he'd been asked to play cricket.

"A few of the lads play," he said. "Just now and again. They've asked me to go along. I can borrow some kit…"

Cricket turned out to be worse than rugby. A car would draw up mid-morning on Saturdays. Sundays too sometimes. Matches lasted all day, followed by the inevitable drinking session. The money they'd so carefully saved up went on the membership fee, cricket whites, and a bat.

"Maybe Mum and Dad can give us the cot as a present," Aaron said. "And your parents could give us a pram…"

Caroline hated the idea of asking them but the alternative—buying second-hand—was even worse. And both sets of parents were keen to help out. Mum rang once a week, and once they'd caught up on what was going on in each other's lives, she would pass the phone over to Dad, whose main concern, naturally, was her health.

"Are you getting enough exercise?" he would ask. "You're not standing for too long at work, are you?" He usually finished with something like, "You know you can come back whenever you like. You don't have to stay up there. This is still your home…"

Aaron's parents rang less often and Caroline had the impression that Aaron wouldn't have minded if they didn't ring at all. But they couldn't afford to alienate them, as it was his parents who had paid the deposit on the rental for the flat; their names were down as guarantors. She knew they'd pay for the cot and anything else they might need. She just wished they didn't have to ask.

Left alone more and more, Caroline found herself wishing that she'd listened to her parents and stayed in Tiverton, where at least she knew people. She hadn't made friends with any of the girls at work but once she'd left, she found she missed their chatter. Helen and Kirstie had stopped contacting her. All the neighbours were out at work. She gazed wistfully at the mothers she saw in the local shops with prams or pushchairs or small children in tow, but although some of them exchanged a friendly smile or nod, or asked when the baby was due, it was a long way from a proper conversation and she could hardly ask where they lived or invite herself in for coffee.

She had hoped she might make friends with someone at anti-natal classes. On the bus there, she pictured herself chatting to the other expectant mothers, exchanging numbers.

Their babies would be due the same time as hers; there would be coffee mornings together; then they'd meet again in the hospital and afterwards, at each other's houses, where they could talk about looking after the babies while they slept peacefully in their prams. But the moment she arrived, she knew it wasn't going to be like that. The room was packed; she squeezed herself in on the end of a row, next to a woman at least ten years older than her, who didn't even turn to her when she said "Good morning". The midwives rattled through their presentation, as boring to listen to as it obviously was for them to present. There was a ten-minute break for coffee and the loo, but even if there had been time to meet someone, she quickly realised most of them seemed to know each other already or had brought friends or sisters along with them. She seemed to be the only one on her own. She didn't bother to turn up for the next session. She was sure no one would miss her.

Aaron was invited to the final session at the hospital. Here, surrounded by other couples in the same situation, he finally seemed to be at ease with her pregnancy. She watched him laughing and joking with the other men, chatting easily about how he would be there with her to hold her hand and stroke her back when she was in labour, and she wished he was always as supportive. This was the Aaron she loved, the "big brother". Aaron who would always look after her and make things better.

At home, he changed back into the man she scarcely knew. He had stopped making love to her once her stomach began to stick out. She knew he had always loved her flat stomach. He used to run his hand over the concave dip, across to her hip bones that jutted out, down to the rise of her pubic bone. Now her hip bones had disappeared and she was one round lump, it was obvious he didn't fancy her anymore. When they were first together she used to fall asleep in his arms and for a while, he went on cuddling her at night. But she sensed his relief when she became so big that it was impossible to lie still long enough for a cuddle.

It was early July when she went into labour; three weeks before the baby was due. At first, she thought it was cramp—she'd had a lot of cramping pains recently.

"Braxton Hicks," her father told her confidently. "Quite common. Nothing to worry about."

But this time the pains didn't go and as the evening wore on, they began to get worse. She rang Dad again.

"You'd better go in," he told her. Aaron had loads of friends who had offered to drive them to the hospital, but it was eleven o'clock at night and they all worked. Also, it might be a false alarm. So he rang for a taxi. Doubled up in pain by then, Caroline scarcely needed to hear them say "You're definitely in labour." when she arrived.

Her parents drove straight up from Tiverton that night. It was the last thing she'd expected, the last thing she thought she wanted, but in fact, she'd never been so pleased to see them in all her life. She had dreaded the idea of Dad turning up, telling them he was a GP, taking over, but now she welcomed it. When she went in, the staff had treated her perfunctorily, as though she was just one more woman in labour making a fuss. With Dad around, they handled her with deference. Mum too seemed quite different. It was the closest they'd ever been, the closest they ever would be. It was as though Caroline had joined some sort of exclusive women's club now she was having a baby.

"It's fine," she kept saying reassuringly every time Caroline winced or groaned. "Perfectly normal."

From the moment she'd started getting her pains, Aaron had retreated into himself, his face set, a distant look in his eyes. He didn't want this to be happening to him, he didn't want to be there. As soon as Mum and Dad arrived, he took it as his cue to leave.

"I don't want to be late for work." he told Caroline. "I'll lose the job."

She nodded weakly. They needed the money, but surely Aaron must have told them about the baby? He could have taken time off, made it up somehow or other? She wanted him with her. She started to cry.

"Don't worry," Mum said to Aaron. "You go on. We'll be fine. First babies always take a long time."

The midwives agreed. "You won't miss anything," they said. "And we can always ring you."

Caroline had always pictured Aaron next to her when the baby was born. She had seen him with his arm around her as she held the baby. Instead, it was Mum who saw Joshua appear in the world; Mum smiling with tears in her eyes, as she said, "He's beautiful. What a clever girl you are."

Caroline was exhausted. She tried to stay awake. She wanted Aaron to be the next person to see him. He would be there any minute, she kept telling herself. But it was mid-afternoon before he appeared. By then, Dad had seen Joshua, so had the other women in her ward, every single nurse had cooed and ahhed over him.

She tried to ignore the tell-tale flush on his cheeks, the slight unsteadiness in his walk that told her he'd been drinking, and concentrate instead on the look of pride she saw in his eyes, and the bunch of cellophane-wrapped flowers in his hand.

"Had to wet the baby's head," he explained, his eyes landing on the cot next to her, rather than on her.

"He's asleep," she said quickly. "But when he wakes up, you can hold him."

She would never forget the expression on his face when she put Joshua rather clumsily into his arms. In that moment, she forgave him everything: the drunken nights, being ashamed to be seen with her, not being there when she needed him, spending their money on his sports stuff. She shifted painfully over to him on the bed, put her arm around him, and lent her head on his shoulder.

"He's beautiful," he said. "Joshua…" He stroked his tiny hand with one finger. "I'll always look after you, little fellow."

For the first few days, she felt like she was on Cloud Nine. Everyone made a fuss of her, everyone loved her.

Cards and presents arrived. She felt like she'd achieved some sort of miracle, as though she was the only person ever to have a baby even though she was surrounded by other mothers with babies. Vicky was the first of her friends to arrive, perching on the edge of her bed, holding Joshua as though she'd been doing it all her life, listening intently to every detail of the birth.

"Wow," she kept saying, "I can't believe it…"

Emma was next, with an embarrassed-looking Robert in tow. If she was jealous at all, as Aaron seemed to think she was, she certainly didn't show it. She took Joshua from Caroline tenderly, gazed down at him with a similar expression to the one Aaron had had, while Robert shuffled uncomfortably from foot-to-foot next to her. The present she'd brought—a soft blue teddy bear—turned out to be Joshua's favourite toy, the one he took with him everywhere, the one he wouldn't go to bed without.

Helen and Kirstie came too with cards, presents, and more flowers to add to the ones she already had crowded around her bed.

With all these people coming and going, Caroline felt like a princess, with her little prince Joshua next to her in his hospital crib.

After a few hours' sleep in the local Travelodge, Dad had driven back to Tiverton, ready for work the next day. Caroline had watched him leave with a strange feeling of pride. She had always taken it for granted that he was a doctor, well-known in the town. She had grown up with it. But that was back in Tiverton. Up here, where no one knew him, she saw him in a different light. The nurses and midwives treated him with respect, rushing out to say goodbye to him, shaking his hand, congratulating him again on his beautiful little grandson.

Mum stayed on until the day Caroline left hospital, then caught the train back.

"You'll want to settle in on your own," she said.

Caroline knew it was her own fault—she was the one

who had wanted to be so independent. Suddenly she wished Mum would stay on to help her with the unfamiliar tasks of feeding and changing and bathing that came so naturally to Mum, but that were so alien to her.

The day Joshua was born was warm and sunny. She would never forget the feeling of elation she had waking up on those warm summer mornings in hospital—the clear blue sky, the sunshine streaming through the windows onto her bed and Joshua's crib. She didn't mind waking up to hear him cry. This was her baby and she couldn't get over it. It was like a miracle having him lying next to her, knowing that she had given birth to this beautiful little creature.

The rain started the day she came home from hospital. Left on his own those few days, Aaron had treated the house like a student flat. She nearly fell over the piles of shoes, trainers and cricket boots that littered the front hallway. The house felt damp; smelt of fried food and cigarettes. There were lager cans, an overflowing ashtray and newspapers on the coffee table. Every surface in the kitchen was strewn with dirty mugs, and plates encrusted with egg or baked beans. A half-empty milk bottle stood on the window ledge.

Her heart sank at the thought of the clearing up she had to do.

"Maybe I should've tidied up a bit," Aaron said, seeing her face.

"Yes," she said curtly. This wasn't the homecoming she had foreseen but she didn't want to argue with Aaron the moment she came back. Joshua was crying, so she had to feed and change him before she tackled the house. That brief feeling of elation—those wonderful few days when she had felt that now she was a mother, nothing else would ever matter—vanished in a moment, replaced by the grim reality of life with a small baby.

There was no paternity leave in those days and Aaron went straight back to work. Joshua, who had seemed like such a good baby in hospital, now cried continually. He woke several times a night to be fed.

"Can't you do something about it?" Aaron would ask. "I've got to be up at four-thirty."

He was home by lunchtime, but he was tired out, collapsing into bed for a few hours' sleep as soon he'd finished lunch.

The wet weather continued for the rest of the summer. Stuck at home with Joshua for day after day, week after week, while the rain poured down outside, the tiny house became a prison. It wasn't at all like she had imagined. From the moment Joshua woke up bawling, every day was one endless monotonous routine of feeding, changing and bathing. There was always something to do and never enough time. In the brief hours between Joshua's feeds, she threw washing into the washing machine, hung it on the airer or over the radiators to dry, took it off again to fold, iron and put away, and cleaned the house. She walked to the shops most days, trudging the grey drab streets of Edgbaston, passing the same houses, the same shops, talking only to the staff who worked in them.

For a week or so after she left hospital, people came to see her: Helen and Kirstie, Barbara and a couple of other women she knew from the rugby or cricket club. But they were all busy. After their duty visit, they never came again. None of them thought to ring her, to ask if she'd like to come over to them.

Caroline had never felt so alone. No one ever knew how unhappy she was; she had no one to confide in, no network of friends like she has now to help her through. The last thing she wanted was anyone knowing what a mistake she'd made, to hear their pity in their voices.

"I'm fine," she would trill to Vicky, Mum and Dad, Emma, the odd few who rang now and again. "Aaron's gone out. Bit of peace and quiet for me..."

As her circle of friends diminished, Aaron's had increased. He was always talking about Mike or Ken or Doug, or someone else—friends he knew from the Post Office or the building site, or from rugby or cricket. She had hoped he might go out less when Joshua was born, but it made no difference. He loved Joshua, she knew he did, but he wasn't the "hands-on" father she thought he would be. He wanted to be free, to be the man he would have been if she hadn't got pregnant and tied him down. When he wasn't playing cricket or rugby, there were training sessions, or he'd go out with one of his mates for a "swift pint", or over to their houses to watch a match or a game. When he was at home he was either asleep or slumped in his chair watching television.

Caroline was so tired all the time—a constant physical and mental exhaustion she had never known before. She was in bed by nine, falling into a deep sleep, scarcely stirring when Aaron came up later, waking only to the first sounds of Joshua crying. She was only too pleased when Aaron made no move on her in bed. She missed the intimacy though, the feeling of being loved; so much so that when he finally did reach for her, she responded fervently.

It was a Sunday morning, Aaron's day off. She lay in his arms for a while afterwards, relishing the feel of his arms around her, the smell of his body. Just as she started to drift off to sleep, Joshua started crying. She climbed out of bed, still naked, and bent over to pick him up and cradle him in her arms.

"My God, look at your stomach," Aaron said.

She looked down and saw what Aaron saw: the soft roll of flabby flesh; the "mummy tummy" she had from giving birth to his son. But Aaron hated it and that was enough. She became determined to lose weight, the start of a problem that was to haunt her for the rest of her life. Even now, with Damian, who would love her whether she weighed eight stone or eighteen stone, she is careful about what she eats. It was harder to lose weight at thirty-four, when she had Harry, than when she had Joshua at twenty. But it's so different. Damian cares about her, encourages her to eat healthily, to look after herself. Aaron made her feel fat and ugly. Desperate to get back the figure he loved, she began starving herself: skipping breakfast because he wasn't there to see her eat it, pretending she'd already had a meal sometimes or putting half the amount of potatoes or pasta on her plate compared to his.

Whenever she had a spare moment, she lay down on the floor and did the sit-ups and other exercises she'd seen in magazines to get her stomach flat again. She took a longer route to the shops, walking further and further every day regardless of the weather. Every morning she stood on the scales, a thrill of pleasure running through her as the needle fell lower and lower.

She didn't stop when she was back to the weight she was before she'd had Joshua and her stomach was as flat as a board. She was too thin. She knew she was anorexic; she knew it was stupid. But it was the only thing she could control in a life that was completely out of her control.

Sometimes she thought she would scream with boredom. Her mind, once so full of learning, so ready to soak up knowledge like a sponge, was now dried up. She had a desperate urge to do something, to go somewhere, to spread her wings and fly, but she was trapped and there was nothing she could do about it.

There must have been days when the sun shone as it had on the day Joshua was born, when she felt alive and full of energy, when Joshua didn't cry and she played with him happily like she did with Harry later on, but the long dark days overshadowed them.

It wasn't that she didn't like children. At any other time, she would have wanted one. But not at that time—she just wasn't ready. Yet looking back now, she can see she was a good mother. The few photos she has of her and Joshua show how proud she was of him: she's leaning towards him, her head close to his; protective, loving. When she had Harry, she discovered that she loved children. She's not surprised Joshua is jealous of him: she planned Harry, she wanted him, she was ready for him. She and Damian bought him everything he needed, the best they could. Joshua had to make do with the cheapest or second-hand. But worse than that, he had been an encumbrance; he'd sapped her freedom, tied her to the house, stole her youth.

On her way back from the shops one day, she walked past a hairdressing shop. She had seen it regularly but on this particular day, there was a new poster in the window: an elfin-faced model with a pixie haircut. *"Under new management"* the sign above read. *"Walk-in appointments available. Come on in."* Caroline stopped and looked. She couldn't remember the last time she'd had her hair cut. It was over a week since she'd washed it. It was always in her way. Whenever she bent over to pick up Joshua, he reached for it and pulled it hard. "Ow!" she couldn't help yelping, jerking away and making him cry even louder. She had taken to tying it back out of her face every day. She glanced down at Joshua, still fast asleep. Before she could change her mind, she manoeuvred the pram through the heavy glass door into the shop.

"I'd like my hair cut," she said to the girl behind the reception desk. She gestured to the poster in the window. "Like that," she went on. "Now, if you can do it."

It was a brand new shop. Of course they could do it now. The receptionist, Amanda-Jane, who turned out to be the hairdresser as well, led her over to the basins. It had been a long time since Caroline had spent money and time on herself. She relished the warm water, the smell of the shampoo, the hairdresser's gentle fingers massaging her scalp, the squeaky-clean feel of freshly-washed hair. She felt a moment of panic as the long hair that Aaron loved fell strand by long, heavy strand onto the floor, but it was too late. The face that emerged looked like a stranger's. Her eyes were bigger, her neck longer. It was grown-up, chic, modern. She walked out feeling lighter and clearer in her head and mind.

It was the last thing she did without asking Aaron. She'll never forget the look on his face when he saw her.

"My God, what've you done?" he gasped

"Don't you like it?" The feeling of elation instantly vanished, replaced by a sick feeling in the pit of her stomach.

"You look awful. Like a refugee. Like you're ill or something. God knows what everyone will think…"

Caroline's hand flew to the wispy strands of hair at the nape of her neck. Her face burned, her eyes filled with tears.

"What made you do it? Are you mad?" He went on.

She was crying in earnest now, great sobs that racked her chest.

"Oh for God's sake, don't be so childish!" he spat out. "It'll grow…."

Every time she looked in the mirror after that, she thought she looked ugly. Ugly and fat with no friends.

The first time she washed her hair, she wondered where it had gone as her fingers slid through the sparse crop. The shampoo lathered quickly and rinsed out in seconds. No standing under the shower for ages with a long thick lank of hair in her hand, trying to get rid of the suds. The hairdresser had used mousse and blow-dried it but Caroline let it dry on its own, ruffling it with her fingers. Despite what Aaron had said, it was tempting to keep it short as it was so much easier to look after. But she let the layers grow out until it was shoulder-length, and then had it re-shaped by Amanda-Jane into a chin-length bob, too short for Joshua to grab hold of, but long enough to please Aaron. Blow-drying it into shape every day though turned out to be harder than when it was long and loose, and she had it cut short again when she started working a few years later, this time with Aaron's grudging approval.

It's easy to see now that she allowed Aaron to control her. He took over where her parents left off. She was his "little girl" even though they were virtually the same age. He led, she followed. Blindly. He was her husband, father, brother. His opinion was hers. He spoke and decided for both of them.

Aaron's job at the Post Office, with its unsociable hours, paid well and he had hoped it would turn into a permanent position. However, it was only temporary—the sort of job usually done by students in the university holidays—and by September, he was again looking for work.

A couple of temporary jobs followed—one at the local council offices, doing odd bits of mundane work that no one else wanted to do, and one in a local factory, working in the packing area. Then one day he saw an advert in a big department store for a Trainee Manager. His heart was still set on a job in a bank or building society, where he could use his Business Studies knowledge, but at least this was a job with prospects.

"I probably won't even get an interview," he told her. But he did, and she watched with a sense of renewed pride as he set off in his suit.

The interview went well. Maybe it was Aaron's experience in the department store in Tiverton, maybe it was the way he spoke, or his eagerness to progress—but whatever it was, he got the job. The money wasn't as good as the Post Office but the hours were a steady nine to five-thirty, with alternate Saturdays off so he could still play his sports. At his interview, he was told he would start off on the sales floor, working in each department to gain retail experience before progressing to the cash office. Finally, he would shadow the manager, ready to cover him in his absence and ultimately take over from him. Aaron was thrilled. He didn't even mind the cheap suit, polyester shirt and clip-on tie he had to wear. This was a job with kudos, the career he'd been looking for.

Joshua at last settled into some sort of routine, and began waking up only once a night. Caroline envied Aaron his freedom and his job but with the steady income, it was the most settled they'd been. Aaron still drank heavily. It seemed to her he was only happy when he was in a bar or pub or with his male friends. Caroline wasn't included. The rugby club bar was no place for a baby in a pram, and although some wives took children along to the cricket matches, where they ran around and played while the fathers were on the field and the mothers did the teas, Joshua was still far too young.

She remembers that she did go along to an away match once. Aaron was a reserve but called on at the last moment to play. Often the club hired a coach, but on that particular time they didn't. Fed up with cadging lifts all the time, Aaron had bought an old Ford Fiesta, which like their previous car was constantly breaking down. There was no time and no money for Caroline to learn to drive but it made it a lot easier for Aaron to come and go as he wished. She can't remember now why she and Joshua were asked along. Maybe Aaron felt guilty leaving her alone again, though that seems unlikely. Maybe it was because it was in Cheltenham and he thought it would be a day out for her. Maybe she nagged Aaron into it. If she did, she soon realised her mistake.

She had been so excited at the idea of going out. She had thought she could watch the match for a while, just to show support. There might be some other wives there that she knew. Then she could wander around the Regency streets in the winter sunshine, find a cafe where she could have a cup of tea and feed Joshua, then go to a park where she could sit on a bench before it was time to go back for Aaron. But it was a cold grey Sunday with a hint of drizzle in the icy wind. As she unloaded the buggy from the boot of the car, she looked around the grey windswept pitch. There was no one there she knew. She remembers now the sudden feeling of desolation and loneliness. What was she going to do for the hour and a half of the match and the several hours in the clubhouse afterwards? She must have been crazy to think it was a good idea. She spent the afternoon wandering around the streets, pushing Joshua's buggy in and out of shops to get out of the cold, browsing through rails of clothes that she couldn't afford to buy until the shop assistants began to give her suspicious looks. As unused to going out as she was, Joshua was amazingly well-behaved. He lay in his buggy looking around, mesmerised by the bright lights in the shops, getting glances of admiration from the shop assistants. He didn't even cry much when she had to change his nappy on a park bench. At last, as the light began to fail and streetlights flicked on one-by-one, it was time to go back to the clubhouse. Here, she felt hopelessly out of place, drinking the cup of tea one of the wives made for her while Aaron held court, laughing loudly with his head thrown back in his characteristic way. She never went again.

If Aaron wasn't playing any sport on Sundays, he would walk to the local pub for a few pints before lunch. These weren't heavy drinking sessions and he was always in a good mood when he came back. Sometimes they made love while Joshua had his afternoon sleep and afterwards, they'd walk around the streets like the other families, following the familiar routes she walked day after day, stopping in the park to sit on a bench and watch the children playing on the swings and slides. Aaron would push the pram and she'd hang onto his arm. These were the times when they felt like a family.

It wasn't always like that though. One day, Aaron came back roaring drunk. She never discovered what had set him off on such a binge but she knew the moment he crashed through the door that he'd had more than usual. She scooped Joshua off the floor to get him out of Aaron's way, but it was too late.

"Don't put him to bed yet!" he slurred. "I never get time to play with him…"

"He's tired, Aaron," she said. "He needs his rest…"

"No you don't, do you son? You want to play with Daddy."

He fell down on his knees next to Joshua on the floor. Joshua had just started to crawl. He loved these boisterous romps with Daddy, but Aaron could scarcely stand and Caroline was worried he'd be too rough.

"Aaron…" she began, "Please, let me put him to bed. He's too tired…" But there was no reasoning with Aaron when he was like this. He began careering drunkenly around the room, shrieking, chasing Joshua, who tried to crawl out of his way. He grabbed him, holding him upside down. Then he suddenly rushed out of the room and Caroline heard him haring upstairs two at a time, then down again, stumbling the last few and landing in a heap at the bottom as he laughed hysterically. She swept Joshua up from the floor, ready to take him upstairs, but it was too late. He was back in the room, grabbed Joshua from her arms,

"Oh no, you don't! We're still playing, aren't we little fellow?" Joshua shrieked with delight as Aaron threw him into the air.

"Aaron please!" Caroline pleaded. "You'll hurt him. Let me have him!"

"We're okay, aren't we Joshy?" He sank to his knees, Joshua still in his arms. Then all of a sudden, he crumpled slightly, closed his eyes. "I feel..." he began. To Caroline's horror, a stream of yellow vomit erupted from his mouth, cascading towards Joshua. Joshua whimpered, his face turning from pleasure to fear and disgust, all in one moment.

"Oh God, Aaron..." Caroline said, scooping up the wailing child. She ran upstairs with Joshua, shushing and rocking him, "Mummy's here. It's going to be all right," she murmured. It took her ages to settle him and when she came back down, Aaron was still where she'd left him, the stinking vomit on his chin and down his front. She got a cloth, shook him awake, cleaned him up, pulled the disgusting top he was wearing over his head as though he was a child, and persuaded him to go up to bed.

"I had a bit too much to drink..." he slurred.

He woke up bewildered, with no idea what had happened. This was part of the problem. He wouldn't take any responsibility for what he was doing, where the money was going.

The small amount of money Caroline had earned when she was pregnant had long since gone. Aaron's income was all they had. She hated asking him for money all the time, having to justify every penny she spent. He didn't bother to hide the bank statements from her: entry after entry showed cash withdrawals—always on Aaron's drinking nights—for booze and cigarettes.

"I work bloody hard for that money," Aaron would say when she confronted him. "Why shouldn't I spend it on myself?"

They argued all the time—bitter arguments.

"You don't know what it's like being left here hour after hour, waiting for you to come home!" she'd shriek at him.

"It's not *my* fault you've got no friends!" he'd yell back.

Aaron had changed. She couldn't remember the last time he'd called her "Little Girl". He didn't seem to care about her at all. She and Joshua were just a millstone around his neck, his marriage and family life something he was constantly trying to escape from. Or maybe she was the one who'd changed

"You're always nagging me," he complained. "Or whining. For God's sake, I'm going out to get a bit of peace and quiet…"

Days would sometimes go by when they didn't speak to each other. Then one of them would apologise, they scarcely knew what for anymore. "I love you," Aaron would say. "I love you too," she'd reply mechanically. But she wasn't sure she did. They hardly ever made love nowadays as Aaron was always out late and usually drunk when he got back. She wouldn't have cared if he had someone else. *Is this my life?* she thought desperately. They'd stopped being nice to each other. Everything Aaron did, annoyed her. She snapped at him. He sniped at her. Every so often, she'd make an effort to get on with him for Joshua's sake. As he grew older, he could sense the tension between them. She didn't want him to grow up with warring parents. But it was already too late. The habits had been set. Any pity she might once have had for Aaron had long since vanished. She had conjured him up as some romantic hero, a man with an undying love for her. His "big brother" behaviour she now saw as bullying. His weakness was drink. She had never known him, she *would* never know him. But there was no escape. She'd made her bed, she'd have to lie in it.

Sometimes she thought of leaving. She'd picture herself packing up, taking the train home. But would she be any better off back with her parents? She still had Joshua. She couldn't expect them to support them both. She'd have to find a job, make friends, start all over again. And what would everyone think of her, turning up back in Tiverton with Joshua in tow? Not only had she been pregnant when she got married, but she hadn't been able to make the marriage work.

Easy to see now that Aaron was unhappy too. That drinking was his only escape from the situation they'd both put themselves in. At the time, all she saw was the unfairness of it all: Aaron could still act like a student. He was free to come and go as he liked. *She* was stuck at home with the baby and the housework. But there was no excuse for the way he treated her: he was overbearing and a bully. She had no say in anything. Everything had to be done his way.

After a year in the department store, Aaron was still on the shop floor, filling in for staff who were absent, working mostly in the menswear department. "I'm just a general dogsbody," he grumbled.

Caroline tried to persuade him to stay. At least it was money coming in. If Aaron would only cut down on cigarettes and alcohol, like he kept promising he would, they might save enough to buy a place of their own. But Aaron started applying for other jobs. He worked in a small menswear shop for a while, the owner promising him that he would be manager one day, but again it came to nothing. After that, he did a stint in another big store. He never gave up on the idea of working in finance though—he sent letter after letter to banks and building societies, and his tenacity paid off when one day he was offered a job.

Caroline hoped this would be a fresh start. It might not be a big banking firm but it was the nearest Aaron was likely to get to the career they had both envisaged for themselves when they went to university. Surely now he had a decent job, one with real prospects, Aaron would give up the boozy nights, the drunken lunchtimes. Surrounded by new friends and colleagues in a professional atmosphere, he'd turn over a new leaf. His colleagues would have wives and families too. She saw babysitting circles, dinner parties at each other's houses, barbecues in the summer, the children playing together, shopping trips with the wives.

But none of this happened. In fact, things got worse. The bank sent Aaron on training courses, meaning he was away all the time. As a junior member of the team, he was the one sent to work in different branches if he was needed. Aaron still played rugby and cricket, but now he also played five-a-side football with the "lads from the office" and was always staying for a "quick drink" after work. Caroline was invited to the work parties but she knew no one to babysit, so she couldn't go.

Aaron brought home course work to do. He would pore over figures and graphs that Caroline remembered vaguely from A-level and university. Now they were like a foreign language. A great yearning rose in her when she saw them. Her own brain was stultified, listening to nothing but baby language all day, concerning herself with little more than what was in the fridge, how much shopping she had to do, and whether there was enough washing to put on another load. She promised herself she'd do an Open University course when Joshua was older; she even sent off for the details, but it all seemed such a long way off.

Every Christmas they went home to Tiverton, alternating between staying with Aaron's parents or hers. Caroline dreaded these trips: the packing up, the long journey home, the ordeal of the Christmas routine with either set of families. The only good thing about it was the fuss they all made of Joshua. Joshua loved it too. Most of the time he hardly saw anyone apart from Caroline and the staff in the shops they went into, so he loved the noise and fuss made by his grandparents, aunts and uncles.

Emma was already becoming the favourite auntie. She and Robert had moved to Manchester and she came to visit them several times a year, always bringing a present. When they graduated, Robert found a position as a pharmacist and Emma had a job in a law firm. Caroline envied them their freedom and their careers, but Emma loved children. She badly wanted a family but Robert wanted to travel first, then buy a decent home with all the things they'd need in it. Contrary to what Aaron had said about Emma being jealous, Joshua had brought her closer to Emma, not driven them apart.

Mum and Dad visited them less often. It was a long way from Tiverton and with both of them still working, it was difficult to get the time off. It was the same with Aaron's parents. They seemed to think she and Aaron should come down to Tiverton instead, but the journey was so expensive.

For the first couple of years, Caroline had managed to hide her weight loss from her parents but the Christmas after Joshua turned two, she had dropped to below seven stone and was the thinnest she'd ever been. She had taken to wearing baggy clothes to try and disguise it, but her parents hadn't seen her since Joshua's birthday in the summer, and she noticed the swift look of concern on her father's face when she took her coat off. She dreaded mealtimes. She'd stopped eating at all during the day, when there was no one around to find out—surviving only on cups of tea. And when Aaron was late back, she'd tell him she'd already had dinner when in fact the most she'd allowed herself was soup or a piece of dry crispbread. Back home with her parents, there were three meals a day to avoid. She had managed successfully to skip breakfast that morning by taking extra time with Joshua, and she had become expert at hiding the amount she ate. She slid the stuffing and the one roast potato she had taken under a slice of turkey. "Phew! I'm so full!" she said. "I don't think I can manage pudding thanks, Mum, I'll just have a satsuma."

That might have worked at Aaron's parents, where no one really noticed what anyone was doing, but Dad was a doctor. After lunch, he called Aaron into his study on the pretext of showing him a new book he'd been given.

"Bit quieter in here," he said, closing the door.

"Let's go for a walk, shall we?" Aaron said when he came out.

Eager to walk off the calories from the roast turkey lunch, Caroline bundled Joshua into a coat and gloves and they set off, Aaron pushing the buggy. These were the times Caroline dreaded seeing Greg. Although his parents lived on the other side of town, he might walk out this way, they might bump into each other.

As if he was reading her mind, Aaron suddenly said, "You still think of him, don't you?"

"What?" she said, reddening guiltily. "Who?"

"Don't be silly, you know who I mean. Greg. Do you think about him? Wonder what he's doing?"

"No..."

But Aaron knew her too well. "I can get in touch with him," he said. "He was my friend too..."

"No," she said quickly—too quickly.

"I'm right," Aaron said. "I knew I was."

She said nothing. They walked along in silence for a while. "Your dad's worried about you," he said suddenly.

Her stomach clenched. She knew what was coming.

"He says you've got thin. He's right. You should eat more."

"I'm fine. You like me slim. You've always said you do."

"Yes," he said. And that was the end of it. As far as Aaron was concerned, she could starve herself to death as long as she left him to get on with his life.

He was right about Greg, of course. She hadn't stopped thinking about him, wondering where he was and what he was doing. When Aaron had gone to work and Joshua was having his afternoon nap, she would write long letters to him, telling him what a mistake she'd made, asking him if they could try again. Her writing would become illegible as she wrote, tears rolling down her face as she sniffed and cried and wiped them away. It didn't matter that no one could read what she'd written. They were never meant to be sent. When she'd finished them, signing them, "Yours forever", she would tear them into long thin strips and flush them down the loo.

Did Aaron, once so in tune with her every thought, pick up now on what she was feeling? He suddenly became obsessed with Greg. The questions would start when he'd been drinking.

"You still love him, don't you?"

"Don't be silly. You know I don't," she lied.

"If you see him again, it'll put it all to rest," he said one day. "Anyway, I'd like to see him. He was my friend before he was yours."

She couldn't believe it was happening. Aaron rang Greg's home and his mum answered. Caroline could tell by Aaron's voice that she was suspicious. Obviously she hadn't forgiven Aaron for taking her away from Greg.

She couldn't stay in the room when he rang Greg. It seemed like ages. He had an odd look on his face when she went back in.

"He's married," he said, watching her face carefully.

"What?" she said weakly. It was the last thing she'd expected to hear.

"Married with a baby," he continued. "Just like you and me."

"You mean…?"

"Yeah, she was up the duff too." He was laughing now. "You should see your face…"

She slammed down the pile of clean clothes she had in her arms, and walked out of the room. In the kitchen, she hung onto the side of the worktop for dear life. So that was that then. There was no chance. She couldn't believe he'd found someone else. Someone he loved as he'd loved her. She fought back the tears that had sprung to her eyes. She knew Aaron would come after her. He was enjoying this.

"I've asked him to come and stay," he said.

"What?"

"Him and the missus and the sprog."

"We can't. We've got no room."

"We've got two bedrooms. A spare bed. They've got a travel cot. It's only a couple of hours."

They were living in Didcot, near Oxford, where Greg had gone to university. Caitlin was three years younger than Greg. She had just finished her A-levels when they met and was working in a bar to earn enough money to go travelling with a friend. Her parents lived in Oxford; her father was some sort of financier in the city. When he found out Caitlin was pregnant, he offered Greg a job with him, but he had always wanted to teach. He found a place in a primary school in Didcot and Caitlin's parents bought them a house there.

"Her mum will look after the baby when he's a bit older," Aaron finished. "So she can go back to work."

The irony of the situation wasn't lost on Caroline. Except for the wealthy parents, this could have been her and Greg.

She didn't know how they would manage in the tiny house with another couple and a six-month-old baby, or how Joshua would take to having another child around. He was used to being on his own.

The week before, she cleared out the spare room, moving the clothes that no longer fitted her so that Caitlin would have somewhere to hang hers. Then she made up the spare bed. On the Friday morning, Aaron helped her dismantle Joshua's cot and move it into their room. Joshua was very excited at the idea of sleeping in with them, even more excited to hear that "Uncle Greg and Auntie Caitlin" were coming to stay.

She wished she could call the whole thing off. It seemed like such a bad idea. Greg must have been mad to agree to it. She had to remind herself that Aaron and Greg were friends long before she came on the scene and they had a right to see each other. And after all, they were all adults now.

While Joshua slept that afternoon, she had a bath and washed her hair, painstakingly blow-drying it into a bob. Then she sat down and took out Aaron's shaving mirror to put on some make-up. Emma had given her a set of eye shadows for Christmas, but the mascara she found smelt stale and left great blobs on her eyelashes that she had to pick off with her fingers. It had been ages since she'd spent so much time getting ready but she was determined to look something like the Caroline Greg would remember. She'd dithered for ages about what to wear. She had so few clothes but there was no money to buy anything new. It was unusually warm for late May and the weekend was forecast to be a scorcher. She had shorts and summer skirts but the sight of her white legs when she tried them on was enough to make her decide on her smartest jeans with a sleeveless t-shirt. When she looked in the mirror, she saw all her worst points: her chest was flatter since she'd lost weight, the jeans were baggy at the waist and hips, the sleeveless top accentuated her thin arms. It was the best she could do though.

Given the warm weather, a salad might have been more appropriate but she'd planned the meal weeks in advance: a beef casserole that would keep warm as long as was necessary. She laid the tiny round table in the corner of the sitting room with four places. Aaron had said they'd be there around seven, but it depended on the traffic. She gave Joshua an early tea and bath and put him to bed.

Aaron couldn't fail to notice how nervous she was. She jumped when the doorbell finally sounded at 7:40 p.m.

"I'll go and put the vegetables on," she said quickly.

"No, don't be silly," Aaron said. "It'll look so rude if I go on my own." And suddenly she realised he was nervous too.

The Greg that stood in front of her looked exactly the same as the one she'd last seen five years ago. Their eyes met and she saw what she felt mirrored in his. Her heart gave a flip. She still loved him. He still loved her. She couldn't believe Aaron and Caitlin couldn't feel the electricity between them. But Aaron was shaking Greg's hand, pulling him towards him in a sort of awkward man hug. Caitlin's head was bent towards the baby squirming and whimpering in her arms. She was a slight little thing, barely reaching Greg's shoulder, the sort of petite delicate type of woman that made Caroline feel like a gawky beanpole.

"Caitlin," Greg was saying, "this is my best friend Aaron and this is Caroline."

Greg couldn't have chosen anyone more different from Caroline. Not only petite and delicate, like a china doll, but olive-skinned with brown eyes and long, jet black wavy hair. Italian heritage perhaps. Certainly not English. Or Irish as her name suggested. She was one of those irritating women who didn't need to wear make-up: her eyelashes and eyebrows were thick and dark and she had no spots, whiteheads or blackheads to hide like Caroline did. Where Caroline would have worn jeans and flat shoes for the car journey, Caitlin was wearing a smart little strappy sundress which showed off her slim brown arms and legs, along with high-heeled white sandals. The baby looked nothing like Greg: he had his mother's olive skin, her jet black hair. As Caitlin jiggled him in her arms, Caroline saw with a stab of pain the glint of her silver wedding ring, that plain silver band that Caroline had searched so hard to find for Greg's eighteenth birthday.

After the introductions, everything seemed to happen at once. Caitlin said the baby's nappy needed changing and asked if there was any possibility of bathing him, while Aaron was offering drinks: a can of beer or maybe, to Caroline's despair, a "swift half" down the road.

"I've got dinner ready," Caroline said quickly.

"Oh, I can bath Matthew later, it's no problem," Caitlin said. "We'd love to eat now, wouldn't we Greg? I'll just sort Matthew out…"

Impossible to believe that Greg hadn't told her about their relationship, but if she was nervous or jealous, Caitlin certainly didn't show it.

She followed Caroline up to the spare bedroom, keeping her voice low so as not to wake Joshua, finding something to praise in every aspect of the house and offering to help when Caroline said she had to put the vegetables on.

"No, it's fine, everything's ready," Caroline said. Greg had followed them up with bags and coats, and she felt suddenly self-conscious with both of them in the cramped space.

It was almost unreal having Greg there, to hear the voice she remembered so well, the laugh she had never forgotten. He was still the same: not taking anything seriously, turning everything into a joke.

He and Aaron talked non-stop during dinner, mostly about old friends and what they were doing now, leaving Caroline to find something to talk to Caitlin about. Caitlin seemed unfazed: she seemed to regard Caroline as some sort of child expert and kept plying her with questions about how she should be looking after Matthew, when she should be starting him on solids, and all sorts of things that Caroline had forgotten about now that Joshua was nearly three.

Caroline was acutely conscious of Greg the whole time, his knees inches away from hers under the table, his hands holding his knife and fork. She couldn't meet his eyes. She knew she'd give herself away.

While Caroline played with her food in the way she had perfected, Caitlin wolfed hers down as if she hadn't eaten for a week and eagerly accepted a second helping.

"Caitlin has a healthy appetite," Greg excused her. "Mum says she's a pleasure to cook for."

Caroline remembered the icy look on Greg's mum's face the last time she had seen her. No wonder she loved Caitlin so much.

They had only just finished eating when they heard a wail from the bedroom above. To Caroline's surprise, it was Greg who jumped up from the table.

"I'll go," he said.

It was something Aaron would never have done. He always left her to deal with Joshua. Ten minutes later, Greg was back, hurtling down the stairs two at a time in a way Caroline remembered from when they were teenagers.

"I've changed his nappy," he announced. "But it's Mummy he needs now. Daddy doesn't have the necessary equipment to provide food."

Caroline felt a stab of jealousy as Caitlin blushed. She'd

tried breastfeeding Joshua but had to give up when she didn't have enough milk. Despite her childlike body, Caitlin was obviously more maternal.

They didn't have the luxury of a dishwasher and Greg dutifully offered to do the drying up. The thought of him next to her in that tiny kitchen was too much to bear, so she sent him in the other room to talk to Aaron. She could hear Caitlin upstairs in the bathroom, talking softly to Matthew, shushing his little squeals of delight as he splashed in the bath.

"Don't worry too much." Caroline had told her. "Josh hardly ever wakes up." If he could sleep through Aaron's drunken rampages, he could sleep through anything.

In the room next door, Aaron and Greg kept up the same easy flow of conversation that had dominated mealtime.

"Sorry it's such a squash here," she heard Aaron say. "We're going to move as soon as we can. Joshua's getting too big for a cot and needs a room we can make his own, with his own stuff."

It was the first Caroline had heard of it. But it was true. Everything here belonged to the landlord and they couldn't change anything. Joshua's cot was crammed next to the double bed in the magnolia-painted bedroom that was clearly meant for visitors. A room of his own. She pictured nursery wallpaper, a little white bed with a mobile hanging above it, a lampshade patterned with trains or cars, shelves and cupboards for Joshua's toys.

She had finished washing up and was packing away the plates when she heard Aaron suggesting again that they go to the pub.

"No thanks," Greg said easily. "Bit late for me. Been a long day."

"Okay," Aaron said. Caroline could hear the regret in his voice. She knew he was itching to escape. "Another beer then?" he went on.

"I think I'll go on up," Caroline said as he reached past her to get to the fridge.

It was a warm night. The house, freezing in winter, was

stifling in the summer, the heat rising as she climbed the narrow stairs. As she passed the door of the second bedroom, she heard Matthew let out a piercing wail. It was still going on as Caroline undressed in the light from the streetlight. Joshua stirred and moaned a bit, reaching for the blue teddy bear that Emma had given him. When Caroline put it into his hands, he murmured something indecipherable that might have been "Thank you" and settled down again. She pulled on her bathrobe, stepped out of the door to go to the bathroom, and almost bumped into Caitlin coming out of the room next door.

"Oh, sorry," they both said almost at the same time.

"Can you ask Greg to come up?" Caitlin was wearing a loose t-shirt and black knickers. Her black hair fell in thick waves down her back. She looked about twelve. "He won't settle without him."

Caroline nodded dumbly. The thought of a baby needing his father like that was alien to her. All Aaron ever did when Joshua cried was to tell her to find some way to keep him quiet.

She crept down, opened the sitting room door a crack and called softy through. A few minutes later, she heard Greg come upstairs and Joshua's cries gradually subsided. The walls of the house were thin: she could hear Greg and Caitlin talking quietly, the mundane conversations couples have about where the toothpaste is, what to wear tomorrow. The thought of them sleeping together so close to her was more than she could bear. The window was open to let in any breath of air. She could hear the usual Friday night sounds of people returning from the pub. From downstairs came the sound of the television—a comedy programme of some kind—and Aaron's occasional roar of laughter. Nursing his can of beer, it would be ages before he came up. Sadness washed over her. Bitter tears of regret dampened her face as she pictured Greg next door, cradling Caitlin in his arms while their baby slept peacefully next to them.

Caroline woke early to the sun searing through the thin

curtains. Joshua and Matthew were both awake: Joshua demanding to get up; Matthew with the piercing wail of a six-month-old needing to be fed.

Despite the early start, it was nearly midday by the time they had all had breakfast and the children were dressed. Joshua and Matthew were far too young to take much interest in each other but both their routines were upset and both grizzled and grumbled. Caroline hadn't given any thought as to how they would spend their time together. Meeting up was Aaron's idea. Her mind had veered away from the details. It was too hot to stay inside but the tiny paved area at the back of the house had no shade from the scorching sun. Aaron was usually out all day on Saturdays and most of the day on Sundays. Caroline was used to finding something to do with Joshua, but she sensed Aaron's restlessness.

"We could go to the park," she said. This was one of Joshua's favourite places. There was a playground area, a pond with ducks, and she was sure they could find a shady place for Matthew in the buggy.

As they walked along with Greg pushing Matthew in the buggy, Caroline wondered if people might think both children were hers. Caitlin, tripping along in another summer dress and different high heels, didn't look old enough to have a child. If Caroline was happier with Aaron, she might have had another baby by now. But the last thing she wanted at that time was another child to tie her down.

Greg treated Caitlin like a Dresden doll, walking at her pace, stopping at kerbs, making sure it was safe to cross before escorting her across the road. Caroline remembered with a pang when Aaron used to do that. Now he strode ahead, dodging the traffic, leaving her to wait on the kerbside until the road was clear enough for her to push Joshua's buggy across.

In the park, Greg and Aaron took it in turns to push Joshua on the swings or roundabout, then they went to the pond to feed the ducks.

Caroline's heart sank when Aaron said on the way home,

"I thought we could go out for a drink this evening."

It had been fine in the afternoon, with Aaron and Greg to help her, but the thought of a whole evening on her own trying to make conversation with Caitlin was more than she could bear. But she was amazed to hear Aaron say, "A mate of mine told me about a good one with a play area for the kids. It's a bit of a way but we could get a taxi…" He had never suggested taking her and Joshua to the pub before.

With two children to feed and get ready, it was quite late by the time they arrived and the pub was crowded. It was still warm, the sun low in a clear blue sky, and there was a festive atmosphere about it, with strings of lights in the garden, the hubbub of people chatting and laughing, the chink of glasses, and the light from the windows of the pub spilling out onto the garden. Aaron and Greg disappeared to queue for drinks while Caroline and Caitlin found a table near the play area so they could keep an eye on Joshua, who had already run off to play. It was such a novelty for Caroline to go out in the evening. The balmy evening made her feel like she was on holiday somewhere. Caitlin must have read her mind.

"D'you get here often?" she asked.

She could have lied, it would have been more loyal to Aaron, but what was the point?

"No," she said with a bitter little laugh. "I never go anywhere."

"I'm lucky, I suppose. I never really thought about it. Having Mum and Dad so close to babysit. Greg takes me out most weekends."

The last thing Caroline wanted to hear was what a perfect husband Greg was. She had seen enough this weekend to see what life could have been like with him. She leapt up from her seat, pretending she'd heard Joshua calling her. He hadn't, of course, and was surprised and cross when she pulled him into her arms and held him close, tears pricking her eyes. Joshua was the only one who loved her as she needed to be loved.

They had another taxi home. Aaron was the biggest so he

sat in the front, leaving the three of them to squash in the back with the children on their laps. On the way over Caitlin had sat in the middle, but on the way back Greg did, leaving Caroline to squeeze in next to him. She was acutely aware of his bare arm next to hers, the heat from his body. Suddenly she felt his fingers reach for her arm, curl around it, squeeze it gently. Her face burned. She stared straight ahead. She crossed her arms casually, took hold of his fingers with hers, and squeezed them back.

Back home, with the children tired and fractious, she wondered if she'd imagined it. But later on, when she went outside to empty the bin, Greg followed her.

"Caro," he said softly. Nothing more. It was enough.

It wasn't difficult to arrange to see each other. She told Aaron that Vicky wanted to see her. "She's having problems with Jason," she lied. "And I haven't been anywhere on my own for ages."

She thought he'd make more fuss, but he didn't. Leaving Joshua on his own with Aaron even for one night was the hardest part. Aaron had so little to do with Joshua, she wasn't sure how he would manage. It would do him good though to find out what it was like to have to stay in for a change. But she should have known better.

"Barbara said she'll babysit," he announced, "so I can play on Saturday as usual."

She could have pointed out that he'd never asked Barbara to babysit so she could join him on evenings out, or that Joshua might be scared to wake up and find a stranger next to him, but she felt guilty enough without dwelling on it. Aaron had driven her to this, she reminded herself. None of this would be happening if he had been kinder to her, if he hadn't brought Greg back into her life to remind her of what she had lost.

She had no idea what Greg had told Caitlin or how he had booked the hotel. As she sat on the train to Tiverton, she tried not to think about the trusting doll-like Caitlin waiting faithfully at home.

Greg was waiting for her at the station. Her heart gave a little lurch as she saw his face light up when he saw her. Closer up, she could tell he was nervous. But so was she.

He turned to her in the car, looked at her, looked deep into her eyes. "Caro," he said again, and she raised her face for his kiss.

They went straight to the hotel. The receptionist, a bored-looking Chinese woman in her early sixties, didn't give them a second glance when Greg gave his surname.

Upstairs in the corporate purple and white bedroom, they fell on the bed and made love. Strange how she can remember so little of it now. It was what she'd always wanted, Greg's naked body on top of hers, his arms around her, and his breath in her ear. He tasted the same, felt the same. But she'd grown used to Aaron's body, the familiar routine of his lovemaking. She felt detached, as though it was happening to someone else. They didn't say "I love you" and it was nothing like she'd imagined. He was like a different person. She felt none of the longing she'd felt for him before.

She remembers Greg lighting a cigarette afterwards, something that brought Aaron so clearly to mind that she felt guilty and grubby.

"You gave Caitlin the ring I gave you," she said, tracing the outline of his wedding ring.

"No," he said quickly, "I lost yours. I'm sorry. I bought another one. That's the one I gave Caitlin."

She wanted so much to believe him, but she knew it was a lie.

"We got married on your birthday," he said. "Caitlin hated that but it was the only day we could get. And her parents... Well, they've been so good to us. They wanted us to hurry so we went with it."

"So she knows about me. I thought maybe..."

"She knows everything," he said. For a moment, she thought he meant she knew where they were now, but he said quickly, "I told her about you, about Aaron. She was very nervous about meeting you."

"She didn't show it."

"No, she's like that."

She heard the pride in his voice, the love.

"The thing is," he said, "when we argue and I say things like we should split up, she starts crying. She's very appealing when she cries. Like a child. I can never leave her."

They made love again later, in that same uninvolved way. It was nothing special. Not like it had been with Aaron, not like it was to be later with Damian. It was a big mistake. They should never have done it.

She was so strung up, she was sure she wouldn't settle, but she'd been so nervous the night before that she'd hardly slept and she fell asleep instantly.

For a moment, she couldn't think where she was when Greg woke her. She had dreamt of this moment for years, the moment when she would wake up in bed with Greg, but it was nothing like she had imagined.

"I didn't book breakfast," he said, getting out of bed and padding naked to the bathroom, "but you can have it if you want. It's in the Beefeater next door."

He didn't gaze into her eyes, he didn't tell her that he loved her, that he'd always loved her. He didn't even kiss her. She waited till she heard the bathroom door close and the sound of the shower running, then she buried her face in the pillow and allowed the sobs to come.

By the time he came out, wrapped in a bath towel, she'd managed to pull herself together.

"Can you drop me into town?" she asked lightly. "I'm going to Vicky and Jason's."

He hadn't asked what excuse she'd given Aaron, like she hadn't asked about Caitlin.

There was no one else waiting for the lift when they left the room and they got in together. Greg gestured to their reflections in the mirror opposite.

"Looks like a couple of adulterers to me," he said.

She never saw him again. Vicky was the only one who knew, who had to know. She was her alibi.

"I must have been mad to think I could resurrect the past," she told her.

She was just as much out of Greg's life as she was before. She tried not to mind but she did—she minded dreadfully. She felt cheap. Caitlin would never do anything like that. All she had done was make Greg love Caitlin more.

Vicky and Jason weren't having problems. That was just an excuse she'd used to Aaron. They were living in Cowleymoor, the only couple she knew who were still together from school and had stayed living locally. They married a few years later with Joshua as a pageboy. Emma married Robert too. Gradually everyone was catching up with Caroline as christenings followed on from the weddings.

Caroline lived in dread of Aaron inviting Greg and Caitlin to stay. Or worse still, Greg and Caitlin inviting them to stay in their perfect little love nest in Didcot. But it never happened. It's a measure of how well she knew Aaron that she never understood exactly what he wanted to achieve by re-introducing Greg into their lives. He never spoke about him again, even in his drunkest moments.

When Joshua started nursery school, Caroline at last found the independence and freedom she'd craved. She had a couple of part-time jobs in shops before finding a job as a receptionist in a Veterinary Surgery, increasing her hours when Joshua started school. It was there that she met Damian. She had long since accepted she had fallen out of love with Aaron. One New Year's Eve, after one of his drinking sessions, she vowed she'd find a way to leave. She didn't know how or when she would do it, but she knew she couldn't go on. It wasn't a purely selfish decision. Joshua had witnessed too many drunken scenes, too many arguments, too many morning-after hangovers. If she stayed, he'd end up just like his father.

Damian was a Vet, a kind and caring man who was as

different from Aaron as it was possible to be. He didn't like sport or going to the pub unless it was for a meal. He liked long walks with his dogs, fine wine, good food. He knew she was unhappy: of course he did, it was written all over her for anyone to read. She tried to tell him about Greg but he waved it away as though it meant nothing.

"First love," he said, laughing. "Always the hardest to forget…"

After years of not being appreciated, it was good to have someone being kind to her, someone telling her she was lovely. It helped that he had money, though in truth, she'd have gone off with a dustman if he'd offered her a way out. She moved in with him less than six months after she'd met him. The first man who showed an interest in her, but another man she didn't know, like she hadn't known Aaron. It was only later that she found out he too could be moody and selfish, jealous and grumpy. On those bad days, when he snaps at her unreasonably or doesn't speak to her at all, she has to remind herself how much worse it would have been if she'd stayed with Aaron. It's all about compromise. Damian makes up for his bad moods by taking her out, treating her well. Here in the cool climes of his safe steady love, she has found refuge from the searing heat of Greg's, the dark oppressiveness of Aaron's.

With Damian, she has security. He was married before but the divorce is long in the past. His wife has had her settlement, his daughter has been educated. He's well-paid. Joshua will be able to go to university, something they could never have afforded if she'd stayed with Aaron.

She thought she might miss Aaron—the man she had shared so much with, the man she lost her virginity to, the father of her child—but she left him without a backward glance. She felt nothing for him, she realised. Any love she might have once felt had been squeezed out of her long ago by his bullying, his drunkenness and his neglect.

If her time with Greg seemed to have been perpetual summer, with Aaron it was always winter: the rain falling on the roof of the car when they first made love; the cold grey day of their wedding; the constant rain of the summer Joshua was born; the long dark lonely days when Aaron was out.

He wrote her two long letters after she left. *"Dear Little Girl"* they both began. The first one asked her to come back. They could start again, he said. It would be different, he had changed. The second one was full of vitriol: he'd worked hard, he told her, to give her a good life. She wasn't the only one to have lost out on her education, and he'd done his best to provide for her and Joshua. Waves of guilt washed over her as she read it. He made it sound like everything was *her* fault. She didn't reply to either of them and after that, he disappeared from her life and from Joshua's, refusing to reply to the solicitor's letters about access arrangements.

Her parents were shocked when she told them about Damian. They had no idea how unhappy she had been with Aaron. Here she was, shocking them again: not only pregnant at twenty but divorced at twenty-nine and living with a divorcé.

Mum took Aaron's side. "That poor boy," she said. "All on his own." She rang him up, told him he could come and see them whenever he came down to Tiverton to visit his parents.

It was ironic that Caroline should see more of Aaron's parents after she left Aaron than she did before: it seemed unfair that the separation should deprive Joshua of his grandparents as well as his father. So in the school holidays, she would drive down from Solihull, where they were living in the sort of house she could only have dreamt of before, in the smart little car Damian had bought her, so Joshua could spend time with Jack and Margaret.

Joshua was ten when she went to live with Damian. Old enough to know and to mind the disruption in his life but too young to understand why she took him away from the father he loved. Joshua didn't like the man who had taken his mother away from his father. He had been pretty easy as a youngster; now he became difficult and surly. By the time he was a teenager, he and Damian scarcely spoke to each other. If one of them came into the room, the other one would go out.

They had nothing in common: Joshua had inherited his father's love of sport. He was already playing rugby and tennis when she was married to Aaron. Damian didn't even watch sport on television. They bought Joshua a TV of his own so he could watch it in his room, and he spent most of his time up there on his own.

When her divorce came through, she married Damian and had Harry a year later. Damian was keener than she was to have another baby. Joshua was fifteen and was going out more: to friends' houses, to play rugby in the winter, tennis in the summer. At last, she was independent. But she found herself looking at babies and young children. And she loved Damian, she wanted his baby. But it made things worse with Joshua: he was a teenager, he was embarrassed to be seen with his pregnant mum, embarrassed that his friends should know his parents had sex. And when Harry was born, he couldn't hide his jealousy.

It was then that he tried to see Aaron. He wasn't hard to find. He hadn't moved on: he was still working in the same bank, still playing rugby in the same club in Harborne, still living in the same little house in Brixham Road. *Still getting blind drunk in the same bloody pubs,* she thought bitterly when Joshua told her.

One thing had changed though: he'd remarried.

"Lori," Joshua told her. "She said you might remember her from the rugby club..."

Caroline nodded dumbly. Barbara's sister, a big-built blonde girl who used to stand at the bar, a half-pint glass of beer in her hand. The type who laughed and joked with the lads; the type who could attract the barman's attention as easily as they could. Aaron could never call *her* his "Little Girl".

"She sounds nice," Joshua went on. "I'm going over on Saturday..."

A stab of jealousy shot through Caroline. She could see Joshua going there regularly, getting the attention he didn't get with her and Damian, moving in with Aaron and Lori maybe, joining the same rugby club, going to the same pubs.

Aaron was already drunk when he arrived. Joshua told Caroline how Lori had made his excuses.

"He's upstairs," she'd said. "He brought a bottle of whisky home from the club. He's probably just a bit nervous about seeing you after all these years."

They sat on the sofa and watched television, he told her. Then she cooked him a meal. Still Aaron didn't appear, though they heard him stumbling from the bedroom to the bathroom a couple of times. Lori went upstairs. In the small house, Joshua could hear their voices from upstairs: Lori trying to reason with him, her pleading voice; Aaron's brusque replies. Even before she came down he knew it was no good. "I'm sorry," she kept saying. It got late. Lori suggested Joshua stayed the night. "You can see him tomorrow," she had said.

So Joshua slept in the room he had slept in as a little boy, with the same slightly grubby magnolia walls and brown threadbare carpet.

The next day, Aaron still refused to come down. "He's really bad," Lori said. "I can't get him out of bed."

Joshua didn't try again after that.

Harry is four now. Caroline tells herself that when he starts primary school, she'll finally do that Open University course, get the degree she's always dreamed of. The dream is becoming more distant though, as her horizon narrows: there always seems to be something to do. With Harry at nursery now, she's gone back to work part-time. She doesn't need to but she's glad of the adult conversation and the feeling that she's useful and needed. Joshua is doing his A-levels and making those decisions about what to do and where to go to university. Damian works long hours. The weekends that aren't taken up with activities for Harry or watching Joshua play sport are spent with friends or visiting Emma and Robert. Summer holidays are usually at Mum and Dad's villa in France with Emma and Robert and their children. She's not sure how much longer Joshua will continue to go with them. Emma's children are much the same age as Harry and the three of them play together. Even with her parents and Auntie Emma there, he is still the odd one out. He's happier with Aaron's parents in Tiverton, where he's the favourite grandchild and gets all the attention.

Vicky and Jason have done nothing with their degrees, settling down back in Tiverton with mundane jobs. But Caroline envies her old school friends on Facebook, the ones that have made something of their lives and now have jobs as bankers, journalists, dentists, opticians.

She reminds herself she has a lot to be grateful for: a good home, two children, a husband who loves her. She means to make a success of this marriage. When things are bad though, she finds herself thinking of Greg, thinking about when they were young and free and the future was theirs to write.

She looked up Caitlin on Facebook: she's still married to Greg, they've had another baby, another little boy. Clearly they're happy together. A life that could have been hers.

If only she'd stayed with Greg. She knows now that all relationships go through bad patches. Behind that easy-going lackadaisical facade lay a steady, single-minded, hard-working man, responsible and reliable. He was never a drug addict. He would have included her in his life if she'd let him. She should have been more patient, waited for the good times to come back. Instead, she allowed herself to be swayed by Aaron, her parents, and what they thought was best for her. You only get one chance at a love like that. She had it and threw it away.

Yet in some ways, she's glad she didn't stay with him. They'd have only ended up like every other couple she knows—bickering about whose turn it is to do the washing up or grumbling about money. This way she can keep their memories unspoiled by real life.

As time goes by, she's almost forgotten the grubby encounter in the cheap hotel, and remembers instead their innocent first love.

She thought she loved Aaron, she thought she loved Damian, but she realises now she's only ever loved one person: Greg. Not the Greg she met later, not even maybe the real Greg, but the Greg she knew when they were sixteen and it was always summer.

Carly

One

Carly likes the new life she's invented for herself. As Caroline Westminster she has a retired doctor as a father, a loving attentive sister, a niece and a nephew, and a successful career. Caroline has everything Carly's ever wanted. She's lived an untroubled life and made no mistakes, unlike Carly Spurway.

Her pre-reg year with Hudson Opticians seems such a long time ago now. The only things she can remember with any clarity are her first real eye examination, and the assessments that made her so nervous she was often physically sick beforehand. Graham was a good supervisor: he checked her work regularly, made sure she was ready for each of those nerve-wracking assessments, gave her the confidence she needed to be a good optometrist. She was lucky: when she met up with other optometry students she heard stories of supervisors who scarcely looked at their work and opticians who used them just as cheap labour, pushing them on to do eye exams more quickly than they were ready for.

Hudson Opticians was a small practice to work in. Everyone knew everything about each other. With so few of them there it was hard to keep anything private. Carly wished Tina hadn't told her about Lucy being pregnant, but luckily she didn't have to keep the secret for long. Graham had only been seeing her for a few months.

"It wasn't something I planned at all," he told Carly later. "I really wasn't ready for fatherhood and all that…"

He didn't show it at the time though. "I've got some news," he said one morning in the staff room—a room that was little more than a tiny back office crammed with filing cabinets. Carly waited for him to say he was getting married but instead, he said, "Lucy's pregnant. I'm going to be a father."

She saw the look that passed between Sandra and Kath. Clearly they'd expected him to say he was getting married too. Andy was oblivious to any underlying story that he was missing. Solidly married to Liz, with two equally solid children, he naturally assumed marriage would follow, if not now, then later. But it didn't. Graham didn't even move in with Lucy.

"He keeps saying he will," Tina told Carly. "When he's ready, he says. But he doesn't feel ready."

It was hard for Carly, hearing Lucy's side of the story from Tina, knowing so much more of what Graham was going through than he actually told her. So when he brought in photos of the scan; when he came in exhausted after the birth, telling them he had a son called Edward Thomas; when he brought in the first photos; she knew from Tina that although he was supporting them financially, Lucy was still waiting for the proposal, the wedding, the house she expected him to buy for them following the birth of their baby.

Carly saw a lot of Tina in that year she spent with Hudson Opticians. It was inevitable really: she didn't know anyone in Reading and after all, the only reason she had gone to Reading at all was because Mum and Dad had wanted her to keep an eye on her. Not that Tina needed it: at that time, she and Joe seemed like the perfect couple. They both worked such long hours, on different shifts, in different departments at the hospital, they had very little time to fall out.

It was through Tina that Carly met most of her friends in Reading. Sandra and Kath at work were both older than her and although she went out with them occasionally, they were both married with kids and she had little in common with them.

There were work parties of course—the first one at Christmas, where she met Lucy, now heavily pregnant. She seemed such a shy girl then, reaching out for Graham's hand at every opportunity, her long fair hair curtaining her face, her hands caressing her baby bump. She adored Graham, it was plain to see: her eyes followed his every move, she laughed when he laughed, agreed with everything he said. Hard to see behind this submissive girl the hard-hearted vixen she turned out to be later, squeezing every penny out of Graham on the pretext that Edward needed it.

Lucy came along to other work parties too, slimmer now, showing off photos of Edward in various stages of babyhood, everyone accepting her as Graham's partner even though they were no nearer to living together. On Graham's day off, Sandra or Kath would gossip about it. "It's shameful." They'd say. "The poor girl. Not even an engagement ring on her finger, let alone a wedding ring." But Carly had seen the way Graham looked at girls who came in; the way he looked at her, even though she was a student. She felt the electricity between them when their fingers brushed sometimes or when he looked over her work. He might feel an obligation, but clearly Graham wasn't in love with Lucy.

Carly had always known there wouldn't be a place for her at Hudson Opticians when she qualified. Even with the branch in Newbury, there wasn't enough work for two optometrists. As soon as she knew she'd passed, she started applying for another job and found a place with Optimum Vision, one of the well-equipped High Street multiples she'd always seen herself working for.

It was a big busy store, with another full-time optometrist, Kate, who was only a little older than her, Ben, the practice manager, and a full team of optical advisers who did everything from helping customers to choose frames and adjusting their spectacles to using some of the pre-examination equipment. Working here was very different from that small independent in Shinfield Road. There was no popping out to buy cakes for the mid-morning chat between patients; in fact, there was hardly time for a cup of tea or coffee in the staff room upstairs.

As a newly-qualified optometrist, Carly was allotted twenty-five minutes for eye examinations, but soon they expected her to do them in twenty minutes. So little time to do everything that Carly had been taught was essential. In Hudson Opticians, it didn't matter if you ran late: the patient's welfare was the most important thing. Here, the optometrist's job was to get through as many eye exams as possible to generate the sales necessary for a healthy profit.

Ben, the manager, was a good-looking man in his mid-thirties with black hair cut short to his head. Always immaculately dressed in suit and tie, he was a stickler for hard work and punctuality. In his spare time, he volunteered for the Territorial Army and he ran the business like a military institution. There was no standing around and chatting when it was quiet like they did in Hudson Opticians: he could always find something for them to do, from tidying out drawers and cupboards to cleaning the spectacle frames on display.

With Carly's new job came a good salary. She moved from the three-bedroomed house she had shared in Cirrus Drive to a brand new one-bedroomed flat within walking distance of work.

Looking back now, this was one of the best times of her life, although she didn't realise it at the time. She was out every weekend: shopping during the day, having lunch, going to a bar or the cinema in the evenings. Jan and Amber, her friends from uni, sometimes came to stay or she'd go up to London to see them, taking in an exhibition or a show together. She went out with a couple of men but it never came to anything.

She and Graham kept in touch for a while. She rang him a couple of times for advice about patients, but gradually she found she could manage on her own. She still saw Tina though, and that's how she heard that Graham and Lucy had split up.

"She got fed up with waiting for him to marry her," Tina said loyally.

It was two years later when she heard that Hudson Opticians had closed down. Carly's fellow optometrist Kate had married by then and was leaving to have a baby. She didn't plan to come back. Graham applied for the vacancy and was accepted. Carly's heart flipped when she saw him. Now that he was free, now that she was no longer his student, it seemed inevitable they would get together. Once he'd had his interview, he waited for nearly an hour for her to finish her last patient of the morning so he could take her to lunch.

Her life changed completely once she started seeing Graham. Gone were her weekends with friends, her trips up to London, her Pilates and Zumba even. Every waking moment was spent with him. The weekends he wasn't seeing Edward were spent driving out to pretty villages like Sonning or Kintbury, or going up to London or somewhere like Stratford-on-Avon, even Paris on one occasion. His friends became her friends.

It seemed to help that Carly already knew about Lucy. Graham didn't need to explain what had happened, when and why. He didn't have to explain either the weekend visits to Lucy's house, the Sundays spent trying to entertain Edward, the Christmases spent as a family.

A year later, they started living together and a year after that, he proposed. She can remember now her surprise. It was a lovely weekend, mid-November, the weather cold, crisp and clear. They had gone to the Cotswolds for the weekend; they'd just been for a long walk in the autumn colour and were now wandering up the High Street in Stow-on-the-Wold, looking for a tea shop. It was beginning to get dark, and light from the brightly lit shops spilled onto the pavements. Every so often, they stopped and gazed idly at the displays in the windows.

"D'you like that ring?" Graham asked suddenly.

The jewellery shop had an array of modern and antique jewellery twinkling in the bright lights. Carly wasn't sure which one he meant. She was hungry and thirsty, her mind on tea and toasted teacake, so she tugged his arm slightly to forge on.

"That one," he persisted, drawing her back. "The diamond solitaire."

She had a sudden inkling of what was going to happen but she quelled it sharply. It was ridiculous.

"I think it's beautiful," he said. "Would you like it? For our engagement?"

It might not have been the most romantic proposal but it must have been one of the most unexpected. She walked out of the shop, the diamond winking on her finger, in a haze of happiness. She'd always thought Graham wasn't the marrying kind. He never married Lucy, so why would he marry her? She had resigned herself from the start to being just his partner for as long as it might last. Now here she was announcing their engagement.

They were staying in Chipping Campden, in a Georgian house which had been converted into a plush spa hotel. She stood at the window, gazing out at the yellow-stoned houses opposite, as she waited nervously for Mum or Dad to answer the phone. She knew her parents didn't approve of Graham.

"Your old supervisor?" her mother had said when she first told them she was seeing him. "Isn't that a bit unprofessional?"

"He isn't my supervisor anymore!" Carly had laughed.

"But he must be a lot older than you."

"Only five years."

"He's been married before though…"

"No," Carly said. "What makes you think that?" Though she had a pretty good idea.

"Tina says he's got a child," her mother said.

"Yes, but he never married her…"

Her mother gave a sharp tut of disapproval.

Graham's parents didn't approve of Carly either. Edward

was their grandchild. Their loyalty lay with Lucy. They thought of her as their daughter-in-law, assumed Graham would do the honourable thing and marry her one day.

Tina's loyalty lay with Lucy too. Lucy was one of her best friends. She treated Carly as though she had done something wrong.

Carly's wedding day was one of the few occasions when Tina didn't upstage her: nine years with Joe, now fully qualified with a salary to match, and she didn't even have an engagement ring on her finger. She couldn't hide her jealousy. The photos show her standing next to Carly in her bridesmaid's dress, a grim smile on her face. It was unfortunate that Graham's sister was the other bridesmaid, a tall, willowy girl with long slim arms. In comparison, Tina looked small and dumpy in the ice pink dress that Carly had chosen especially for her colouring.

Carly was proud to be married to Graham, to have her name linked with his: 'Mrs. Carly Anderson' on the door of her consulting room. Graham had a good professional reputation and his patients from Hudson Opticians followed him to Optimum Vision. If he was too booked up, they would sometimes see her.

"Oh, *Mrs.* Anderson," they'd say. "Well, you must be all right if you're Mr. Anderson's wife."

Sometimes they'd see her next time rather than go back to him. She and Graham made a good team: some patients preferred a young newly-qualified or female optometrist. Some preferred an older, more experienced man.

But Graham was a flirt. He couldn't help himself. Working with him made it a hundred times worse. Carly would rush through her patient if she saw a pretty girl waiting for an eye exam, desperate to take her in herself, eaten up with jealousy at the thought of Graham in a darkened room with her, talking to her, leaning close, smelling her perfume, putting his hand on her forehead when he did ophthalmoscopy.

The spectre of Lucy was always in the background.

Determined to prove she'd got there first, she changed her name by deed poll to Mrs. Anderson, saying it was so she could have the same surname as Edward. She wore a ring on her wedding finger and told Tina that Graham had given it to her, though he swore he hadn't.

Edward was five when they got married. He came over every other weekend. Graham's parents often came over to see him. They would ask Edward how Mummy was, what she was doing. Carly felt like an interloper. There was Edward's birthday, Christmases, holidays, all times when Carly had to see and be polite to Lucy. And the times Carly wasn't included: parent evenings at school, where Graham and Lucy were treated as a married couple; school plays, sports days. She told Graham how she felt. In those days, she thought she could tell him anything. She soon realised there were things he didn't tell her, so she began keeping her thoughts and feelings to herself.

It wasn't easy being a stepmother. Edward wasn't exactly a bad little boy but Graham spoilt him. Carly knew that children should have a set routine. Edward should eat what she put in front of him, have a bath and go to bed at a set time. But Graham let Edward have everything his own way: he could stay up late, his table manners were appalling, and Carly wasn't allowed to tell him off.

"He won't want to come at all if you keep going on at him," he said.

They were still living in the two-bedroomed Victorian house in Caversham that Graham had bought when he first moved to Reading. When they were first married, Graham promised he would put it on the market and that they would buy a house together but every time she brought up the subject, he always had an excuse that meant they had to postpone it. When they divorced ten years later, the house was still in his name. It was always Graham's house, never hers. A Victorian semi, with a fireplace, a log burner, high ceilings, wood floors. He loved it. He was blind to its bad points. It needed re-decorating. The kitchen was outdated, the rugs tatty, the sofa sagged. They were both working: the log burner took ages to light and the room was only just beginning to warm up when it was time to go to bed. Logs needed to be bought and stored. Carly missed her bright modern apartment in Kennet Side, where she had chosen her own colour schemes, her own furniture, her own decorations. Everything here had been chosen by someone else, Graham presumably, but maybe Lucy had chosen the cushions, the curtains even, the pictures on the wall. This was the house Lucy had hoped to live in. She had slept with Graham in the big double bed upstairs, gazed up at the sloping ceiling above Graham's shoulder as they made love. Other girls had slept there too. The house held memories, it had secrets, whispered promises, never meant, long since broken.

There were only two bedrooms, the second one was Edward's, decorated the way he wanted and re-decorated at his every whim. Carly wasn't allowed to touch anything. She could scarcely clean it, or she was accused of moving and losing precious items. Maybe if she'd had a baby, a little girl so they would need another room, it would have forced them to move house. His proposal had been so much of a surprise, she had been so overwhelmed, so happy and grateful, that she had never thought to ask him about children. She just assumed that one day they'd have them. Meanwhile, Graham assumed she was a career girl. It was her own fault. She'd been so keen to impress him when she was his student that she had told him how she wanted to build up her professional reputation, continue going to lectures and seminars at the university, write articles for professional magazines. He saw her as someone different from Lucy, who had been happy in her work at the hospital where she did little more than mop-up vomit or take temperatures, looked for nothing more than marriage and children. But Carly wanted both: a career and children. And she knew it was possible. She was well-paid. She could go back to work part-time, hire a nanny. Other optometrists did it. It was one of those things that had attracted her to Optometry in the first place.

Having Edward so young though, unplanned and unprepared, had put Graham off the idea of having another one.

"Not yet," he kept saying. "We're tied down enough with Edward. And you've got your career to think about. You don't want to give up when you're not even established. Let's have some fun first. We can have holidays, weekends away. Babies put an end to all that."

And it was true—having Edward around had put her off children. When he was there, the house was in chaos. The floor was littered with toys and games that she was always falling over, and he threw a tantrum if she tried to tidy them up at all or limit them to a specific area.

"Mummy lets me!" he'd say defiantly, looking up at Graham.

The television was on the whole time at full volume, whether he was watching it or not. They always had to find ways to amuse him: visits to parks or children's amusements. Mealtimes were a battle, bedtimes were worse. And he'd wake early and barge into their bedroom, oblivious to any state of undress she might be in.

It's easy to see now that she should have been more assertive, told Graham they had to have rules and boundaries. But at the time, Carly was so besotted with Graham she would done anything, gone anywhere, as long as she had him.

Six years after they were married, just at the time when Carly was beginning to feel ready to ask Graham again about starting a family, something happened that turned her world upside down and put the idea totally out of her mind. It started, as everything always did, with Tina.

Carly was cooking dinner one night when Graham came in. "Your sister's on the phone," he said, passing it to her. "But I can't understand what she's saying. She's hysterical."

Carly sighed. Since she'd married Graham, she'd hardly seen Tina, who hadn't forgiven her for taking him away from Lucy. But she still rang when she was desperate. This was one of those occasions and it was obviously a problem with Joe. Usually, after an hour or so on the phone, she'd be calmer. Joe would come back from wherever he'd stormed off to and everything would be back to normal. This time, however, it was more serious. Joe had gone. Really gone this time. Not just an argument, but an affair with a fellow doctor. Tina was inconsolable.

"I'll have to go and see her," Carly said.

Graham shrugged. "Okay."

Tina and Joe had moved from their flat share to a house in Earley, not far from the hospital. It was November 4th, a Friday evening. As she drove over, Carly could hear fireworks going off in the distance, see occasional bright bursts of light and colour. She passed a group of people huddled up in warm clothes and wellies, small children tugging at their arms, obviously on their way to a firework display. She and Graham had arranged to take Edward to one at the recreation ground the next day.

Tina's house in Earley was everything Carly would have liked for herself: bright, modern and warm, decorated by Tina without any input from Joe, who had no time and no interest in anything domestic. The last time Carly had been here was their housewarming party. Tina had stood with her arm around Joe, so proud of their new place. Now she opened the door in her dressing gown, her face red and blotchy, a tissue balled up in her hand.

"Mum and Dad are coming up," she said.

"What? Now? Tonight?"

It was eight o'clock on a dark, foggy night and they would have a four-hour journey at the very least. Only Tina could expect her parents to drop everything and come up.

"I don't want to be alone," she said.

"I can stay," Carly said. Even to her own ears, her voice lacked conviction.

"But you don't want to, do you?" Tina said. "You want to go home to lover boy."

"He's my husband," Carly said defensively. But the word 'husband' set Tina off crying again. Carly knew she should put her arm around her, but they'd never been like that. She sat next to her on the sofa, patting her back awkwardly with one hand.

"I don't know what I'm going to do…" Tina wailed. "I love him so much. I gave up everything for him."

"I know, I know…" Carly said because she didn't know what else to say.

"*How* do you know?" Tina snapped.

"I just meant…" Carly began.

"You don't understand!" She burst out. "Graham goes to work with you, comes home with you. You've got evenings, weekends. Joe's always so busy. But I was here for him. Always here. How can he do this to me? Oh, I wish Mum would hurry up. She'd understand…"

Carly doubted if she would, as Dad worked a steady nine to five-thirty, but she wanted their parents there too. Tina could rail at them instead of her, and she could go back home.

At ten o'clock, they turned the television on to watch the news. They kept the volume turned low; neither of them really watching it. Carly was tired. Her eyelids dropped. Then suddenly, she was wide awake:

"*News is coming in of a crash on the M5 earlier this evening…*"

Tina had the controller. She turned the volume up.

"Don't be silly," Carly said quickly. "It won't be them…"

The rest of the night is something of a blur to her now. Graham turned up, though she can't remember whether he rang her or she rang him. Tina kept saying, "It's my fault, it's my fault" over and over again, even though they hadn't heard anything yet. "Don't be silly." Carly kept saying. "It'll all be fine. They'll be here soon." But as time dragged on and still they didn't come, Carly knew they were gone.

The memories that followed are kept in a box in her mind marked "Do not open". There was the inquest, the blame and counter-blame: their father was upset and not concentrating, he was driving too fast, it was a foggy night, and there was smoke from a bonfire blowing across the motorway. Carly can't remember much of it now. She can't remember the funeral either, except for the pressure of Tina's hand on her arm, the sea of white faces, the sympathetic murmuring voices. It was as though it was happening to someone else. She and Tina were both dosed up on anti-depressants. They both had counselling.

Guilt came with the grief. She could have gone to see them more often, Carly thought. She was sharp with them sometimes on the phone, she hadn't involved them enough in her life.

Tina's guilt was worse: she blamed herself for asking them to come up. On top of Joe leaving, it could have been too much for her. But Tina had a core of steel. This was the girl who had run away at thirteen, had an abortion at sixteen, left home at eighteen. It took a while but she pulled through. Carly was grudgingly proud of her. At this time, they were the closest they'd ever been, probably the closest they ever would be.

Joe had come to the funeral to support Tina, and Carly wasn't surprised to hear he had gone back to live with her. It didn't last though. Before long, he had returned to his doctor lady friend.

Presumably Tina, too, had hoped for a baby. She was thirty and had been with Joe for years. Maybe she'd been waiting for the right time. Now it would never come. But she was entitled to a settlement: not enough to stay in the three-bedroomed house in Earley but enough to buy a smart little one-bedroom apartment in the same area.

She might be managing well, but outwardly Tina kept up the helpless little girl act that had stood her in such good stead all these years. With no Joe to turn to, she latched on to Graham, asking his advice for every problem. Carly thought that working in a hospital would cure her hypochondria but it only made things worse. If a patient complained of a symptom, she'd find she had it too. Joe was a doctor. He had reassured her. Graham might be only an optometrist but he had some medical knowledge. Carly could have pointed out that *she* was an optometrist too, she knew just as much as Graham, but she had no patience with Tina and Graham seemed to love this helpless little female telling him her catalogue of symptoms, asking his advice on every single issue in her life. She'd be on the phone for hours describing any tiny ache and pain, every cold and sniffle. Carly would hear Graham saying, "Yes, of course. Yes, I see. Yes, I know. I'm sure it's nothing serious…"

"Can't you just tell her to go to the bloody doctor?" Carly would say afterwards.

"I'm just trying to help," he'd explain.

Then there were the problems with the car, the phone, the internet, or work. Carly knew Tina was perfectly able to sort these things out for herself. She just liked the attention.

When Tina saw the advert for the job of Diabetic Retinopathy Screener it was Graham she rang to ask about it, Graham who went around to her flat to help her prepare for the interview.

To begin with, it was good to see them getting on so well. Tina had never forgiven Graham for leaving Lucy and Edward, and for years she had been nothing more than icily polite to him. And Carly was so pleased to see Tina smiling and happy again—doing well in her new well-paid responsible job, standing on her own two feet—that she was blind to the reason behind her sister's newfound confidence and happiness. Graham was always speaking to Tina on the phone. He'd pop around to see her to help with things in the new apartment or offer advice about the new job. But after a while, she began to resent it. Graham was always there under some pretext or other. When Tina rang up one night, she lost her temper with Graham.

"You're not going there *again*. I'm fed up with it. For God's sake, just tell her to grow up and stand on her own two feet."

Graham reddened. Carly thought it had worked. He stopped going.

"I'm thinking of joining a gym," he said one day.

"What a good idea," Carly said. Graham always grumbled when she went to Pilates. Now he'd have something to do as well. She didn't even mind when he texted her sometimes to say he was going out for a drink afterwards, as it meant she could join Kelly and Ruth in the bar after their class. Sometimes Graham would go for a run. The time they now spent apart, with separate hobbies and friends, seemed to suit them. Graham was much nicer to her. Suddenly she could have anything she wanted: clothes, things for the house, a holiday. It was only later, looking back on it, that she realised why.

It was Tina who told her. Carly was telling her about Graham's keep-fit fad, laughing about it actually. "I don't know what's brought it on," she said.

Tina was silent for a moment. Then suddenly she said, "You know what's going on, don't you?"

"No, what?" Carly said.

"Graham and I are having an affair."

Graham denied it. He said she was lying. "She's mad, your sister," he said. "She lives in a world of her own."

But Carly didn't believe him. Why would Tina lie? To get attention? It was the sort of thing she might do. Or to make trouble between her and Graham so he'd go back to Lucy and Edward? No, too many things added up. Carly realised what a fool she'd been. She moved into Edward's room, sleeping in his narrow single bed under his Transformers duvet, and only moving back in with Graham when Edward came to stay, sleeping as far away as possible from Graham's naked body. She slept badly, tortured by visions of Graham and Tina together, Graham kissing her, his tongue in her mouth, his hands on her naked body. She'd get up the next day to go to work, tired and groggy, and then make polite, stilted conversation with Graham at the breakfast table and in the car on the way to work. There, no one would have known anything was wrong. They were so professional, looking through their list of patients each day, consulting each other as usual.

Carly started looking for jobs in the Optometry Today magazine. She'd make a clean break, she thought, far away from here, back in the West Country, away from Graham and Tina, Lucy and Edward. Bath or Bristol maybe, or Taunton or Exeter. Not Tiverton—the memories were too painful and she'd have to see all those aunts and uncles who would remind her of Mum and Dad.

After more than a year on the market, her parents' house had finally sold. The furniture, their clothes, everything they had ever known was given away or disposed of. Carly and Tina were left with boxes of photographs and paperwork. Neither of them had been able to face going through them, and they had been up in Carly and Graham's loft since then.

If she was moving though, she should sort them out, give Tina the stuff she might like to have before she went away. Graham was still trying to persuade her not to go, but he was being so polite to her, on such good behaviour, that he took out the ladder and dutifully brought the boxes down when she asked him.

She sat on the living room floor one afternoon when Graham and Edward were out in the park, a knot of dread in her stomach as she sliced through the packing tape with the kitchen knife.

It was a job that would have been made easier if she could share it with Tina, but she couldn't bear to see her.

In fact, to start with it wasn't as bad as she'd expected it to be. There were a lot of bills, bank statements and car documents that could be shredded now that probate was finished. The next box held photo albums: Mum and Dad's wedding photos. As the eldest, she would keep these and pass them on to her children if she ever had any. Then came albums of her and Tina as babies and small children. This was easy too: there was a whole album dedicated to Carly before Tina came along; she would obviously have that one, and the others she could divide between them. The holiday ones were harder: camping holidays in France with her and Tina on the ferry, villa holidays in Italy with them in the pool. Tina should have been there with her to laugh at their funny haircuts, their dreadful swimming costumes, Dad in his shorts, Mum with her old-fashioned hairstyle and her long-since-outdated summer dresses. Her throat tightened and she shoved the album in her own pile. Tina could have them when Carly was dead too. At the bottom of the box lay a pile of loose photos. Carly picked them up: school photos of herself and Tina at various ages; snaps of the garden that Mum and Dad were so proud of; more recent holiday photos, just Mum and Dad, that hadn't made it into an album. She sifted through them, dividing them up equally between her and Tina.

She slit open the final box: at the top were their school reports, divided into two separate bundles, one for her, one for Tina. She glanced through some of her own: *Carly works hard, Carly shows progress this term.* She knew without looking at them what Tina's would say. *Tina needs to apply herself* was the usual comment.

Underneath were wedding invitations, including her own; cuttings from newspapers and magazines, and the odd bill. She was shredding them one at a time when she saw the top edge of a document she hadn't noticed before: the distinctive salmon pink of a birth certificate. Puzzled, she pulled it out. She and Tina had both had their birth certificates for years— why would there be another one?

Tina's name was on it and their parents'. But the date at the top wasn't Tina's date of birth. Then with a jolt, she saw the words: "Date of adoption and description of court by which made." *Tina was adopted.* Suddenly everything slotted into place. Amazing how Tina looked so much like Mum and Dad. But she had none of their characteristics. And none of Carly's.

A thought suddenly occurred to her: she searched feverishly through the other pieces of paper, checked the bottom of the box, the bottom of the other boxes, but there was nothing. So *she* wasn't adopted. Just Tina. Mum and Dad must have wanted her to have a little sister, a little sister to play with, to love, to look after. She hadn't made a very good job of it.

She sat on the floor in front of the shredder with the piece of paper in her hand. How easy it would be to get rid of it. No one would know. Maybe Mum and Dad would want her to. It can't have meant much to them or it wouldn't have been shoved in haphazardly with everything else. They had done all they could to bring Tina up well, to make sure she'd never know she was adopted.

But even as Carly's hand hovered over the top of the shredder, she knew she couldn't do it. Tina had a right to know, to search for her birth parents if that was what she wanted to do. She looked at the clock. Graham and Edward wouldn't be back for another twenty minutes or so. She reached for her mobile phone and pressed Tina's name.

"I'm sorting out Mum and Dad's stuff," she said as casually as she could. "Can you come over and help me with it?"

They hadn't spoken for weeks. Tina was surprised but came straight over.

Carly tried to behave normally when she opened the door but Tina knew her too well. "What's happened?" she asked. She looked at the empty boxes on the sitting room floor, the neat piles next to them, the shredder. "You've done it all," she said. "You don't need me…"

"Sit down," Carly said.

"For God's sake, tell me what's going on," Tina said. "Is it Graham? Has something happened to Edward?"

Carly handed her the certificate. She couldn't look at Tina. Tina stood with it in her hand for a long time. Then Carly heard her mutter something under her breath.

"What did you say?" She asked.

"Changeling," Tina said. "*I'm* the changeling. Brought by the bad fairies. *You're* the princess. At least—" She broke off. "Unless—"

"No," Carly said quickly. "I've looked through everything. But we can check properly. Both of us. Make sure there's no mistake."

"No," Tina shook her head. "I mean, *you* can check. But you don't need to. You must see. I do. You're like Mum and Dad. Just like them. *I'm* the odd one out. *I'm* the one that doesn't fit in. It's obvious, isn't it?"

Tina was right. It all made sense. The way Mum and Dad treated her like she was special, the way they let her get away with so much, the way they favoured her so she would never think they preferred their natural daughter to her.

"When I was little, I asked Mum one day where I came from," Tina said. "She told me she'd gone into a big room full of babies and she'd chosen me especially out of all of them. She was telling me the truth, wasn't she?"

Carly said nothing. She remembered Mum's dream about rescuing Carly from the water before she knew she was pregnant. Maybe Tina was right. Mum *was* trying to tell her she was adopted. If Carly had been the sort of sister she would like to have been, she would have put her arm around Tina, they would have held each other close. Instead, she sat awkwardly next to Tina while she cried and sniffed and wiped her nose until she was calm enough to go.

So now they were right back where they were before. Tina was her responsibility again—the little sister, who wasn't a sister at all, who needed looking after even though she could manage perfectly well on her own. Nothing had changed. It was as though she'd made a promise to Mum and Dad to look after Tina when she found that adoption certificate. They only had each other now. Oh, there were uncles and aunts in Tiverton, an aunt in Ealing even, that they could turn to if they really needed.

"D'you think they know?" Tina asked. "Auntie Louise, Auntie Sharon—all of them?"

"They must do, I suppose…"

"And no one ever said."

"Well, they wouldn't, would they? Not if Mum and Dad didn't want them to. Maybe they thought they'd tell you one day."

Carly was sure that if it had been her, she'd have wanted to look up her birth parents, but Tina didn't want to. She must have confided in someone—Lucy probably, as they were best friends—but she never mentioned it to Carly again.

Graham didn't seem to notice anything wrong when he came back with Edward that day. If he thought it was odd that Carly and Tina were suddenly seeing each other again he didn't ask why. He just accepted it.

Carly still intended leaving him. Just because she had to look after Tina didn't mean she couldn't move out: she could stay nearby. But her plans became gradually more distant. She stopped packing up stuff, she didn't grab the optician magazines each week to look at the Jobs page.

Things were still far from right. Graham behaved as though he was the injured party and Carly felt like she was the one making all the compromises, tiptoeing around his bad moods and hurt silences just to keep the peace. But there was no doubt they were getting on better and one weekend when Edward went home, she didn't move back into his bedroom.

She never knew whether Graham and Tina actually had an affair. She didn't question him, she didn't question Tina. Like Tina's abortion, her running away, their parents' death, her adoption, it became one more thing they didn't talk about.

They had been very good to Carly at work when her parents had died. Their manager Ben had allowed her time off to go to the inquest, arrange the funeral, sort out her parents' legal affairs and generally recover from the shock.

At the start of the following year, Optimum Vision took over EyesRight, one of the other multiple opticians. Managers were moved around, re-located, promoted or demoted as necessary. They lost Ben, who had run the place like an army platoon, replaced by Diane from the branch of EyesRight fifty yards down the road.

Diane was a big built sporty-looking woman with

shoulder-length blonde hair and severe black-framed glasses. She was the sort of woman who seldom smiled. She was brisk, efficient. She couldn't have been much older than Carly but she looked about fifty. Like Andy in Hudson Opticians, Ben was a qualified Dispensing Optician. He had been more retail-orientated than Andy had been: this was a business with sales figures, not a professional practice offering a service. All the opticians were expected to take an interest in the figures, sales were important, and they all had targets. But being qualified, Ben knew and understood the problems patients could have. The new manager, Diane, wasn't qualified and wasn't interested in professionalism. She crammed as many eye examinations as possible into the day, expecting Graham and Carly to rush through each one, however complex they might be, not realising that certain eye conditions needed more care, older patients took much longer to examine. And if someone couldn't get on with their spectacles, she always assumed it was the optometrist's fault. She had no idea about the technical side of dispensing the spectacles: that it could be the fit of the frame that was at fault, that a small adjustment to the spectacles might be all that was needed.

To Diane, the weekly sales were paramount. Despite his military approach, Ben had had the knack of encouraging his staff to perform and to think of themselves as a team, acting together to get the best performance. He got the best out of his staff: his weekly staff meetings were an opportunity to discuss issues and find ways to improve things. Diane ran her meetings like a headmistress in charge of unruly children. If the weekly takings were less than expected, she would pounce on individual members of staff, challenging them to come up with a good reason for it. She expected everyone to memorise the daily figures. If they couldn't recite them, she held them up to ridicule in front of everyone else. The optometrists weren't exempt. They had to come up with a good excuse if they hadn't reached their targets for converting eye exams into spectacle sales. There was no encouragement to come up with good ideas to improve the running of the business: everyone was too terrified to speak.

One week, Graham called Diane into his room after the meeting. Carly, in her room next door, heard him say, "I wonder if I could give you some feedback."

Diane closed the door and the rest of the conversation was muffled. Graham's face was like a thundercloud when Diane went out. He never told Carly what went on: "That woman is impossible," was all he said.

The amalgamation of Optimum Vision with EyesRight made them into a big business—the second-largest multiple opticians in the country—and there was a myriad of rules and regulations. There were the security rules: there were lockers in the staff room and they weren't allowed to carry cash or personal belongings on the sales floor; certain areas were out of bounds during the day; there were staff doors with security codes. Then there were fire regulations, manual handling, Health and Safety rules. Carly had worked there longer than Graham, she was used to them. But Graham had only ever worked in small private opticians like Hudson's. He dutifully signed all the various documents he was given, he paid lip service to what he perceived as ridiculous rules, but as far as he was concerned he was an optometrist, he was above all that, they simply didn't apply to him.

Like many optometrists, Graham considered himself superior to the other staff. He was always telling Carly not to be too friendly with them.

"We're professional," he told her. "We need to keep ourselves separate."

Even at Hudson Opticians, where they were more like a family than a team, he would take his sandwiches and cup of tea into his examination room to have on his own. The only person he sometimes talked to was Andy, and that was because he was a Dispensing Optician. But Carly had never been like that. She would sit and chat with Sandra and Kath. They went out for a drink sometimes after work. It was the same in Optimum Vision, where she was friendly with all the optical advisers, especially Lynsey and Tanya, who used to ask her to join them for a drink after work before she was married.

Ben had recognised that Graham was an important member of the team, that he had a big following, patients who would only see him and who would have the spectacles he recommended. So he turned a blind eye to Graham leaving by the customer door rather than the staff door like everyone else, carrying money in his pocket on the sales floor instead of putting it in his locker, and not bothering to complete the annual Fire Prevention and Health and Safety training.

Diane, however, was a martinet. Everything had to be done correctly. Carly warned Graham he would have to take more care.

"They'd never get rid of me," Graham said confidently. "I'm an optometrist. They need me."

"You're just one of a number to them, Graham," Carly said. "They could replace you just like that." And she clicked her fingers. But she knew he didn't believe her.

The Health and Safety and Fire Prevention training was done online. It was an easy enough process but deadly dull. Every time Carly reminded Graham about it he'd say, "I'm too busy." And it was true: they were busier than ever, patient after patient every twenty minutes. There were still the odd times it could be squeezed in: some examinations were quicker than others: a child, for example, or someone with perfect vision who had come in because they were getting headaches, more likely due to stress than to poor eyesight. And it was early December, when people began to think about Christmas and forgot their annual eye exam. Graham would use this odd fifteen to twenty minutes to dash up to the staff room for a cup of coffee or read a motoring magazine, but Carly stayed in her room to work through the tedious online training.

As the date for completion drew nearer, Diane kept asking Graham if he'd done it yet. "I haven't had time," he'd say heavily.

Carly was worried: Graham was the highest paid member of staff in the business. It was obvious that before long, the small branch of EyesRight would shut down, the staff moved to other branches or made redundant. Graham might think his job was safe but he had only worked in the private sector, he didn't understand how the big companies worked. Someone like Diane would find any excuse to get rid of higher-paid staff to keep salary costs down.

The next time she had a free fifteen minutes, Carly logged on with Graham's staff number and whizzed through the Health and Safety module, using the same answers she'd used for hers. Then she did it again the following day with the Fire Prevention one. Afterwards, she felt like a huge weight had been lifted off her mind. A fizz of excitement ran through her as she thought of how she'd thwarted Diane's plan. Oh, she probably had other ways of getting rid of him—performance management, targets he couldn't possibly reach—but at least Carly had stopped this attempt.

She was so pleased with herself that she was humming a little tune as she came out of her eye examination room.

"You're happy," Tanya said, laughing.

Everyone else was busy with patients. "I've just done Graham's online training," Carly said quietly. "That'll please Diane."

"What?" Tanya said, but she didn't sound particularly interested.

"Graham's online training," she repeated. "He never does it. I've done it for him."

She remembers Tanya suddenly putting down her pen and picking up a pile of forms from the desk. "I'm just going out to the office," she said. "I need to take these to Diane."

"Okay," Carly said.

Graham was right. She should never have been so friendly with the other staff. Tanya was also afraid of losing her job and needed to keep in with Diane. Carly had thought she was her friend but maybe all this time Tanya had resented the high salaries paid to Graham and Carly, the BMW Graham drove to work, Carly's smart little sports car, the expensive holidays they went on. Whatever her reason, she must have gone straight out and told Diane.

Carly sensed the atmosphere immediately when she and Graham arrived at work the following Monday. No one would meet her eyes, especially Tanya, the one person who had always greeted her with a smile and some little joke about the day ahead. Graham, of course, noticed nothing.

"You're being paranoid," he laughed.

But when Carly popped up to the staff room to get a drink of water, she saw a manager from one of the other branches sitting reading a newspaper. Alarm bells rang in her head. "Hi Tony," she said as casually as she could manage. He looked up, his eyes slid away from hers and his face reddened as he mumbled "Good Morning." A knot of dread tightened in her stomach.

Back downstairs, she found her ten o'clock and ten-twenty patients had been cancelled, as had Graham's ten-forty and eleven a.m. She glanced at Graham's door, but he had already taken his first patient in and although she heard his voice droning next door and glimpsed him twice between patients, she didn't get a chance to actually speak to him.

At ten o'clock, Diane knocked on her door. "Can you come into the staff room please, Carly?"

Carly saw the look of malicious triumph in her eyes. She knew something bad was coming.

Tony was already sitting at the desk, a pen poised over a pad of paper.

"Mr. Hart will be taking notes," Diane said. She glanced at her watch. "The meeting started at five past ten." She nodded her head and he dutifully wrote it down.

"I have a statement here that I'd like you to read." She slid a piece of paper across the desk. Carly's eyes slid across the scrawled words to the signature at the bottom: Tanya Baker.

"You are alleged to have completed Graham Anderson's

online Fire Prevention and Health and Safety modules," Diane said. "This is extremely serious. It constitutes a breach of company rules."

Words flew into Carly's brain: *But Graham's never done them, no one's ever been bothered.* But this was what Diane wanted: an admission of guilt, one she could use to get rid of them both.

"No," Carly heard herself say. "It's not true." She was amazed at her own clear steady voice. She never knew she could lie so convincingly. Only her flaming red face might have given her away. She saw Tony write down her words.

Diane was thrown. Clearly this wasn't what she'd expected. With all this formality, like a police investigation, she thought Carly would give way and confess. She hesitated. "I see," she said finally. "Well, this isn't the end of the matter. I'll have to investigate it further. Please ask Graham to come in now. But you are not to tell him what it's about."

Carly's legs trembled as she stood up and walked out, the palms of her hands were damp. She only had a moment to speak to Graham. She had to make the most of it.

"Diane wants to speak to you. It's about your online training. You *have* to lie," she whispered urgently.

Graham was confused. "What?"

"It's an investigation," she said quickly. "The Health and Safety stuff. You did them. All of them. Yourself."

Graham was often slow on the uptake but in this case, he seemed to pick it up quickly. "I don't like to lie," he said.

"It's that or lose your job."

She didn't see Graham when he came back out; they never had the same lunch hours and there was no chance between patients to speak to each other. The atmosphere that afternoon was electric: every time Carly came out of her room she saw the optical advisers with their heads bent together, conversations stopped suddenly, no one would meet her eyes. Diane was so unprofessional, she couldn't keep it to herself. Everyone knew.

Graham said nothing to her on the way out. Only when they were in the street did he turn to her and say, "What the hell is going on?"

"I did your online training..." Carly began.

"Yes, I know. Why, for God's sake? I'd have done it..."

"You wouldn't, Graham, you know you wouldn't. You never have."

"That woman and her petty little rules. What the hell does it matter? I don't need to know their Health and Safety rules to do my job."

"I know, but..."

"Well, it'll blow over," he said confidently. "She has to wave the flag I suppose. Set an example. New manager and all that..."

Relief washed over Carly. Of course, Graham was right. She hadn't done anything wrong. It would be fine.

But it wasn't the end of it. Staff from Head Office came in. They searched through the records of Fire Prevention and Health and Safety records, checked Graham's examination times and the times of the online training. Carly was sure it would be hard for them to prove anything.

"You have to say you did it," she told Graham. "And you've always done it. It's your word against theirs."

"I don't see why it matters," Graham said.

Carly and Graham were asked to attend disciplinary meetings just before Christmas. The word *'disciplinary'* sent a shiver of dread through Carly. Graham was still brazenly confident. "Is this just a clumsy way to try to get rid of us?" he asked Diane.

"Of course not," she said. "It's company procedure, that's all."

But she couldn't conceal her air of triumph. The rest of the staff were still awkward with Carly. Gone were the little chats on the reception desk between patients. Now they avoided her as much as possible.

Mid-December brought the Christmas Party. She and Graham still had to go. Carly was nervous. Never having had much to do with the other staff, Graham was still blissfully unaware of any awkwardness. This year, the staff of EyesRight were coming as well. The moment they arrived, Carly knew they shouldn't have come. The staff had brought husbands and wives. They all knew each other. Staff she was used to seeing in the uniform of a navy skirt and white blouse were now decked in short skirts and high heels or party dresses. One man wore a shirt open almost to his navel. He had a gold chain around his neck and a funny little trilby hat perched on the back of his head. Another wore a t-shirt that said "Fcuk Xmas" It was a smart restaurant. Graham wore a suit and open-necked shirt; Carly wore a black fitted knee-length dress and high heels. She felt so out of place. The only places left were right at the end of the table. She sat down next to Eve, one of the optical advisers from EyesRight, who scarcely turned to say "Hello" before turning back to talk to the others.

After the first course, Eve picked up her bag and nudged Carly. "Fag break," she said. Carly nodded weakly and managed a smile. Ten minutes later, Eve was back, her breath and her long black hair stinking of cigarettes. "Bloody cold out there," she said, putting her hand on Carly's arm. "And icy. I nearly slipped down." She nudged Carly. "What would Health and Safety say about that then, eh?"

A knife plunged through Carly. She knew. Everyone knew. As far as they were concerned, she and Graham were getting their comeuppance for thinking that they were better than them. And she thought they all liked her. She could have cried.

By the end of the meal, everyone was pretty drunk. Carly, who was driving, was stone-cold sober. The man with the trilby hat instigated some sort of silly game where he passed his paper serviette down the table in his mouth from one person to the next. There was a huge cheer as each person took it in their teeth and passed it to the next. By the time it reached Carly, it was smeared with moisture and the bits of food from people's dinner. She couldn't bear the thought of taking it in her lips, even for a moment, but if she refused she'd be ridiculed. Then Graham leant forward. "Let's stop this shall we?" he said easily, taking the serviette from Eve's mouth and screwing it up in his hand. "Silly game."

Carly felt like flinging her arms around him and kissing him. Instead, she reached under the table and squeezed his hand.

"You worry too much," he told her in the car on the way home. "No one knows a thing. It's all harmless nonsense."

He still thought he was safe, no one would get rid of him.

Carly woke the next morning with a blinding headache, even though she'd had nothing to drink. She still had it on Monday morning and for the first time in years, she rang in sick. By Wednesday she was better, but she couldn't face going into work. It was unprofessional to let her patients down because of some silly upset with the manager, but the thought of seeing Diane made her heart race. She was scared of her. It was ridiculous.

Then there was Tanya, Lynsey, and all the others who knew she was being investigated as though she had committed some heinous crime.

The next day she went to the doctor. "Your blood pressure is very high," the doctor said. "Are you going through some sort of stress?"

Carly tried to answer but her throat had closed over. Tears ran down her face. Somehow between sobs, she explained what had happened.

"Recession brings out the worst in companies," the doctor said. She signed Carly off for two weeks.

Graham was still unconcerned. "I never did it before," he said blithely. "No one was ever bothered."

"If you tell them that, you'll land Ben in trouble," Carly said. Ben had been promoted to one of the big London branches. "It could ruin his career."

Carly rang her old friend Amber from uni, who had worked for Optimum Vision in Wimbledon since she had been qualified.

"Honestly, I wouldn't worry," Amber said in her no-nonsense Northern accent. "It sounds like she's just trying to make an example of both of you. Not doing your Health and Safety training isn't a sackable offence. I know loads of people who never do it. But I'll tell you what, you can have as many attempts at those modules as you like. You can even do them at home. Get Graham to log on and do them himself tonight."

Relief washed over Carly again. It was going to be all right.

But it made no difference. Diane had the full force of Head Office behind her. She'd been told to find a way to get rid of their highest-paid staff.

The investigation had tried to prove that Graham had patients with him at the time he had been logged onto the computer, so he couldn't possibly have been doing his online training. But the clocks on the computer were never set to the correct time. They couldn't be completely sure that the timing was accurate. So Tanya had signed a written statement to say that Graham was fully booked, that he was in his room all the time, he couldn't possibly have done them himself.

The procedure was thrown into turmoil when Graham told them he had done the training again "Just to make sure I knew it all properly."

The interview was halted and Graham said he could hear Diane and the Head Office staff discussing it in urgent voices in the room next door. Quiet confidence surged through him.

When they came back in, however, they began to ask Graham instead about the previous two years that Graham had been with the company.

Graham's confidence vanished. "I told them I couldn't remember," he told Carly. "I asked Diane if *she* could remember what *she* did a year ago and two years ago."

Carly's heart sank. "What did she say?" she asked.

"She said she remembers doing her Health and Safety

Training…"

It was Graham's attitude that let him down. That cocky self-assurance that he knew better than anyone else, that he was always right, that they were lucky to have him, that they wouldn't dare get rid of him.

He was devastated when it happened. He came home and threw the letter down on the kitchen table. "I can't believe it," he kept saying. "Well, it's not the last of it. I'm not just accepting it. It can't be right. I'll go to a solicitor. It's not right. I'm an optometrist, for Christ's sake. They can't sack me for *this*."

Carly felt dreadful: the shame and the guilt. It was all her fault. She had dragged Graham into this. She couldn't sleep, she couldn't eat. She went back to the doctor, who signed her off for a further two weeks. If she went into work she'd have to go through the same disciplinary process as Graham and she couldn't face it. Graham collected her stuff from her locker, cleared her room, and emptied his own desk.

Diane couldn't have timed it better if she'd tried. It was a week before Christmas. This year it was Lucy's turn to have Edward for Christmas. She was spending it with her family which meant that Graham and Carly were going to his parents for the day.

"What are we going to tell them?" Carly said. "They'll have to know. Everyone will…."

Graham came up with a version of the truth: a clash of personalities, he said, he and Carly didn't get on with the new manager. They were given targets they couldn't meet. It was unprofessional. They had decided to leave. They might take a sabbatical for a while before deciding where to work.

Graham was entitled to appeal and in early January, he went for another interview with a manager from a different branch. He and Carly had talked it over and over before he went in.

"*You* did it," Carly kept saying. "Whatever they ask you, that's what you must say."

But whatever he said wasn't enough. He lost his appeal.

They went to a solicitor. "You could take it to court," she advised him. "But as long as the company has followed correct protocol, you're unlikely to win. And it's an expensive process…"

So there they were, she and Graham, two people who had loved their work, trapped together at home, both feeling like they'd committed some dreadful crime. Graham became convinced that everyone knew, that they were looking at him. He wouldn't go out anywhere, didn't want to see anybody.

He sat on the sofa all day, watching trashy daytime television or DVDs. At night, he stayed up drinking whisky long after Carly had gone to bed. She was so stressed that it took ages for her to settle down and she'd usually only just drifted off when he came up to bed. She'd then find herself wide awake again, the same thoughts circling around her mind. With Graham now snoring drunkenly, she'd go downstairs, make a cup of tea and try to read, her mind usually wandering to what a mess she'd made of things and how she wished she could turn back the clock. When she went back to bed, it was Graham's turn to wake up, and she'd drift off to sleep to the sound of the television downstairs again.

Carly was worried about him. She tried to persuade him to come with her to the shops or go for a walk.

"I don't feel like it," he said. "You go if you like."

She felt so bad. She'd lost Graham the job he loved, taken away his self-esteem. It was all her fault.

"Don't beat yourself up about it," Amber said on the phone. "Diane wanted you out. If it wasn't that, it would have been something else. Performance management. Not making the grade. It's happening everywhere…"

Now it's easy to see it was all part of a grand plan. She and Graham were replaced by newly-qualified optometrists, probably paid a fraction of their salary. But at the time, she couldn't see the wood for the trees.

She told Tina the same version she'd told everyone else. "We fell out with the manager," she said. "We just walked out..."

"Bit more to it than that though, isn't there?" Tina said.

"What?" Carly asked weakly. Did everyone know? Kelly? Ruth? Her other friends at Pilates? Had rumour spread that far?

"Lucy told me," Tina said smugly. "Graham told her..."

Carly knew then, if she hadn't known before, that her marriage to Graham was over. She didn't blame him for confiding in someone. After all, she'd told Amber. But why couldn't it have been one of his mates from the gym? But no, it had to be Lucy, the mother of his child, the woman who had shared his life before Carly. She could see him sitting on Lucy's sofa while Edward watched television, or played on his phone or computer upstairs. Lucy probably nodded her head sagely when he told her, comforted him, agreed that Carly was a silly bitch. Maybe she put his arm around her, maybe they kissed. The thought was unbearable.

The weeks Graham had spent sitting on the sofa feeling sorry for himself, Carly had spent re-doing her C.V. and applying for jobs. At the time, she hoped Graham would be working with her again.

"We could go anywhere," she had told him. "Start again, somewhere new. Somewhere no one knows us. Abroad even: New Zealand, Australia, America...."

She told Mark she chose Pender and Brown, but the truth was, they chose her. All that stuff about wanting to be in the West Country was rubbish. She'd have gone anywhere: Scotland, the midlands, it didn't matter, as long as she could get away. Pender and Brown just happened to be the first to offer her an interview—they really needed an optometrist, they didn't even glance at her references.

This time Graham didn't beg Carly to stay. He watched her pack up without a word. He blamed Carly for what had happened. She blamed herself.

Tina stared at her unbelievingly when Carly told her she was going. "What about me?" she asked.

"You're a big girl now," Carly thought. *"You can*

manage without me."

Out loud, she said as gently as possible: "You've got lots of friends here now: Lucy, Elaine, Jenni..."

"And Graham," she added in her mind.

"But I can come and see you?" Tina asked, still in the small tearful voice she used to use on Dad.

"Yes, of course," Carly said. "As soon as I'm settled in..."

Carly could have stayed with Graham. They might have made it work. People do. Marriages last the most amazing upheavals: infidelity, dishonesty, crime. But now that she's met Mark, Carly knows what love is really like. She can't say what Graham felt for her, but what she felt for him was more like hero worship. If she'd really loved him, she would have stayed and fought for him. But she gave up and Lucy won.

Two

Carly reads the text message through again and presses the send button. She hates herself for doing it. She should speak to Mark, explain herself properly. It's a cowardly thing to do, sending a text message to end a relationship.

"I think you should give your marriage a fair chance," she had written.

She had said something similar in the car on the way back from Stratford. But Mark was driving and she hadn't wanted to upset him.

"It's too soon," she had said as well.

"I'm not suggesting you move in tomorrow," he had said easily. "There's a lot to sort out. But I mean it, Caro, I love you. I want a future with you."

"It's not as easy as that, Mark. I *know* what divorce is like. It's messy. You start out thinking you'll be fair to each other, polite and pleasant and adult. But it doesn't last. Soon you're arguing over the house, the settlement, or some vase you never liked that some distant aunt gave you for your wedding. And we didn't even have kids. Have you thought what it'll do to Chloe and Sam? The hurt, the not-understanding-why. The custody arrangements, weekend visits, Christmases, Birthdays, school holidays..." She stops, realising she makes it sound likes she *does* know. "Can't we just stay like we are, Mark?"

"You're not the one trying not to get caught out," Mark

says. "Feeling guilty every time you make an excuse, every time you come back. I don't want that anymore, Carly. I don't care what it takes: I love you and I want to be with you."

"I love you too," she says.

This wasn't supposed to happen. She didn't mean to fall in love. It was all just fun. And it seemed so simple. Now it's out of control. Even if by some miracle she could have a future with Mark, she'd be back in the same position as she was with Graham: an ex-wife demanding financial support, and step-children coming and going. Love isn't enough in that sort of situation: you have to have patience, understanding, tolerance, empathy, blind faith. She just isn't up to it.

Mark's reply to her message comes immediately. *"We need to talk."*

She hesitates. If she agrees to see him, even if she hears his voice on the phone, her resolve will weaken.

"No," she replies. *"I'm sorry Mark but I've made up my mind."*

The hurt goes deep, like a knife in her chest. Nothing to look forward to now, just day after day of work. Everything the same—like one monotonous chore. The tears fall down her face. She wipes them away, willing herself to be strong, but once she's started, she can't stop. Big heavy sobs wrench her chest. Her phone rings again but she ignores it. She knows it will be Mark and she can't speak to him, can't speak to anyone until she's calmed down.

She misses him more than she thought possible. It's a struggle getting up in the mornings, getting through the day. Then there are the long dark lonely evenings and the sleepless tear-filled nights. It doesn't seem long since she was missing Graham like this. She reminds herself this is all her own fault; she must have been mad to fall from one relationship straight into another.

Work is the only thing that keeps her going, the only

thing she has to cling on to. The need to get up every day; patients and staff depending on her, needing her advice and knowledge. It's what she missed during those long empty months after the fiasco with Optimum Vision.

She checks her phone a dozen times a day, staring at the blank screen that used to have so many messages and calls waiting for her. Her own fingers itch to type "I love you" or "I miss you." But it would only make things worse for both of them so she puts her phone away.

Christmas approaches, the shops decked with baubles and greenery, the endless Christmas music, the streets filled with people. Everyone tries to be jolly: some must be looking forward to it but many seem to wish it was just over. Hannah and Rachel are at the age when the build-up to Christmas is quite fun, but the day itself—with parents and elderly relatives—is just a duty. Lesley won't talk about it, muttering something about a family crisis. No one dares to ask any details. Only Bob, with his three children, is genuinely excited, regaling anyone who will listen with stories of going to see Father Christmas, school plays and hand-made Christmas decorations. Carly can't avoid the usual question of "What are you doing for Christmas?"

"I'll be with my sister," she says. Tina invited herself in mid-November. But of course, they all assume she's going up to the fictional Emma and her family in Manchester.

"You're not going over to France to see your parents?"

"No," she manages to laugh easily. "They've got a house full of other relatives this year…"

There must have been a time when Carly enjoyed Christmas—when she was a child; the first Christmas she and Graham were together—but nowadays Christmas only brings bad memories: that first Christmas her parents died, the Christmases shuttling Edward between their house and Lucy's, the awful Christmas party with Optimum Vision, the excruciating Christmas Days with Graham's parents, the Christmas when Graham was fired and worst of all, that last Christmas with Graham when everyone knew she was leaving but appearances had to be kept up. Now it's just her and Tina. God knows how they'll get through the day.

Knowing that Bob and Lesley want to be with their families, Carly offers to work right up to the 23rd.

"I'm driving up to Manchester on Christmas Eve," she lies.

Valerie has time off as she has teenage children, so it's just Carly, Rachel and Hannah working that day. They're fully booked but no one wants to choose frames until "after Christmas" and other than that, there's just the odd person needing repairs or adjustments to their glasses.

Rachel has done her best to make things fun: there are mince pies and chocolates, and in between patients they do puzzles in magazines, sing Christmas songs and tell silly jokes. It reminds Carly of her pre-reg year in Hudson Opticians with Sandra and Kath—a far cry from her time with Optimim Vision—and it's hard not to get caught up in the festive atmosphere. By the end of the day, she feels quite Christmassy as she walks back to her car through the streets adorned with winking multicoloured Christmas lights and beautiful decorations. It would be better still if it was cold and frosty, if she could see her breath in the air, feel the bite of cold in her lungs when she breathes in. But although November brought sleet and ice, it's unusually mild for late December and the decorations look out of time and place. She drives home, past rows of houses, their curtains not yet drawn, Christmas trees and Christmas cards visible through the sitting room windows. She envies the families waiting for Daddy to come home from work, looking forward to Father Christmas coming. The garden centre she passes every day has a tiny Christmas tree perched high on top of what looks like a maypole. A handwritten sign says: "Christmas Trees For Sale."

Carly wasn't going to bother with a tree at all, but Tina had sounded so disappointed when she told her that she had gone into Argos and bought the smallest she could find and some baubles and gold beads. She wonders whether she should leave it for Tina to decorate. She's the artistic one, the one with the flare. When they were little they used to argue about it but as she grew older, Carly realised that Tina was much better at things like that. But Tina will be tired when she arrives and she probably won't want to start decorating a tree. So Carly does the best she can.

The health farm is closed for Christmas: the gates pulled together slightly, the usually brightly lit house in darkness, the car park at the front deserted as Carly drives past.

She spends Christmas Eve getting the flat ready, making up the bed, preparing the vegetables, working out the cooking time for the turkey crown she bought in the supermarket.

Tina arrives just after seven o'clock, fizzing with excitement. She whirls into the flat, leaving a trail of coats, scarves, bags and presents; wheeling her suitcase into the middle of the room like she did in the summer.

"I've met someone," she bursts out, her eyes shining. "Oliver. He's... Oh, he's wonderful, Carly. Like no one I've ever known before..."

Carly's heard this before but she tries to be happy for Tina, who's had a pretty bad time, first with Joe and then with a trail of boyfriends since. So she listens patiently to Tina's story of how they met the day before at a party.

"I wasn't going to go. Neither was he. It was meant to be..."

Tina doesn't pause long enough in her monologue to ask how Carly is, how her work is, whether she's still seeing someone. In a way, Carly is relieved. She might start crying if she told Tina about Mark. She's jealous, though, of the constant texts, the way Tina smiles and reddens when she looks at her phone, that first euphoria of a new relationship.

She wakes up on Christmas morning to the sound of Tina talking in a low, lovey-dovey voice on the phone. Carly picks hers up: several messages from friends but nothing from Mark. Silly of her to think he might text her, just to wish her Merry Christmas. But she's disappointed anyway.

Carly edges past the sofa bed where Tina is sitting wrapped in her dressing gown.

"Oliver says Happy Christmas," Tina says, laughing. She doesn't wait for a reply and carries on chattering while Carly makes coffee and passes a mug to her.

"What would you like for breakfast?" she asks her when she's finally finished. "Only, I'll have to start the lunch soon."

"Oh, I don't mind. I'm not very hungry. You haven't got any bacon, have you?"

"I'm not cooking bacon and egg, Tina. We're having a big lunch."

"Oh, okay." She shrugs easily. "I'll just have toast then."

Carly knew Tina wouldn't help but it would have been nice if she'd offered. She washes up the breakfast things, lays the table and peels the potatoes. Tina, in the meantime, showers and washes her hair, peers shortsightedly into the mirror to do her make-up, and checks her phone every five minutes.

Even with the sofa bed returned to a sofa, it's a squash in the flat with Tina's stuff piled in one corner and the Christmas tree next to the dining table.

Tina waits impatiently for Carly to sit down and take off her apron, then she raises her glass. "To absent friends," she says. Carly assumes she means their parents but the blush on her face shows she's thinking about Oliver, while Carly's mind flies to Mark, sitting at the head of the Christmas table, Paula at the other end, the twins either side.

After lunch, there's a flurry of phone calls from aunts and uncles making sure they're all right.

"Auntie Louise wants us to go down and see her tomorrow," Carly says as she presses the button to end the call. "I told her you had to get back."

"We can go if you like," Tina says.

"What? Are you sure?"

"Oliver says I have to stop feeling guilty. I have to move on."

"You've told him a lot already, haven't you? What is he? A psychiatrist?"

"No, a surveyor." She laughs.

"So, you want me to ring her back and say we'll go?" Carly says quickly before Tina starts talking about Oliver again.

"Yes," Tina says. "That's fine."

Auntie Louise is thrilled of course. "I'll ask Sharon and Hugh to pop over too," she says.

Carly wakes the next morning to clear blue skies and sunshine, a day borrowed from the summer. Tina is quiet on the way down, nervously fingering her phone, fiddling with the car heating, adjusting the visor so that the sun doesn't shine in her eyes. But once they arrive, she doesn't stop talking. Carly knows it's so that no one mentions their parents.

"And how are you?" Auntie Louise asks when Carly takes the plates out to the kitchen.

"I'm fine," Carly says carefully.

Auntie Louise lowers her voice so that Tina can't hear. "I know it's been hard for you both."

"Hard for all of us," Carly says. Auntie Louise is their father's older sister, Auntie Sharon their mother's younger one. They've suffered too.

"We thought we'd go for a walk if you'd like to," Auntie Louise goes on. "It's such a lovely day. We could go down by the river."

Auntie Louise and Uncle David's children—their cousins Maurice and Annette—are both married now with children of their own. Their place has been taken by two little Scottie dogs, Dylan and Bertie.

"Who's coming for walkies with Mummy and Daddy?" Auntie Louise coos.

"Better put their coats on," Uncle David says.

"Oh no, it's too mild for that, isn't it boys?" Auntie Louise says.

Auntie Sharon catches Carly's eye and smiles.

They stroll through the streets with their tightly-packed terraced houses, catching glimpses of sparkling Christmas trees through the windows, past the rows of shops, down the slope to the riverside walk.

It's beautiful down here and other couples and families are out enjoying the unusually warm sunshine. Dylan and Bertie scurry along on their little legs, straining at their leads, yelping and growling at any other dog they pass.

Tina is still keeping up her cheerful chatter, though she does seem a little more relaxed now. She talks about Oliver as though she's known him for years rather than just one day, and Uncle Hugh is confused.

"I thought his name was Joe?" he asks.

"Oh no," Tina laughs. "That was ages ago..."

"Do you keep in touch with any of your old school friends?" Uncle Hugh asks.

"Not really..." Tina replies. "Only on Facebook, you know..."

Carly smiles inwardly as Uncle Hugh nods, though probably he doesn't know anything about Facebook.

As they head back through the still-busy streets, they move to one side to let a family pass: a mother and grandparents with two boys; a tall broad-shouldered boy with thick dark wavy hair, and a small, fair-haired boy of about four or five. The older boy walks slowly, earnestly talking to his grandmother. The younger one stops to stroke one of the dogs, then races on.

"Don't run too far ahead!" The mother calls out. She catches Carly's eye and smiles.

"Do you know her?" Tina asks.

"No, I don't think so..." Carly says but she turns around anyway to take another look. The woman has turned around too. Their eyes meet again, then she's gone.

Tina is as quiet on the way home as she was on the journey there. The first time Carly risks taking her eyes off the road, she sees her scrolling through her mobile phone.

The next time, she's fallen asleep, her head to one side, her mouth slightly open. She looks like she did as a child and for a brief moment, Carly feels something like the pull of sisterly love. It vanishes though when Tina wakes up, stretches, and grumbles about how hot it is.

"I thought you might be cold when you were asleep," Carly says, turning the heating down again. "I *wasn't* asleep," Tina snaps.

Carly drives up the long dark drive, no lights from the health farm to guide her. The security lights flash on as she enters the car park and with a shock, she sees Mark's silver Audi parked where she always parks. Tina has heard her sharp intake of breath, senses her alarm.

"Who is it?" she asks.

If Tina had been the sort of sister who she told everything to, the sort of sister who had bothered to actually ask her whether she was seeing anyone, Carly wouldn't have had to prevaricate.

"A friend," she says quickly. "Look," she fumbles in her bag for the keys to the flat and thrusts them at Tina. "Can you go on in? I won't be long. I just need to…"

But Tina has summed up the situation pretty quickly. "Of course," she says. "I'll let you and your *friend* have a chat. Take your time. I'll be fine. I'll give Oliver a call…"

Mark has got out and is standing by the car. He nods awkwardly to Tina, who gives a cheery little wave. "Hi," he says to Carly. "Can we talk?"

He doesn't ask who Tina is—presumably he thinks she's a friend. He opens the passenger door and Carly gets in. The moment he gets in next to her, they're in each other's arms, his lips on hers, his tongue in her mouth, his breath hot in her ear. "I love you, I've missed you…" They're both saying the same.

"I thought you might be away," he says. "I thought I wouldn't see you. I've been waiting for hours, just in case…"

"What're you doing here?"

"I need to tell you. Paula. Me. It's over."

"What?" Christmas is not the right time to end a relationship. "What's happened?" she says.

"It's not you," he says quickly. "It's her. She's been seeing someone else." He gives a small ironic little laugh. "For ages, apparently. Chloe knew. She came home and found them together."

It could so nearly have been them.

"Anyway, she wants a divorce. The kids are fine about it."

"Of course they're not. It's not that easy, Mark. It can't be. It won't be."

But Mark doesn't want to hear another long diatribe about how difficult divorce is, however mutual it might be, however civilised it starts off.

"We can be together, Carly," he strokes her hand gently. "This is *our* year. A new start."

Carly shakes her head. "No, Mark."

"Why? I don't understand. I thought you loved me…"

"I do."

"It'll be fine…" he says reassuringly.

"No." She says again, more firmly this time. "You think you know me but you don't. You don't know a thing about me. I'm not Caroline Westminster. I'm Carly Spurway." In the dim interior car light, she can make out the frown on his face. "You see?" she bursts out. "You don't even remember her. You haven't loved *me* since I was sixteen, you've loved Caroline." The words end in a half-sob but she forges on. She *has* to. And there's a certain relief in the truth coming out. "I don't have a perfect sister," she says. "And my parents don't live in the Dordogne. My parents are dead." She senses his shock. "And my sister, Tina…" She gestures towards the flat, where Tina is probably still on the phone to Oliver. "Well, Tina's nothing but a pain in the bloody neck." She manages a slightly hysterical half-laugh. "And she isn't even my sister. She's adopted. I'm not the perfect person you think I am, Mark. I've lied to you. I lied at work. I lost my husband his job. *That's* why he divorced me. And I didn't *leave* my job. I was fired..." She's run out of steam now, and she's crying uncontrollably.

Mark sits silently next to her. He let go of her hand when she started explaining and he doesn't touch her now, doesn't move towards her or put his arm around her like she wants him to.

She opens the car door, starts to get out.

"Wait," he says. "Caro, Carly, please, don't go."

"There's no point, Mark," she sobs.

"I don't know what's been going on," he says. "And I don't understand it. But I do know I love you. Whatever you've done in the past, it makes no difference. You're still the person I love. Your sister, well, I didn't know her anyway. But you don't know mine either. Your parents..." He softens his voice deferentially. "That's dreadful. I'm so sorry." He pauses. "As for work," he goes on. "I just can't believe you'd do anything wrong. And if you have, well, we all make mistakes. It doesn't make me love you any less. Look, there's a lot you don't know about me. There's plenty of time. We can get to know each other..."

Carly gets back in. "Are you sure?"

"Yes. Yes, I'm sure. Come here." He pulls her towards him. She leans her head against his shoulder, tears still trickling down her face. *Our Year.* Mark had said. *A new start.* That's what she'll make it. She can be herself again. No more pretending, no more lies. Her mind veers away from the complicated details. As Mark said, there is plenty of time.

THE END

About the Author

Bethany Askew is the author of seven other novels: The Time Before, The World Within, Out of Step, Counting the Days, Poppy's Seed, Three Extraordinary Years and The Two Saras.

She has also written a short story, The Night of the Storm, and she writes poetry.

Bethany lives in Somerset, where she was born and brought up. She is married and has four children and seven grandchildren.

www.bethanyaskew.co.uk

Printed in Great Britain
by Amazon